RED WEEK

An Inspector Cruz Investigation

Frank Broughton

Copyright © Frank Broughton 2013

Frank Broughton has asserted his right under the Copyright, Designs and Patents Act 1988 to be identified as the author of this work

NOTE TO READERS

All profits from the sale of this book will be donated to LUPUS UK to help fund the research urgently needed for improved diagnosis and treatment of this presently incurable auto-immune disease.

RED WEEK

1. Monday: Green or Red?
2. Monday: Police Headquarters
3. Monday: Golden Gate Bar
4. Monday: *Gato Negro*
5. Tuesday: *Casa Cruz*
6. Tuesday: Police Headquarters
7. Tuesday: *Piso Montez*
8. Tuesday: *Gato Negro*
9. Tuesday: *Casa Albañez*
10. Tuesday: *Casa Albañez*
11. Wednesday: *Piso Montez*
12. Wednesday: Police Headquarters
13. Wednesday: *Piso Montez*
14. Wednesday *Asilo Rio Blanco*
15. Wednesday: *Universidad Nacional*
16. Wednesday : Golden Gate Bar
17. Thursday: *Casa Cruz*
18. Thursday: Coastal Freeway
19. Thursday: *Gato Negro*

MONDAY 1: *INDEPENDENCIA*

Inspector Amalio Cruz swore under his breath as he approached the *14 Julio* intersection. The lights on the high gantry stretching across four lanes of traffic had just flicked to red. It wasn't so much the delay that bothered him. Every morning on his way to headquarters he played a little game with the lights. If he got through both *14 Julio* and *Constitucional* on green then his shift would go smoothly. If it was 50/50 he could expect just the usual degree of aggravation but two reds was definitely an ill omen. He was already halfway to having a bad day.

He pulled a handkerchief out of his pocket and wiped a trickle of sweat from the back of his neck. Eight in the morning and already the temperature in the streets of the capital was climbing towards the sticky heat of mid-day. The air conditioning on his elderly Peugeot had ceased to function months ago and the electric window mechanism on the driver's door window was equally defunct. Not for the first time, Cruz promised himself that he would definitely get the car fixed this week.

With a squeal of brakes a *micro* bus pulled up on the inside lane alongside Cruz. At the same time a flash of movement in his offside mirror caught the corner of Cruz's eye. A face pressed against the car's side window and a fist rapped sharply on the glass. Unable to wind down the window, Cruz had to open the door to hear what the face was mouthing at him.

"Hey boss, be careful, you nearly knocked me over!" It was Nesto the legless beggar who usually worked this intersection, propelling himself everywhere on his tiny wooden cart. For some reason he had risked life and what were left of his limbs by pushing himself into the thick of the traffic to reach the Peugeot.

"What do you want Nesto?"

Nesto's wrinkled walnut face split into a grin. "Lucky I spotted your car Inspector. El Chico, he wants to see you. Golden Gate Bar, noon today."

"About what?" Cruz queried but Nesto was already gone and the cars behind were blaring a reminder that the lights had changed again. He slammed the door and accelerated across the intersection, wondering what was so urgent that El Chico couldn't wait until the evening. A police and military liaison meeting was scheduled for ten that morning. They had a habit of dragging on forever but when the big man asked to see you it was unwise to raise objections. He would have to think up some excuse for missing the meeting. Cruz cursed again, more loudly this time as he saw the next set of lights start to change. He slammed his foot on the throttle and sped through, missing a taxi that was heading across his bows by a hairsbreadth. He gave a finger to the driver and as he drove on down *Avenida Libertad* tried to forget that he had started the week with two reds.

MONDAY 2: POLICE HEADQUARTERS, *INDEPENDENCIA*

In February 1980 a military coup toppled the corrupt and widely unpopular civilian government of the *Republica Pacifica*. The only fighting in the capital took place around the Ministry of Justice where a small band of Government loyalists held out until air force jets bombed and rocketed it to rubble. Dust had hardly settled on the ruins when, in a neatly symbolic act, the generals who had taken control commissioned a new police headquarters on the site of the Ministry building.

Nearly five years later, ten storeys of concrete and glass rise like an exclamation mark above the elegant if rather dilapidated baroque frontages lining the remainder of the *Avenida Bolivar*. Within weeks the tower had been christened "Pepe" by the city's criminal fraternity, a neat abbreviation of *Pinga del Puerco* "The Pig's Prick." Today in a large office on Pepe's top floor, three immaculately uniformed men sit at a conference table. Each has a sheaf of buff-coloured files in front of him. The oldest, his florid face contrasting with iron grey hair, glances at his watch.

"Gentlemen, just one more I think, then we should break for lunch. Who's next Alvarez?"

The younger officer on his right consults a typed list. "In order of seniority, Inspector Cruz is next, General."

Each man riffles through his papers until he finds the right file. The General stares at the photo clipped to the front page of his copy. A clean-shaven face with hair longer than would be acceptable in the military stares back at him. The creases in his forehead deepen slightly.

"*Comisario* Fuentes, perhaps you could read out the summary. This one shouldn't detain us long."

"Certainly Sir." The third officer, lean-faced and with a permanently gloomy expression, clears his throat.

"Cruz, Amalio, Inspector. Age thirty-eight. Joined the service September 1964, transferred to Investigations Division and promoted Agent-Detective 1967, promoted Sub-Inspector 1973, Inspector 1979, so that makes six years in his present grade."

The senior man nods. "Not exactly a meteoric rise. Just give me the summary from his annual report."

Fuentes looks down at his file. "Inspector Cruz is an experienced officer who has from time to time made an important contribution to the work of Central Division. His judgment of priorities can sometimes be called into question and he needs to show more consistent application in his fulfilment of routine but important tasks. He does not always appreciate the necessity of communicating effectively with his superiors." Signed, Ignacio Delgado, *Comisario.*

The General glances at his colleague. "Any comments on political reliability?"

Alvarez shakes his head. "Nothing in writing sir. We had a verbal complaint from the Military Police last year about his lack of cooperation. It was during our joint investigation of a communist cell in the workforce at the *Colinas* Power Plant."

The General closes his copy of the file. "I've heard more than enough. Not recommended for promotion. All agreed? Mark the file for review after two years. Time for lunch gentlemen."

MONDAY 3: GOLDEN ~~GATE~~ BAR

The seedy drinking den near the *Estacion Central* had been the Golden Gate for as long as Cruz had lived in the city but there had never been much golden about it. The bar occupied the street level corner of a building that had started life as an office block before deteriorating into a nest of grimy storehouses and workshops.

Cruz pushed open the swinging half doors, installed by the first owner, a *Yanqui* from California, in the style of a cowboy saloon. Inside it was so dark by comparison with the fierce sunlight on the street that Cruz was temporarily blinded. When his eyes had adjusted enough to make out his surroundings, he found himself staring into the pock-marked face of a heavily-built individual with greased-back hair. Despite the heat, El Chico's muscle was wearing a buttoned-up dark suit. "Hello Caiman" he said. "Your boss is expecting me."

Caiman, never in Cruz's experience a man to waste words, nodded and led the way towards an unobtrusive door at the rear. As Cruz followed, he took a quick glance around the bar. A T-shirted barman was polishing glasses and a couple of dedicated drinkers were slumped on bar stools, staring glumly into their half-empty glasses. Maybe they were wondering how to pay for the next bottle.

Not a problem to worry El Chico. He owned half a dozen bars and the most profitable casino in *Independencia.* Most lucrative of all, he ran the dealers in *Sector Norte,* the highest class residential area in the capital. If the Junta's wives, sons or daughters snorted coke, smoked dope or stuck needles into their arms, Miguel Torres, universally known as El Chico, was their supplier.

El Chico "The Kid" had gained his nickname in ironic reference to his massive physique. His first career had been professional wrestling but he had put on some weight since then. Nowadays an extra chin wobbled when he laughed, often at things his business associates didn't find all that funny. At their first meeting he had told Cruz what had happened to his previous casino manager when the operation's profits had failed to live up to expectations.

"He told me he had no head for figures" the big man had said. Then he guffawed heartily "Two days later they found him in a storm drain with no head for anything! Somebody must have got carried away lookin' for his brains!"

Not that threats were El Chico's style when he was dealing with the *Independencia* Police Department. He smiled genially when he saw Cruz step through the door and waved him an invitation to sit down. El Chico felt comfortable dealing with Inspector Cruz. He didn't like him personally, because affection for people who weren't family was not something he ever indulged in. He didn't trust him, because he didn't trust anybody. But he respected him, if respect was a word you could use about a policeman who was ready to do favours. Cruz didn't try to flatter the big man like some of his colleagues or patronise him as a gutter rat made good. He simply listened to what El Chico wanted, then either said yes straight away or occasionally explained why what was being asked for was something he couldn't deliver. And when he did promise to do a thing he did it, in other words a man you could do business with.

El Chico wondered how the Inspector spent the generous payoffs the big man gave him. Certainly not on his appearance. Today he was wearing his usual creased linen suit and a Panama hat rapidly turning grey from the effects of city smog. Together with his pale complexion, broad forehead and high cheekbones they gave him the appearance of a somewhat scruffy academic rather than a policeman.

The big man glanced at the gold Rolex on his wrist. "Inspector, good to see you. And right on time." A young waitress, her hair permed into a mass of black curls, brought a tray to the table, smiled at Cruz, then placed a glass in front of the Inspector and poured from a jug clinking with ice cubes.

"My favourite cooler on a hot day Inspector" El Chico raised his own glass, drained it and nodded for a refill. "*Pisco*, dry ginger and lots of ice."

Caiman remained standing next to the door, arms folded in the style favoured by bodyguards who may need rapid access to a shoulder holster. Cruz, who had unsuccessfully been trying to ignore the waitress's generous cleavage as she bent to pour, watched the girl retreat behind the small private bar that occupied the far corner of the room and took a pull at his drink. Only then did Cruz notice another man seated at a table next to the bar, a face he didn't recognise, a younger man, late twenties maybe, with a narrow, pinched nose and an effeminate rosebud mouth. He wore a sharp suit with a bow tie and looked more like a bandleader or a nightclub compère than a gangster. El Chico jerked a thumb towards the stranger. "My son Hector."

Cruz wouldn't have guessed: he didn't see any family resemblance between the massively built gangleader and the dapperly dressed figure in the corner. He nodded an acknowledgement and waited for an explanation as to why he had been summoned at such short notice. But when El Chico finally spoke, it was not what Cruz was expecting.

"Tell me, do you have children Inspector?" Cruz nodded, wondering where this was going.

"Yes, I have a girl. She's nine years old."

"Ah, the best years of childhood! When they get older children can be a worry, getting into bad company, going off the rails."

El Chico took another drink then fished in the breast pocket of his shirt and pulled out a photograph. It showed a young woman with long hair and big dark eyes smiling into the camera.

"Pretty girl. Who is she?"

"My niece. Keep the photo. You'll need it. I want your help to find her."

Cruz stared at the photo. "Her face seems familiar"

El Chico nodded. "Maybe you've seen her on TV. She did some acting before she went to University. She had a small part in a soap, did a couple of adverts."

Cruz turned over the photo. Written on the back was a name; Coretta Sanchez Mendoza. "How come she's lost? And why do you need me to find her?"

"She's lost because she ran away. Last night. She was at a party, a house in *Las Fuentes*, with Hector. Lots of young people there and somebody offered her a line. Maybe they cut it with something they shouldn't have. When she sniffed it she went berserk, Hector tried to restrain her and she stabbed him in the arm with a bread knife she picked up from the kitchen table then ran off. Ten minutes later the party got busted, not by your boys, by the army"

"The army?" queried Cruz. "You mean the military police?"

"Yeah, those bastards in the black helmets. They found Hector in the kitchen patching himself up. They dragged him off to the Officers' School."

Cruz sucked in a breath. The Officers' School was a place no civilian entered by choice. Too many had come out of its interrogation cells feet first. Still Hector didn't look as though he'd been roughed up.

"I was clean when they searched me and I told them this was an accident." Hector flexed his right arm carefully. He spoke quietly, an educated voice. Cruz guessed some of El Gordo's money had been spent on an expensive education for his son.

El Chico nodded. "The boy kept his mouth shut and when I heard what happened I made a couple of phone calls and this morning they let him go. That's when I put the call out for you."

"So Coretta didn't show up at home last night?"

El Chico brushed a fly from the rim of his glass. "No. Maybe she's scared of me and maybe she's scared more about what those army police might do. Those bastards could charge her with attempted murder but that's not all. She left her bag behind when she ran and the cops are saying they found nearly half a brick in it, more than a hundred grammes of pure coke. Enough to make a dealer charge. She'd get ten years mandatory."

"That's a lot of stuff. Was it hers?"

Cruz's question was directed at Hector but it was El Chico who answered.

"No way. Why should she carry that much around with her? She's no dealer and if she wanted a little snow, she could get it anytime. No, those Black Helmet pigs planted it on her to get at me. Now you got to find her before they do. Just let me know where she is. Don't tell her you're working for me, that might scare her off after what she did to Hector. I need to talk to her, tell her everything's OK. Then I'll get her over the border and she'll be safe until the heat's off."

El Chico leaned over the table and slid an envelope across to Cruz. "Five hundred U.S. You find her, there's five thousand coming to you."

Cruz slipped the envelope into his jacket pocket. "You'll be looking as well I guess?" he queried.

"Sure we'll be looking." The big man nodded towards Caiman. "He'll be my man on the case. Talk to him if you need to but you know my guys aren't welcome in some places. You got contacts everywhere. I'm counting on you Inspector."

El Chico's eyes, black, utterly opaque, held Cruz's for a moment, then he sat back in his chair. "Caiman, show the Inspector out."

MONDAY 4: *EL GATO NEGRO*

An hour later Cruz was sitting in a bar of his own choosing, a cup of dark Colombian coffee in front of him. He needed to think. He couldn't do that at his desk in headquarters or at home where Felicia would be complaining about the shortcomings of the new maid or wheedling him again about the new set of dining room furniture she was after. Here in the *Gato Negro,* the Black Cat, no-one would bother him.

His mind drifted back to his first meeting with El Chico. How long was it since they'd first met? Two years or was it three? Not, he suspected, that he was the only one doing favours for the big man, although El Chico never let slip who his other contacts in the Department were. But he had his sources, Cruz was sure. If not, how would the El Chico have known when to make the first approach to the desperate-for-money Inspector Cruz?

Cruz had been, what was the *Yanqui* saying? "Between a rock and a hard place." A wife with expensive tastes and a mistress who had just told him that she needed an abortion. When Cruz had found out how much that would cost at the discreet private clinic Adriana had insisted was the only acceptable option, he had almost cracked up and confessed everything. As a good Catholic Felicia might not have demanded a divorce, but she would certainly have made his life hell.

Then had come the phone call from El Chico's tame lawyer. All the big man wanted in return for enough greenbacks to pay for Adriana's operation was to make sure that El Chico's son, the same Hector currently recovering from last night's encounter with the wrong end of a kitchen knife, escaped a conviction for dangerous driving. He'd been arrested after his sports car had careered onto the sidewalk and put a woman walking home from her night shift as a ward orderly back into the hospital she had just left.

Cruz had served a stint in traffic early in his career and knew who to contact. A couple of discreet phone calls and an envelope slipped into the right palm meant Hector walked free to continue his career as a boy racer. El Chico was pleased, showing his gratitude via another, thicker envelope. Adriana was also delighted when she found out that the clinic she could now book into had recently been patronised by a female newsreader with the highest profile and lowest cut dresses on the Republic's most popular TV channel. Cruz persuaded himself that he had acted as nothing more than a go-between. To ease his conscience, he had anonymously posted a percentage of his take to the cleaner.

That had been the start of what El Chico, who liked to be diplomatic when dealing with officialdom, referred to as his consultancy arrangement. Since then, Cruz had been approached no more than two or three times a year to smooth out some problem affecting El Chico's operations. The extra income kept Adriana sweet and paid a good chunk of the fees required by the private school his wife insisted their daughter should attend.

Which didn't leave much for him, Cruz reflected ruefully as he lit a Marlboro' and inhaled gratefully. Surely he deserved something? After all, for ninety percent of the time he was an honest cop.

Back to the present problem: the niece who couldn't be trusted with a bread knife. Cruz took her photo out of his wallet and stared at it thoughtfully. The face was a perfect oval, the lips full and slightly parted, the nose just long enough to give character.

"You are a looker, Coretta" he whispered to himself. "Nobody would guess you're related to El Chico. Are you really his niece or just his latest piece of action?" That was one question, but there were other things about the story the big man had told him that bothered Cruz. For a start, giving adulterated coke to any member of El Chico's family was a fairly reliable method of suicide. But if it wasn't dodgy coke that had sparked off Coretta's homicidal tendencies, what was it?

Then there was the question of the half brick of C found in Coretta's bag. El Chico was surely right. There was no good reason for his nearest and dearest to walk around with enough raw coke to earn an automatic ten year stretch. Cruz was willing to bet the brick had been planted where the military cops found it, but why?

And then there were the cops themselves. Why had the Black Helmets recently developed such an interest in illegal drugs?

This was the third raid Cruz had heard about in the last month. Up to then the military had confined themselves to hunting down the remnants of the ELR opposition and arresting anyone else brave or foolish enough to criticise the Junta in public.

The *Ejercito de Lucha Revolucionario*, or "Army of Revolutionary Struggle", had never been much more than a rabble of idealistic students, whose enthusiasm for the doctrines of Fidel and Che, spiced with a dash of anarchism, hadn't roused much enthusiasm amongst the poverty-stricken masses in the shanty towns that surrounded *Independencia*. Most ELR members had quickly been rounded up before disappearing into the grey concrete building that housed the Officers' School. Unlike El Chico's Hector, their disappearance had been permanent.

Although the newspapers and telecasts were still full of exhortations to be on guard against the "Red Menace" Cruz suspected they were mainly intended to ensure continuing middle class support for the military regime. The Cubans had enough to do trying to keep their economy afloat and regime intact now that Gorbachev had cut the Soviet aid programme and the *Yanqui* President Reagan was throwing millions of US dollars at every counter-revolutionary group in the Americas.

Whatever the reason, the Black Helmets had begun to squeeze the drug traffickers. Cruz had heard plenty of grumbling about that. Up until recently things had run smoothly enough on traditional lines. The civil police anti-drugs unit had maintained a reasonable working relationship with the more important dealers who, after an initial bloody period of infighting, had established a stable cartel. Every so often a middle-ranking player in one of the gangs would get greedy or mess up the arrangements for a shipment. The police would be alerted resulting in a speedy arrest followed by a flurry of headlines trumpeting "Another Victory In The War On Drugs." The impact of these arrests was reinforced by the cartel's willingness to permit the police search squads periodically to "discover" modest consignments of whichever drug was most in the news at the moment. Now this comfortable arrangement appeared to be under serious threat. A quick call had confirmed that Cruz's drug unit colleagues had known nothing about last night's raid.

Well, Cruz told himself, his first step had to be finding Coretta. Maybe she could attach some answers to the questions bothering him. So, where to start looking? El Chico's men would obviously have checked out her home address, her relatives and any of her friends that their boss, or Hector, were aware of. El Chico had come to him because he could make enquiries in territory outside of the big man's control, places such as the south side *barrios*. If Coretta had wanted to stay out of El Chico's clutches, that might be a good place to start looking but to do that he was going to need some help.

Cruz had first met Detective Tomàs Caldera as a fellow cadet on his training course at the Police Academy. They were allocated adjacent lockers and soon found they had more in common than surnames starting with "C." Both raised in small provincial towns distant from the capital, both found themselves friendless in the big city. But Tomàs had more handicaps than just a provincial accent. Small, stocky and dark skinned he was quickly nicknamed *El Indio*. Discrimination, more subtle but just as pervasive as in the southern states of the USA and a basic schooling barely sufficient to scrape through the police entrance exam would bar his way to promotion. Despite these handicaps, his dedication to the job and nose for detective work had eventually impressed his seniors sufficiently to allow him to make the coveted switch to plainclothes policing.

In their younger days Cruz and Tomàs had been partnered and Tomàs had become as close a friend as Cruz had in the world. Then Cruz had been promoted, soon after got married and they inevitably saw less of each other. But they remained *compadres* and Tomàs was the one person on the force Cruz could open up to about his worries, including the favours he did for El Chico. So far as Cruz knew, Tomàs was on nobody's payroll but he was well enough aware of how things worked in the Department. He just did his job and kept his mouth shut.

Now Cruz needed his *compadre's* help. He went over to the phone booth at one end of the bar and rang headquarters. As he had hoped, Tomàs was still at his desk. "Hey *amigo*, how goes it? I need to talk to you. Yeah, right now, *Gato Negro*. I'll have a cold beer waiting, don't let it get warm."

TUESDAY 1: *CASA CRUZ*

Cruz glanced at the luminous dial of the clock sitting on his bedside table. Three a.m. but he couldn't sleep: it was too hot and sticky, even under the cover of just a single sheet. Felicia was having no trouble. She lay on her back alongside him making just the lightest whiffle of a snore through her nostrils. Cruz carefully pulled back the sheet from his side of the bed and swung his legs onto the floor. He picked up his lighter and cigarettes, crept quietly to the French windows in the wall facing the bed and with the skill of long practice, very gently turned the handle. Opening the door just enough to slip through, he emerged onto the tiny balcony and took a deep breath.

Outside, the air was just a little cooler. Cruz's house backed onto the sports field of the school that his daughter attended and in clear weather it was possible to see the high peaks of the Andes, even at night if there was moonlight. But not tonight; the smog had been gradually thickening through the last hot and humid week and when he looked up, Cruz could not make out a single star.

He lit a cigarette and leaned against the balcony. It had been a long, trying day and it hadn't ended too well. His *compadre* was not the problem. After Cruz had promised to square it with his sergeant, Tomàs had agreed to spend a couple of days chasing his contacts in the south side *barrios* to see if he could pick up any trace of the girl. No, Tomàs was not the difficulty: it was El Chico. Just after Cruz got home that evening he'd had a phone call. Not from the big man himself: he never used the phone to make contact. When Cruz picked up, he heard a hoarse voice which after a moment he identified as Caiman's.

"You found that package we mislaid yet?"

"Tomorrow morning I'll be on to it. I had arrangements to make first."

"Well the management is getting impatient. They need results fast."

"I told you I'm on the case. I'll let you know as soon as I have anything."

Felicia had called out from the kitchen asking who was on the phone and Cruz, worried she might pick up the extension, had put the receiver down before Caiman could say anything else. Now he was wondering whether it was just concern for his missing niece, if she was his niece, that had the big man worried. He had never hassled Cruz like this before. It strengthened the detective's hunch that what he had been told about Coretta was far from being the whole story.

Cruz stubbed his cigarette butt on the balcony rail. As he did so he remembered tomorrow, or rather today, was Tuesday, Adriana's day off, his regular afternoon at her flat. For some reason he didn't feel the usual flicker of anticipation when he thought about that. Maybe he was getting too old for a double life he reflected gloomily as he slid quietly back into bed, closed his eyes and began to tense and then release the muscles in his legs, arms and torso.

He had been taught the technique at a Yoga class Felicia had dragged him along to years back and it often helped when sleep was hard to come by, but on this occasion, just as he began to feel drowsy, a sudden flash of memory jerked him wide awake. Coretta: his vague recollection that he had seen her before. Now he remembered! It wasn't on TV, it was another photograph, not so flattering and using a different name but definitely her -a police mug shot! Where and when had he seen it? He struggled without success to pin down time and place until he felt a hand on his arm.

"Hey *amor,* can't you keep still? You woke me up!"

"Sorry my love." He leaned across and kissed his wife's ear. She turned over and went back to sleep but Cruz could not follow her example. He had just remembered why the girl had a police mug shot: she had been arrested on suspicion of being a member of the ELR. Was El Chico's niece a red terrorist?

TUESDAY 2: POLICE HEADQUARTERS, *INDEPENDENCIA*

Cruz spent the morning alternating between his desk and the criminal records office. He'd read that in the U.S. the FBI had transferred their records onto computer disk but in the *Policia Nacional's* archive, dog-eared card indexes and dusty files remained the order of the day.

Cruz found nothing under the name Coretta Sanchez Mendoza, which didn't surprise him. Virtually every member of the ELR he'd had dealings with used an alias. He switched to the arrests record which was in chronological order and included a copy of the mugshot taken when a suspect was first interrogated, whether or not they were subsequently charged with an offence. He was fairly confident he had first seen Coretta's picture on a weekly compendium of arrest photos on circulation sometime towards the end of the previous year.

It didn't take long to track her down. After no more than fifteen minutes trawling through the arrest cards, he saw Coretta's face staring at him again. Despite the sullen expression and tied-back hair it was definitely the same girl as in the photo he took out of his wallet and laid alongside the mugshot. The arrest card recorded her name as Corazon Silva Moran, the same initials, he noted, as her real name and gave her age as twenty-one.

Armed with her alias, Cruz quickly found her main file, where he learnt that Corazon/Coretta had first been pulled in for taking part in a protest against the imprisonment of union leaders involved in a strike at the main post office. A couple of weeks later she had been arrested during a police raid on a flat in a run-down area no more than a few streets away from the Golden Gate bar. Apparently there had been a tipoff that the flat was used as an ELR safe house. No arms or explosives had been recovered but fake identity documents and passports in a variety of names had been found in a cardboard box hidden under a loose floorboard in the lounge.

Cruz read that Coretta and another girl, a Marta Albañez, lived in the flat and were arrested there when the police moved in.

Both girls were students at the National University and told their interrogators that the box must have been hidden by one of the many students who slept a night or two on their sofa while searching for more permanent accommodation. Cruz glanced at the bottom of the page. The box for the arresting officers' names had been left blank and the brief file note concluded "Suspect released after questioning."

The note was dated the same day as the arrest, 2 November 1984. Cruz raised his eyebrows. Arrested, questioned and released on the same day? And after incriminating documents had been found in her flat? The girl was fortunate she hadn't been handed over to the Black Helmets or sent to the bleak gaol at *Puente Alto* in the Andean foothills where the Junta held those of its political prisoners who survived interrogation. Another piece of this jigsaw that didn't seem to fit, reflected Cruz as he went back to the Record Clerk's desk to ask for the file on Marta Albañez.

"Your men must be busy Inspector, having to dig out these files yourself." A sharp-nosed clerk with a pencil moustache glanced at the name on the file he had found under "1984/A" and eyed Cruz curiously.

Cruz shrugged, he was tempted to tell the clerk to mind his own business but held to his rule of never antagonising colleagues who could be useful later. "You know how it is, shorthanded and half the team out on surveillance. Somebody has to keep the routine stuff moving." The clerk smiled sympathetically as he handed over the file then booked his customer's name in the ledger. Cruz hoped that no-one would want to check why he had borrowed the files on the two girls: if they did he would need a cover story. He had a flash of inspiration: both girls were students at the *Universidad Nacional.* He could tell anyone who asked that he was following a lead on another of his cases. One that *Comisario* Delgado had been chasing him about for weeks: a series of thefts of valuable manuscripts from the University library. Checking up on students with arrest records could be a plausible explanation for his interest in Sanchez and Albañez.

Back at his desk, Cruz opened Marta's file. Her photo showed a thin-faced girl with short-cut hair and the eyes of a scared rabbit. Like Coretta she was recorded as studying literature and drama. Again there was no detail on who the arresting officers were and the file note ended with the same wording as Coretta's. "Suspect released after questioning." There was one additional piece of information. As well as the location of the flat where the girls were arrested, another was given: a house in *Sector Norte*. In brackets afterwards was annotated "father's address."

    Cruz decided that it would be worth checking out the house. El Chico would surely know about the girl's flat but might not have the address of Marta's family home. He would pay the place a visit tonight and take Tomàs along with him. He grabbed a pen and on a scrap of paper wrote G.N. 18.00 then folded the paper and made his way towards the stairway that led to the big open-plan office where Tomàs had a desk. To get to the stairs he had to pass *Comisario* Delgado's office. Usually the door was shut and Cruz was able to sneak past unobserved but this time he was out of luck. Delgado's door suddenly swung open and a heftily-built figure, shoulders bulging under his tight-fitting suit, almost cannoned into Cruz.

    "*Perdon, amigo*" said the apparition, throwing out a meaty hand to steady Cruz then grinned "Inspector Cruz!" adding in English "How ya doin' pal?"

    Cruz smiled back rather wearily at Brad Daley, the FBI liaison officer. Daley always crackled with so much energy and bonhomie that just to look at him made Cruz feel tired. "I'm well thanks. And you?"

    "Great. I'm great, just been catching up on the gossip with your boss."

    As if the words had summoned him from his lair, *Comisario* Delgado suddenly appeared in the doorway. "Ah, Cruz! Just the man. I need an update on those manuscript thefts, Professor Bello is pressing us for results and he's a good friend of the General's. I can see you tomorrow, 8.30 sharp before the monthly programme meeting. I'll expect full details and something positive to report."

    Delgado vanished as quickly as he had appeared. The door slammed shut behind him and Daley raised his eyebrows at Cruz. "Looks like you're in the hot seat tomorrow Inspector" said the FBI man as they walked along the corridor. "If you get any hint that those missing manuscripts might have gone to the States, give me a call. Maybe I can help."

Cruz nodded his thanks and shook Daley' proffered hand as the *Yanqui* glanced over his shoulder then yelled "Hey! Hold that!" before disappearing through the already closing door of the lift. Cruz, who had only one floor to descend, made for the adjacent stairs in gloomy mood. Now he had not just the tedious monthly progress meeting to attend tomorrow: even before that he would have to face Delgado with precious little progress to report on the manuscripts case. The curse of the two red lights definitely had him in its grip.

After dropping his cryptic note on Tomàs's desk, Cruz had to pass the typing pool on the way back to his office. A thought occurred to him as he was about to walk past. He went into the pool and edging past the girls sitting at their rows of machines, he entered a small glass cubicle at the far end of the room.

"Hello Natalia." The plump good-looking woman checking a pile of typescripts looked up and smiled.

"Amalio! I haven't seen you in a while."

"I've been busy, you know how it is."

Natalia Hernandez had been married to a police sergeant killed in a car smash while chasing a getaway car. She had got over her loss quickly enough to become known throughout Investigations Branch as the Merry Widow. She and Cruz had enjoyed a couple of one-nighters and she hadn't seemed to bear a grudge when he stopped seeing her after he met Adriana.

"So what is it Inspector? You always want something when you come in here."

"Two things *bonita*, first to see your pretty face..."

Natalia scrunched up a piece of waste paper and threw it at him.

"And second to ask whether you've had the promotion letters in yet?"

"I knew it, you terrible man!"

Cruz did his best to put on an appealing face. Natalia laughed and began to search through several piles of paper sitting on the table in front of her. "Here you are. I haven't checked it yet and it's not signed so you can't take it away."

Cruz glanced down the one page letter. Natalia saw his expression change. "I'm sorry. It's not good news is it?"

Cruz shook his head. "Thanks anyway. I wasn't really expecting anything else. In any case if I'd got the nod they'd have moved me and what would happen to my reports? Nobody can make sense of my handwriting like you Natalia."

Natalia smiled. "That's true enough. How about inviting me to dinner some time as a thankyou?"

"Sure, that's a date, I'll call you."

Cruz escaped from the typing pool before Natalia could pin him down any further then hurried downstairs and extracted a plastic cupful of what the machine in the corridor claimed was coffee. The machine had recently replaced a venerable lady who used to push her battered trolley from floor to floor in search of custom. Back in his cubby hole of an office, he put his feet up on the desk, sipped the pale, lukewarm liquid and decided that it was even worse than the stuff the *vieja* used to sell.

He lit a cigarette to disguise the taste of the coffee and checked his watch. It was already past mid-day and he had a decision to make. He could ring Adriana, tell her that he had an urgent job to deal with, then spend the afternoon working up a convincing story on the manuscripts case or, he could stick to plan A. As he hesitated, the wording of the letter he had just read floated into his mind. "...therefore we regret to inform you that your name has not gone forward to the next Chief Inspector promotion board."

"Screw the bastards!" he exclaimed aloud, got to his feet, grabbed his jacket and walked out, slamming the door behind him.

TUESDAY 3: PISO MONTEZ

Cruz stretched luxuriously then rolled reluctantly out of bed, narrowly avoiding coming a cropper when he put his foot on an empty wine bottle lying on the carpet of Adriana Montez's bedroom. She was still dozing, only half covered by a sheet, the lovely curve of her rump too inviting not to stroke. Her eyes opened at the touch of his fingers and she smiled up at him and lifted the sheet. "A little more *dulce* amor?" He smiled back, then his expression suddenly changed as he caught sight of the bedside clock. "Shit, I'm late for a meeting. I'll have to run!"

Adriana leaned over to check the time. "My God! I'll have to hurry as well. I need to be at the airport in two hours. Señor Gonzalez is taking me with him on his trip to Caracas. Don't look at me like that *amor*. No need for you to get jealous, it's strictly business."

Cruz was buttoning his shirt at the same time as he hunted for a missing sock. He perched on the corner of the bed to pull on his trousers then ducked to look in the mirror while he dragged a comb through his hair. "When do you fly back?"

Adriana was head down picking out underwear from a chest of drawers. "Thursday. Call me on Friday we'll see if we can fix something up for the weekend." In reply Cruz squeezed the most accessible part of her anatomy. "Not now *amorcito*" she protested then turned swiftly to plant a kiss on his cheek. "Save it for later my love."

Cruz ran down the first flight of stairs in Adriana's apartment block before noticing a trailing shoelace that threatened to send him flying headlong. "Police Lothario Found Dead Outside Illicit Love Nest" would make a great tabloid headline. He sat on the stairs for a moment to tie up the lace then continued down at a more sensible pace.

As usual after an afternoon with Adriana, Cruz felt twinges of guilt. But he knew that a couple of days without seeing her would change that. After all, what was there to be guilty about? True, Felicia was what they called "a good wife" but the romance in their marriage had over the years gradually faded into routine and a preoccupation, on her part, with suburban respectability. Adriana was attractive, adventurous between the sheets and ten years younger. That, Cruz assured himself, helped to keep him younger as well.

TUESDAY 4: *GATO NEGRO*

Cruz raised both hands in apology as he entered the *Gato Negro* and saw Tomàs seated at their usual table in the corner of the bar. "Hey *Compadre* I'm sorry, I got held up."

Tomas signalled the waitress to come over, raising his empty beer glass and holding up two fingers. Then he pointed at Cruz's chest. "Maybe you should have stopped by the men's room on the way."

Cruz glanced down and saw that his shirt was buttoned up askew, he must look like a clumsy kid hurrying home from school after games. He waited until the girl had brought their drinks then fumbled with buttons until he appeared more presentable.

Tomàs took a pull at his beer "You should get your girl friend to check you over before she lets you out onto the street" he grinned.

Tomàs was the only one of Cruz's colleagues who knew the full story about Adriana. He smiled sheepishly. "Let's talk some business. How did it go today?"

"Not a peep from any of my snouts. No whispers about a nicely spoken young student who ought to stick out in the *barrio* like a whore in a seminary. Maybe she went a lot further than the Southside"

"El Chico's boys are keeping a watch for her at the airport and the stations. I've got a feeling she hasn't left the city. Perhaps we've been looking in the wrong part of town. Anyway I've got a lead that might help."

Cruz told Tomàs about the alternate address he'd found for Marta. "My bet is that after the police bust on their flat Marta would have hurried straight back home. That could have been where Coretta headed as well when she had to make a run for it. I don't think El Chico knows where Marta's parents live. If he did he would have had the place checked out when Coretta first went missing."

Tomàs looked unconvinced. "Maybe he did and she wasn't there."

Cruz finished off his beer and stood up. "Only one way to find out. Let's go and have a look."

Tomàs didn't move, he stayed sitting at the table, eyes fixed on his glass of beer. "I'm not coming with you. This time you're on your own."

Cruz repocketed his car keys and sat down again. "What's the matter? Are you pissed off because I turned up late?"

Tomàs shook his head. "I talked to my snouts like you asked, that's one thing. But interviewing an attempted homicide suspect in a case that we're not assigned to is different. If the Black Helmets do find Coretta it's bound to come out that we've interrogated her and we'll be deep in the shit."

"I don't want to interrogate her, just find her and let the big man know where she is. That's no big deal. "

"No big deal to you maybe" said Tomàs more loudly. The waitress, who was carrying a tray of glasses to the bar, glanced curiously in their direction.

"Keep your voice down" warned Cruz. "It's just a favour for the big man. You've never said no before."

"Maybe I should have done" said Tomàs, more quietly but for the first time looking Cruz in the face. "You may be able to get by nicely on what El Chico pays you but if I'm going to eat I need to keep my job."

"So that's it!" Cruz grinned. "You want a percentage of the beef! Why didn't you just come straight out and say so? I'll slice you off a piece."

For a moment Tomàs sat quite still then he jumped out of his chair, swept his arm across the table and stalked out, leaving Cruz staring at a glitter of broken glass on the floor. The waitress, clucking her tongue in dismay, hurried over with a broom to sweep up the mess. "You heard of the male menopause?" Cruz asked her as he extracted a couple of notes from his bill fold and dropped them on the table. He couldn't raise a smile when he said it and she didn't laugh.

TUESDAY 5: CASA ALBAÑEZ

The Albañez house proved to be a substantial two-storey villa on a quiet street in the older part of *Sector Norte*. The house had a garden fronted by a low stone wall. A wrought iron gate stood open onto a short driveway empty of cars. Cruz had found a good position to park about fifty metres past the house on the opposite side of the road, giving him a view of the front door as well as the driveway. There was no sign of activity and despite the gathering dusk, there were no lights showing.

Cruz looked at his watch: seven-thirty. It would be sensible to wait for a while and see if anybody turned up before he attempted to gain entry to the house. His stomach was rumbling and he was glad he'd given in to temptation and stopped at a street vendor's stall on the way from the *Gato Negro*. He'd bought an *empanada* and only wished he'd ordered beef instead of the melted cheese filling which was already seeping through a corner of the pastry and threatening to drip into his lap.

Rummaging under the dashboard, Cruz found a piece of rag that looked as if it had been used to wipe the dipstick and spread it over his pants. He bit hungrily into the *empananda* and when it was finished brushed away the crumbs then settled back in his seat and tried to relax. It wasn't easy: the argument with Tomas replayed in his head, Tomas, who he'd always been able to rely on. Now that familiar ground had shifted under his feet.

The hands on his watch crawled round the dial. When it showed seven-fifty he reached under his seat and pulled out the snub-nosed revolver he preferred to the heavy standard-issue police automatic. He checked the safety and tucked the gun into his waistband. It was a tight fit: he must be putting on weight.

"No more *empanadas* this week" he said aloud and as he did so his eye caught the flash of headlights at the far end of the avenue. A small Citroen drove towards him, turned into the Albañez driveway and stopped.

A woman got out of the car and after a moment's hesitation Cruz jerked open his door, ran to the gateway and hurried up the drive after her. The woman, a heavy shopping bag in one hand and her key already in the front door lock, looked back as she heard him coming. A security lamp over the door had switched itself on, giving enough light for Cruz to see a terrified face that he recognised from her mugshot. "Marta, don't be scared!" he yelled. He pulled out his identity card and waved it in her direction. "I just want to ask you a few questions. It's nothing..."

Marta, who had seemed frozen to the spot, suddenly turned, shouldered the door open and bolted into the house. Cruz, intent on getting to the door before she had a chance to lock it again, grabbed the handle. The door swung under his weight and as it did so he tripped over the shopping bag Marta had dropped in the doorway. Cursing freely he hauled himself up, rubbing his shin. The hallway was too dark to see much but there was no sign of the girl. He called out again. "Marta, my name is Inspector Cruz. I just need to talk, ask you a few questions. Where are you?"

"In here. I'm in here." The voice, little more than a frightened squeak, was coming from a room on the right hand side of the hall. Cruz glanced through the doorway. A table lamp was switched on and he could see Marta sitting in a big leather chair opposite the door, her hands were grasping the arms of the chair and she looked petrified. He stepped into the room. "There really is no need for you to be frightened Marta" he reassured her.

As he stepped into the room what felt uncomfortably like the muzzle of a gun jabbed into the small of his back. Another voice, female, from behind him. "No, you're the one who should be frightened *puerco*. Lie down on the floor."

Cruz raised his hands slowly to show they were empty. "I'm a police detective. Civil not military" he said as reassuringly as he could manage. "There's no need for this."

"I told you to lie down" said the voice more urgently. "Do it slowly or I'll paint your brains over that wall." The threat sounded convincing. Cruz dropped to his knees then spread himself on the floor. A hand patted him down and his revolver and cuffs were swiftly extracted from his pocket.

He tried again. "Listen please. I really am a policeman, my identity card's in my wallet. I promise you you're not in any danger. Just let me..."

Something hard cracked against the side of his head. "Shut up! Get your hands behind your back!" Dazed, Cruz complied, felt metal scratch his wrists then heard the click as his handcuffs were locked. The unseen girl spoke again. "Marta, turn the light on and see if you can find his I.D. I'll keep him covered." Fingers scrabbled in his jacket and pulled out his wallet. There was a pause then the voice spoke again. "OK Inspector Cruz, you can turn over."

Cruz tried but it wasn't easy with his arms pinned behind him. Finally a hand grabbed his jacket, rolled him over and he found himself looking up at Coretta Sanchez. Glowering from behind the barrel of a gun, she looked a good deal less appealing than in the photo in his wallet. Behind her Marta sat on the arm of the chair she had occupied when he first entered the room. She was holding his gun in both hands but she didn't look any happier.

Coretta, keeping her eyes fixed on Cruz called out "Marta, just go and check outside, front and back. We'd better make sure Mr Inspector Man is on his own."

Coretta settled herself on the arm of the chair her friend had just vacated. Cruz tried to wriggle himself into a more comfortable position but the girl warned him to keep still. Time passed, very slowly as far as Cruz was concerned, until eventually Marta came back to report that all was quiet outside. "There's an old car parked across the road but I couldn't see anyone in it."

"Yours?" queried Coretta looking at her captive. "Yes" said Cruz. "But please don't call it old, it's my pride and joy."

His attempt to lighten the tone fell flatter than a punctured tyre. Coretta gave him a cold stare.

"So Mr Inspector, tell us why you're here."

"As I tried to explain to your friend, I'm investigating an incident at a party in *Sector Norte* a couple of nights ago. A man was injured, a Señor Hector Torres. A number of witnesses identified you as the assailant. I need to talk to you, get you to tell me what happened."

"You're lying, Mr Inspector. Think of a better story."

"Why should I lie to you? You've seen my I.D. I work in Investigations Division."

"Maybe you do or maybe that I.D. is fake. Marta, look again in his wallet. Let's see if it all checks out."

Marta who had been standing by the window came over and picked up his wallet, her hands shaking so much that she scattered the contents onto the floor. Her eye caught Coretta's photo. "Hey, look at this" she exclaimed, holding it up "It's you!"

Coretta glanced quickly at the photo, then grabbed it and examined it more closely "Where did you get this?" she demanded.

"From police files" Cruz replied.

"This isn't a police photo, you're lying again you bastard!" She stood up and kicked him hard in the ribs. "And the rest of your story is crap. You pigs work in twos. If this is an official police visit where's your partner? Who **are** you working for, the Black Helmets or El Chico?"

Helpless on the floor, Cruz protested his innocence. Coretta ignored him and telling her friend to watch him closely, she left the room. As soon as she'd gone, Cruz tried an appeal to Marta. "Please believe me, I'm just an ordinary policeman investigating a crime. The key to my cuffs is in my trouser pocket. Unlock them and I'll forget your part in this. If you don't, you'll be in trouble as deep as Coretta."

Marta bit her lip. Her shoulders shook and she waved his gun around so wildly that Cruz was scared she would pull the trigger by accident. "I can't stand this anymore" she moaned. "I just want to be left alone."

"Don't be frightened. Come and get the key" urged Cruz. "Then we can sort all this out without anybody getting hurt."

"Still trying to fool us Mr Inspector?" He was too late. Coretta was back, carrying a hand towel. With a sudden lurch of his stomach Cruz saw her wrap the towel carefully around the muzzle of her pistol. Christ she was going to shoot him!

Coretta looked up and saw the expression on his face. She smiled "Don't want to alarm the neighbours do we? Now Inspector Cruz, let's see if you can tell the truth for once."

She jammed the wrapped muzzle of the gun against his right kneecap. "Who are you working for?"

Cruz had seen a couple of victims of kneecapping, drug runners who had made minor mistakes in carrying out their bosses' orders. One of them managed to get about with a stick, the other was permanently on crutches. A trickle of sweat ran down the side of his forehead and stung the corner of his eye.

"All right, don't shoot! I'll tell you. I'm doing a favour for El Chico. Your Uncle just needed to know where you were. He's worried about you and he wanted you to know everything's all right. Hector's recovering fine and he won't give evidence against you."

Coretta laughed but it wasn't a happy sound. "My uncle! What makes you think El Chico is my uncle? That's what he told you is it? Well, it's true we're related but about as distant as you can get and not by blood thank God. His wife is my father's cousin. As far as El Chico's concerned I don't count as family. The only worry he has about me is that I'm still breathing. You don't make a very convincing hit man but then all you have to do is to let him know where I am and he'll fix things. So how do we stop you telling him?"

Cruz's guts felt as if they had turned to water. He was helpless and this was a girl who had thought nothing of sticking a knife into the son of the most dangerous criminal in *Independencia*.

"Please, I swear I didn't know he meant you any harm. He told me he just wanted to look after you."

Coretta's eyes drilled into him. "And now I've got to think of a way to look after you."

"No Coretta! No! We can't kill a policeman! We'd never get away with it." Marta tugged at her friend's arm.

"For Christ's sake!" yelled Cruz, terrified Coretta's gun was about to go off.

"Calm yourself, it's okay" Coretta reassured him, shaking herself free of Marta. "Look," she unwrapped the towel from her gun. "The safety's on!"

Marta collapsed weeping on the floor. Cruz felt like joining in. Instead he watched as Coretta relieved her friend of the gun she was still holding then led her back to the leather armchair where she curled up into a ball and began to sob quietly. When Coretta came back to Cruz, she squatted down holding both guns, the policeman's weapon pointed at his stomach and stared at him thoughtfully.

"So what next Mr Policeman? If we let you go you're going to tell El Chico where to find us and Marta doesn't want me to shoot you. I wish I could think of another option."

A voice from behind offered her some good advice. "How about you just put those guns down?"

TUESDAY 6: CASA ALBAÑEZ

Cruz had never seen a more welcome sight in his life, Tomas was standing in the doorway, his automatic clasped in both hands in the regulation firing position and aimed directly at Coretta.

"Drop your weapon and get down on the floor." Tomas's voice hardened. "I'll count to three and if you're still standing I'll put you down with a bullet. One..."

Coretta dropped her guns with a clatter on the bare floorboards and lay flat. With practised speed Tomas cuffed her, then slipped Cruz's keys out of his pocket and released his friend. Cruz rubbed his wrists and carefully fingered his temple. Tomas grinned "That's quite a bruise amigo. Looks like she packs a good left hook."

Cruz tried to smile back but found his face hurt. "She packs a good pistol you mean. Thanks *compadre*, I owe you."

Tomas shook his head. "You have a bad habit of getting yourself into trouble with women. When I calmed down I decided Uncle Tomas had better keep an eye on you."

Cruz picked up his gun and ignoring Marta's shrieks of protest he cuffed her as well. Then he came back to where Coretta lay on the floor, rolled her over and propped her up against the wall. She stared back at him, holding his gaze steadily but he could see how scared she was. Her eyes flicked round to look at Tomas.

"So that's your hit man! He certainly looks the part more than you do."

Cruz raised his eyebrows at Tomas. "Which of us do you think she's trying to insult?"

Tomas grinned back at him. "Both I think." He leaned against the wall opposite Coretta and holstered his automatic.

Coretta turned to face Cruz who had dragged a wooden chair from the far end of the room and sat down with his arms resting on the chair back, staring at her. "Stop playing games" she said. "If you're going to shoot me, just do it, you bastards."

Cruz pulled a pack of cigarettes out of his pocket, lit one and offered the pack to Tomas who shook his head. "Coretta, what I told you was the truth. I didn't know El Chico meant to harm you. And I certainly don't. Now I've got a few questions myself. First, why did you stab Hector Torres? El Chico said you were high on coke. Is that true?"

Coretta shook her head violently. "I don't snort, I don't use dope, I don't even smoke filthy cigarettes."

Cruz blew a trail of smoke towards the ceiling. "Easy now, if you're trying for sainthood you better stop hitting cops on the head with a gun. So what did make you stick Señor Torres?"

Coretta stared down at the floor and said nothing.

"Coretta, if we meant to harm you we would have done it by now. Just tell me why you took a knife to the guy. I can think of reasons, mostly to do with you being a good looking woman and him being a prick but I need you to tell me."

"Why?" She was looking at him now. "Why do you want to know? You've told me you're here because you're doing a favour for El Chico. Now you've done it. You can tell him where to find me and he'll do the rest."

"He lied to me. My deal with the big man is off, I'm telling him nothing."

"So, take these cuffs off, walk away and leave us alone. You don't have to get involved."

"Let's just say I'm curious. It's an occupational hazard for detectives. I might even be able to help you. It sounds as though you need all the help you can get. On the other hand, if you won't talk to me I'll have no alternative but to lock you both up."

Marta whose sobs had started to quieten down let out a wail. Coretta glanced at her friend, shook her head then sighed. "OK, I'll tell you. What have I got to lose? There's nobody else I can talk to outside of a confessional and it's a long time since I went to mass."

"So what had you got against Hector? He may be an asshole but if you go round stabbing every asshole in *Independencia* you're going to be a very busy girl."

"Hector's deep in daddy's business."

"And that's why you went for him? A business argument?"

Coretta shook her head. "How much do you know about the Black Helmets?"

Cruz was puzzled. "What have the Black Helmets to do with this?"

"If you've checked me out on your records you'll know I was arrested last year, Marta as well. They raided our flat."

"Yes, then they released you after questioning."

"They did, but not until I agreed to cooperate."

Cruz nodded. The story on Coretta's file was beginning to make sense.

"A guy came and talked to me after my interrogation. He didn't tell me his name, just said he was military police. He told me the cops had found some stuff in our flat, false papers, enough to bring us before the anti-terrorist court. He said we'd get fifteen years at least but if I agreed to help them they'd let us both go free. What choice did I have?"

"What kind of help was he looking for?"

"He knew I was related to El Chico, I'd been to his house, been seen in night clubs with his daughter a couple of times. He told me the Black Helmets were running a big new anti-drug operation. Everyone knows the police are taking pay-offs from the big man and not just from him. The *Yanquis* have lost patience, they told the Junta they wanted to see some real action or they'd cancel the military aid programme, so the Generals ordered the Black Helmets to get to work. This guy told me they wanted information about El Chico and Hector."

"What kind of information?"

"Nothing too difficult at first. I'd admitted I knew Carmen, Hector's younger sister. He told me to visit her more often. Find out more about Hector, his friends, places he liked to go, let them know if he was away for a while, that kind of thing."

"So how did you report back?"

"I had a contact, at the university, another student. We'd meet up once at week and I'd pass on anything I'd heard."

"And what went wrong last Sunday?"

"It was a party, a birthday party, some friend of a friend of Hector's. I went with Carmen. It was crowded, we had a drink, danced a little then I noticed Hector and two other guys talking together. I recognised one of them. When I was released from gaol I was taken to the Officer's School. They did that just to scare me I think, to make sure I did as I was told and I saw him there. Carmen had met him before. She told me his name was Araya, Captain Araya and that the other man was his boss, Colonel Diaz. I was going to say hello to Hector but before I reached him he and the others went outside and sat round a table on the patio. Whatever they were talking about it looked like business not pleasure so I decided to find out what was going on. I got into the back garden. There were lots of bushes and shrubs and I was able to get close enough to hear what they were saying without being seen."

"You were taking quite a risk though. Why should you do that? Were the Black Helmets paying you by results?"

Coretta almost spat out her denial. "No! What do you think I am? One of your dirty informers? I wasn't just trying to save my skin. I have a friend who's held in *Puente Alto*. It's bad up there. My contact promised that if I could find out how El Chico was bringing the gear into the country they'd release him."

"This friend of yours, he must be a real good friend" said Tomas.

Coretta turned her head away without replying.

"OK, so you got close to Hector and his two pals" Cruz continued. "What did you find out?"

"I found out plenty, but not what I expected. They were talking about some kind of drug deal, the Black Helmets were looking for a payoff."

Tomas let out a low whistle and Cruz leaned forward in his chair, bringing his face close to Coretta's. "You're telling me that Hector was trying to fix a deal with a senior officer in the Black Helmets?"

Coretta stared him out. "Yes and why not? Everybody else in this country is on the take so why not them? What they were talking about was whether Diaz and Araya would be paid in cocaine or in dollars. They were insisting on cash."

"So did you hear anything about where the stuff was coming from?"

"I didn't get the chance. A couple came out of the house. They were both pretty drunk and the guy was fooling around. He must have lost his balance and he fell right into the bush I was hiding behind. When he saw me he started shouting his mouth off, "Who've we got here, a little girl lost in the woods!" and he grabbed me and dragged me out onto the patio right in front of Hector and the others. They all jumped up and one of the Black Helmets pulled a gun but I managed to get free from the drunk guy and ran back into the house.

"Hector came after me. The place was crowded and the lights were down. I was trying to get to the front door but I got lost. I found myself in the kitchen and Hector was behind me blocking the doorway."

"So what did you do?"

"There's only one door into the kitchen. I had to get past him to get out so I picked up a knife someone had been cutting bread with. He just laughed and made a grab for it. I stabbed him in the arm and he yelled and tried to grab me so I kicked him in the balls. He fell down and I ran and managed to find the front door and just kept running. It was dark and every time I heard a car coming I hid until it went away and at last I got here and Marta took me in."

Cruz stubbed his cigarette out on the floor. "That's quite a story" he grinned. "They should make a film of it."

Coretta shook her head angrily. "Are you calling me a liar? That's what happened. If it's funny to you, it wasn't to me."

"Calm down. I was just a little overwhelmed meeting a girl who sticks a knife into the nearest and dearest of the Pacific Republic's Number One Drug Lord then kicks him in the balls for an encore." Cruz fingered the swelling on the side of his temple. "I should be grateful you let me off so lightly."

Coretta tossed her head, looking for a moment like a fourteen year-old accused of smoking an illicit cigarette.

"Now" said Cruz. "A couple of things I need to clear up. Did you leave anything behind at the party when you ran for it?"

"Yes, my coat and a bag with my purse in it. There was a little money, not much."

"Did you know the Black Helmets raided the party just after you left?"

Coretta's look of surprise seemed genuine. "No I didn't. Why would the Black Helmets raid a birthday party?"

"Maybe one of the guys Hector was talking to called them in. Anyway they pulled in Hector and they searched the place, including your bag and they found something interesting."

"Interesting? All I had in there were a few pesetas and a lipstick. Oh!" Coretta gave a cry of dismay."My pocket diary was in there as well, with my friends' addresses!"

"Well they're all likely to get a visit. Let's hope they're cleaner than you were."

Coretta looked puzzled. "Cleaner than me? What are you talking about?"

"I'm talking about the half brick of cocaine they found in your bag."

"You're lying again! There was none of that stuff in my bag!"

Cruz nodded. "Half a brick is what they found. Ten years minimum."

Coretta was shaking with what seemed to Cruz genuine anger.

"That wasn't mine! Some bastard planted it in my bag!"

Cruz sat back and gave her a long stare without saying anything, before he nodded. "Even El Chico agrees with you. He thinks it was planted to get at him, but maybe he's wrong. Could be one of Hector's buddies dropped it in your bag. What I don't understand is why the party was raided by the Black Helmets just when two of their guys were trying to make a deal with Hector and the big man."

"Sounds like our outfit isn't the only one where the left hand doesn't know what the right hand is doing" Tomas suggested.

"Yes, could be this Colonel Diaz is running a private operation the Black Helmets bosses know nothing about."

Cruz turned back to Coretta. "One more thing, where did you get the gun you stuck in my back when I came in here?"

"It belongs to Marta's father. He's on the committee of the Athletics Club." Seeing Cruz's puzzled expression, her lips curved. It was the first smile she had shown him and even though it wasn't a friendly smile it caused an odd lurch in the pit of Cruz's stomach.

"It's a starting pistol. Check the magazine, it's full of blanks!"

Tomas coughed to hide a chuckle. "What happens now boss? Do we arrest these two?"

Cruz caught Coretta's sudden look of fear. He pointed a finger to indicate to Tomas that he wanted a private word and led the way back out into the hall.

"If we take them into Police Central or any other police post in this city, El Chico will hear about in within the hour. I wouldn't lay a bet against him getting to them while they're in custody and if not he'll certainly be waiting for them when they come out."

Tomas nodded. "So what else can we do? Just leave them here?"

Cruz spun round as a bright light invaded the hallway. It was coming through the glass panel at the top of the front door. The light moved slowly along the ceiling: car headlights. They stopped opposite the gateway to the Albañez house. Cruz ran back into the lounge and made for the front window. As he reached it and peered out, an engine revved and a vehicle accelerated away into the darkness.

Tomas appeared at Cruz's side. "It may be nothing" Cruz said, not quite convincing himself.

"Maybe, or it could be a sign that we'd better not hang about here much longer. Would they recognise your car?"

"I'm not sure. Maybe."

"Too many maybe's *compadre*. Time to make a decision."

Cruz turned to face Coretta. "Have you any relatives or friends you could stay with?"

She shook her head. "El Chico knows all my relations and the cops, I mean the Black Helmets, they've got my diary with my friends' addresses in it."

"Including this one? Asked Cruz. Coretta nodded. "Which means you can't stay here."

"What about Marta?" Tomas asked.

Cruz had almost forgotten Marta who had remained huddled in her chair, as if trying to pretend that she was somewhere else. She raised a tear-stained face when Tomas spoke "I took Coretta in last night, she's my friend so I helped her, but I want to get away from all this."

"What about your parents?" Cruz asked.

"My mother died two years ago and my father is away. He's an archaeologist excavating a site in the jungle. But there's my boy friend, Alejandro, I can go to his flat."

Coretta shook her head. "That's no good, his address was in my diary and El Chico's probably got his hands on that by now. Marta, why don't you go down to *Costa Azul*." She glanced up at Cruz. "Her father has a *casita,* a small villa, on the coast. She should be safe there. It's not much more than a couple of hours drive from here."

"Do you want to come with me?" asked Marta in a scared voice.

Coretta shook her head. "I've caused enough trouble for you already. You'll be safely out of it at *Costa Azul."*

Cruz saw from the relieved expression on Marta's face that she wasn't going to argue the point.

"It wouldn't be wise to use her car" he said, thinking of the pickup he had seen driving past. If that was El Chico's men they would have spotted Marta's vehicle in the driveway.

Tomas broke into his thoughts. "She could get to *Costa Azul* by train tonight. There's a late mail train I used to catch when I was on detached duty down there last summer."

Cruz nodded "Right. OK Marta you'd better throw a few things into a bag."

Tomas uncuffed Marta who hurried out and up the stairs to her bedroom. Coretta looked at Cruz but said nothing. He knew she had run out of options. So had he except for one. Adriana was away and he had the key to her flat.

"You have a toothbrush here?" he asked. She nodded. He took out his key and unlocked her cuffs. Coretta rubbed her wrists then climbed to her feet. "Get what you need upstairs then bring Marta back down with you. We can drop her off at the station then I can take you to a place you can stay safe, at least for tonight." He glanced at his watch. "We need to be away in ten minutes."

As Coretta followed her friend upstairs, Tomas glanced quizzically at Cruz. "If you don't mind me saying so *amigo*, you're getting yourself in a little deep here."

"What could I do? Leave her here waiting for El Chico's boys to smash the door in?"

Tomas shook his head. "Maybe it would have been better if we'd stayed in the *Gato Negro* tonight and got drunk."

Cruz groaned as he remembered what the morning held in store. "Not for me it wouldn't *compadre*. I've got an appointment with Delgado first thing tomorrow and I've a feeling my balls are the first item on his breakfast menu."

WEDNESDAY 1: *PISO MONTEZ*

By midnight Cruz was beginning to feel like a taxi service. First he had driven to the station to see Marta onto the mail train to *Costa Azul*, then he dropped off Tomas before heading for Adriana's flat. He pulled into a parking space opposite the front entrance of the apartment block.

"This is it" he told Coretta, who had not spoken a word since she said goodbye to her friend at the station. Cruz leaned across and opened the door for her. "Time to get out."

She still didn't move. "Who does this place belong to?"

"Just somebody I know who's away."

"And what's the rent?"

Cruz was puzzled. "Rent?"

She held his glance steadily.

"Yes, how do you expect to be paid for taking me in like this?"

Cruz got the message. "No charge, no strings."

"You don't look much like a fairy godmother so why are you doing this Inspector Cruz?"

"Call me Amalio"

"So you do expect a payment Mr Inspector!"

Cruz shook his head. "Nothing like that. It's just that it's late and my head hurts where you smacked me with your gun and my ribs hurt where you kicked me and a little friendliness might help. That's all I expect." He didn't add that in the dim light of the lamp illuminating the entrance to Adriana's apartment block, Coretta's eyes looked larger and darker than ever and that however stern her expression, her mouth was so evidently designed for kissing that if she smiled, it might be too much for him. Fortunately for Cruz's self control she didn't smile, she just pushed open her door a little wider and climbed out of the car.

Cruz led the way up the dark stairs to the door of Adriana's flat and after a struggle managed to find the right key. He opened the door, clicked on the light switch and Coretta followed him into the lounge. Adriana had evidently left in almost as much of a hurry as Cruz. A dress was draped across the back of the settee, two wineglasses still stood on the coffee table and he stumbled over a discarded pair of shoes left on the carpet. When Cruz checked in the bedroom he saw that the bed had not been made, the sheets lying in a jumbled pile on the floor. He sniffed the mingled odour of stale sweat, perfume and sex then closed the door.

"Better if you sleep on the sofa" he advised. "If I get you a blanket and pillow you should be comfortable enough."

Coretta dropped the shoulder bag that was her entire luggage onto the settee and gave the room an appraising glance. "This place belongs to a friend you said?"

"I didn't, but as it happens, it does."

"I think I can make a guess at what kind of friend."

Cruz didn't rise to that, he walked over to the window, drew the curtains then bent down to open the cabinet under the windowsill. "Want a drink?"

"Nothing alcoholic. I'll have a soft drink if there is one."

Cruz pulled out a bottle of dry ginger and hunted around for an opener before remembering he'd left it on the bedside table. Was that only this afternoon? It felt more like a year ago. He retrieved the opener, flipped the cap of the bottle and handed it to Coretta. "Hope you don't mind. If you insist I'll see if I can find a clean glass."

The girl shook her head. "This is fine."

Cruz squatted to check out what was left in the cabinet and found a half-full bottle of whisky. He went over to the coffee table, picked up one of the wineglasses and emptied the remaining dregs of red wine into the other glass before pouring himself a generous measure. Then he sat down on the settee and raised his glass to Coretta who was at the window peering down into the street.

"*Salud!* And don't worry. Nobody knows about this place. At least nobody who matters to you. Come and sit down."

Coretta turned to look at him but stayed by the window.

"Listen, I promise I'm not going to make a pass at you. Just come and sit down for a moment. You're making me nervous pacing around."

Coretta shrugged and sat down in a chair facing Cruz. "I'm still trying to work out your angle on this."

"My angle? Why should I have one?"

"Because you seem to me, Mr Policeman, like a man who would have things all worked out before he made a move."

Cruz laughed and almost choked on his whisky. "Coretta, you could not be more wrong. I'm the kind who jumps first and works out afterwards how far he has to fall. This situation is a perfect example."

"And what situation is that?"

Cruz was too tired, physically and mentally to indulge in any fancy storytelling.

"The situation of me sitting in my absent mistress's flat with a beautiful woman who's mixed up with some very questionable people, who almost fractured my skull two hours back and who I would very much like to kiss except," Cruz paused a moment for dramatic effect, thinking he was doing quite well, "I've promised not to."

Coretta raised her eyebrows. She looked solemn but Cruz had the feeling she was trying hard not to smile. "So you have a mistress. What about a wife?"

"Sure I have a wife and before you ask, a daughter as well. Also I own an old car you've already ridden in and I'm thinking of getting a dog. Is there anything else you want to know?"

"Well at least you're being honest about that, even if you do a little dirty work for El Chico on the side."

"And how about you?" Cruz countered. "How did you get mixed up with the ELR?"

Coretta stood up, her smile vanishing abruptly. "Forget it. I've told you why I agreed to work for the Black Helmets but there's no way I'm going to inform on my comrades."

"Calm yourself Coretta and please sit down. I'm not trying to get information out of you. I'm just interested to know why a girl like you entangled herself with a bunch of adolescent revolutionaries like the ELR. You don't look or sound as if you come from the *barrios.*"

Coretta shot Cruz a look cold enough to skate on. "Those "adolescent revolutionaries" are the only people willing to fight this fascist Government, the *hijos de mierda* that you're so happy to work for Mr Policeman."

Cruz raised a hand but she brushed aside his excuses. "It's true I don't come from the *barrios.* My father was teacher. He had a well-paid job in the American school teaching rich kids and diplomats' children but he had a conscience. When the generals took over he was one of the few who marched to Independence Square to protest. Where were you that day Inspector Cruz? Firing teargas grenades at citizens who had the balls to stand up to the army?"

Cruz knew it would be futile to point out that the detective branch didn't man anti-riot barricades. "What happened to your father?"

Coretta brushed a wisp of dark hair from her forehead.

"He got hit on the head by a baton, then the army dragged him off to the barracks at Los Nogales. That's where they beat him up some more, fractured his skull. He died in the cells there. Then last year I lost my mother. It said cancer on her death certificate but she didn't fight it too hard."

Cruz shook his head. "I can see why..."

Coretta slammed her bottle of *mineral* down onto the coffee table so hard that Cruz jumped in his chair. "No you can't see anything or you wouldn't be working for those thugs!"

Cruz wished to God he'd kept his mouth shut about the ELR.

"Look Coretta, I'm just a civilian police detective. OK I do the occasional favour for El Chico but nothing bad" he added, pushing the thought of Hector's hit and run to the back of his memory. "Most of the time I'm solving crimes or trying to. I was a cop long before the generals made their move and I don't like them any more than you but what could I do? I have a family and I don't claim to be a hero. I do my job and wait for better times."

"And how do you think we'll get to see these better times? By keeping quiet and doing what the fascists tell you?"

"Not by robbing a few banks and scrawling graffiti" Cruz was tempted to retort but he managed to bite the words back. "Look, can't we call a truce? Maybe my first impression was that you were a spoilt rich kid playing at being a revolutionary. I was wrong and I'm sorry. Now I understand why you do what you do. And please believe me, I am trying to help you."

Coretta sat down again in the chair opposite Cruz and took a sip of what was left in her bottle. As she drank her eyes never left Cruz's face. They had lost the frigid glare she had given him earlier but Cruz found the appraising look he was getting now even more unsettling. He felt like a man trying to swim a river whose current was too strong for him. He could hear the thunder of the waterfall downstream and there was nothing he could do about it. He wasn't even sure he wanted to. Dressed in jeans and sweatshirt and without a trace of makeup she looked more beautiful than any girl Cruz had ever sat so close to.

"You still haven't told me why you're going to all this trouble to help me."

Cruz shrugged. "Maybe it's because I don't like being made a fool of by El Chico and then..."

"And then what?" Cruz suspected that she hardly needed to ask.

"I'm thinking how little that mugshot did you justice."

Finally Coretta smiled: Cruz could feel his heart rate accelerating.

"And I'm thinking it's time you went home to your wife. What was the motto on that badge of yours I saw earlier "Honour above all?" Let's see if it means anything."

Cruz nodded and with an effort, hauled himself out of his seat.

"You're right. I'll get back here as soon as I can tomorrow. There's a place I know where you should be able to lie low for a while. And before you ask it's very respectable, almost too respectable for me. I'll make a call in the morning to the lady who runs it but I'm sure she'll take you in."

Coretta gave Cruz a doubtful look. "How can you be so certain?"

"Because taking in waifs and strays is part of her job description. She's a nun."

When Cruz got home he unlocked the door as quietly as he could and took off his shoes before creeping up the stairs. He undressed on the landing in the dark and tiptoed into the bedroom hoping Felicia was asleep. He felt exhausted: if he could just lie down and close his eyes he would be able to forget his worries but as he tried to disentangle enough of the sheet to cover his nakedness, Felicia turned over and slid her arms around him. "*Querida* where have you been till this time? I've hardly seen you for two days." A hand slid down his thigh and her lips nibbled at his neck. Sleep would have to be postponed for a while.

WEDNESDAY 2: POLICE HEADQUARTERS

Delgado's piercing eyes, beak-like nose and pointed chin invariably reminded Cruz of a picture of one of the *conquistadores* in the history textbook he had read at school. At present the *Comisario* was glaring at Cruz in the way Cortes or Pizarro might have confronted an uncooperative mule.

"So Inspector, what it comes down to is that you've identified a dozen possible suspects for these manuscript thefts, everyone from the library janitor up to and including Professor Bello himself but so far you haven't found a scrap of evidence to suggest who actually did it."

Cruz shuffled uneasily in his chair. "Sir it's been difficult. My sergeant's off sick and I've had a lot of paperwork to catch up on. These new reporting guidelines...."

"So now you're blaming me for the fact that you've achieved practically nothing on a case you've supposedly been giving top priority to for the last fortnight? I want you to get down to the University right now and I'll see you back in this office same time tomorrow with some results, not excuses. And just remember, Inspector, the road from uniform to Investigations Branch isn't one way. If you're not careful you'll find yourself in charge of border post in the jungle with nothing but mosquitoes for company. Now get out!"

Cruz got out, back to his cubbyhole of an office. He had no intention of reminding Delgado that he had been meant to attend the *Comisario's* weekly progress meeting. The morning saved by missing that should give him just enough time to get to Adriana's flat and drive Coretta to the place he had in mind where she could hide safely from El Chico's hard men. Once he'd organised that, he could concentrate on cracking the manuscripts case and saving his job. He pulled his notebook out of his pocket, checked a number and dialled. He was in luck, a familiar voice answered.

"Erica, it's me, Cruz. Listen, I need a favour..."

WEDNESDAY 3: *PISO MONTEZ*

When he got to the flat, Coretta was eating toast and finishing a mug of coffee. "I hope your girlfriend won't mind me helping myself but I was starving. Do you want a cup?"

Cruz shook his head. "We need to leave straight away."

Coretta drained her mug and stood up. "So where is this mysterious hideout you've got lined up for me? You said there were nuns. Is it a convent?"

"Well to be exact, sisters not nuns and no it's not a convent. It's a place up in the hills, well outside El Chico's territory and before you ask, it won't cost you to stay there. It's a womens' refuge. They look after battered wives, pregnant girls, that kind of thing. I know one of the sisters there, know her from way back, she'll take you in."

"So which category do I fit into, battered woman, or immoral teenager?

To hide the unsettling effect of her smile, Cruz turned away and made for Adriana's bedroom where he opened a door and began rummaging through the contents of the wardrobe. He pulled out one of his mistress's trouser suits then picked up a pair of shoes from the bottom rack and called out to Coretta.

"I think it would be a good idea if we change your appearance a little. You and my friend Adriana are about the same size I guess, try these on. Just until we get you to the refuge."

Coretta came into the bedroom and stared at the suit Cruz was holding out to her.

"You want me to wear that?" she giggled. "People will think I'm auditioning for a part in "Life and Love!""

Cruz, who was not a fan of the most popular soap on *TV Pacifica* grimaced then had another inspiration. He pulled open a drawer and produced a blonde wig that Adriana kept strictly for party wear. "Put that on as well and let's see what you look like."

Still laughing Coretta hustled him out of the room. When a few minutes later she re-entered the lounge, Cruz gave a low whistle. "Here, let's complete the picture."

He picked up one of Adriana's many pairs of sunglasses from the window sill and gave them to Coretta. "That's perfect. I'd never have recognised you."

"Perfect except for the shoes. These are a little tight."

"You won't have to wear them for long, just till we get in the car. Have you enough money to get by for a few days?"

"Marta lent me some. I've just got a few things I need to buy."

Cruz wasn't happy about giving El Chico's men another opportunity to spot Coretta, even in disguise, but she was adamant that she needed some women's necessities that Cruz wasn't too keen to enquire about. At least she would be a lot harder to recognise now she had discarded her universal student T-shirt and denim look. Different but to Cruz's eyes, even more attractive. Adriana's pale yellow suit complemented her honey coloured skin and the blonde wig added an exotic touch she was beautiful enough to carry off. She glanced at Cruz then smiled in a way that meant she knew what effect she was having on him before picking up the capacious but rather threadbare bag she had brought with her to the flat.

"I'm ready, let's go."

"I'll carry the bag, it doesn't match the rest of your outfit."

Cruz locked the door of the flat with his own key then led the way down the stairs. When they got to the hallway he told Coretta to wait then opened one of the glass double doors and took a quick look around.

"It seems clear but you stay inside while I get the car." Still carrying Coretta's bag, he made his way back down the hall and then along a narrow corridor to the rear of the building. Before he left headquarters he'd taken the precaution of swopping his Peugeot for one of the Division's pool cars which he'd left behind the block of flats.

Outside he scrambled through a gated and fenced-off yard littered with bottles, cans and empty metal drums that stank of cooking oil. His car was still safely parked at the near end of the short cul-de-sac leading to the yard. Cruz slipped a fifty peseta note to the toothless old janitor who doubled as car minder for those inhabitants of the flats who didn't rent a secure garage.

"Now Paco, if anyone asks, you haven't seen me today."

"Sure Senor, my lips are..." he made a zipping up gesture across his mouth and grinned.

"Let's hope nobody offers you more than a fifty" Cruz muttered as he drove round the corner to the apartment block's front entrance.

WEDNESDAY 4: ASILO RIO BLANCO

Coretta bought the things she needed in a new up-market mall on the outer fringe of *Sector Norte*. As she progressed from shop to shop Cruz trailed fifty metres behind her, keeping a wary eye out for signs of anyone who might be El Chico muscle. Only after they were back in the car and heading towards the mountains did he begin to feel a little more relaxed. Half an hour later they had left the city behind and the road began to climb, steadily at first then more steeply via a series of giant hairpins towards the nearest rocky shoulder of the mountains.

Coretta, wound down her window. "The air's clearer already: it's good to get out of the smog." As they rounded the next bend they saw *Independencia* spread out below them, almost filling the wide shallow basin between the Andes and the lesser range of mountains that fronted the Pacific Ocean. The morning sun was catching fire on the summits of the coastal hills. They seemed to float over the grey blanket of smog smothering the metropolis.

"To think we're breathing that stuff everyday" Coretta exclaimed. Can we stop? I'd like to get out and taste some real fresh air."

"I can't stop here, it's too steep" Cruz replied. "This rustbucket is struggling as it is. Anyway there's not far to go."

He jammed the gearlever of the beaten-up Chevette the car pool had given him, into second and kept his foot hard down on the accelerator. Slowly, the car's engine whining in protest, they ground their way up the next stretch of one in four, then on around yet another hundred and eighty degree bend to find themselves on the flattish top of a ridge peppered with scrawny bushes of dark, thorny scrub. From there the highway headed on upwards towards the ski lifts and imitation Swiss chalets of the *Las Nieves* winter sports resort but to their right a minor road forked off and descended into a narrow valley leading towards the nearest cluster of snow-clad summits. Silhouetted against a deep blue sky they now looked much higher and more intimidating than they did from the balcony of Cruz's bedroom.

Cruz swung the car onto the side road. When they reached the valley floor the road deteriorated to a dirt track running alongside a swift mountain stream, its bed a crazy jumble of giant boulders. The sun glinted so brightly off the water that it was almost blinding and they could hear the roar of the torrent over the noise of their engine. Here and there, where the valley bottom yielded an area of flatter ground, they passed farmsteads surrounded by a patchwork of tiny irrigated fields. The houses and barns were built of rough planks weathered dark in the sun under roofs of rusty galvanised sheet.

"This feels light years away from the city" Coretta laughed.

"Hard to realise its less than fifty kilometres" Cruz agreed. "Look, we've arrived." As they turned the next bend a series of flat-roofed breeze-block huts came into view.

"Sorry if you were expecting something more picturesque but *Asilo Rio Blanco* isn't exactly a colonial foundation, there was nothing here ten years back. I'm not sure even now that the archbishop approves."

"Not as far as spending money on the place, I can see that" Coretta replied.

Cruz drove carefully between two rows of huts through a space thronged with children and drew up in front of a white-painted church. It was slightly bigger but no grander than the other buildings and had a large blue cross painted on the front wall.

Cruz got out of the car and greeted a tall, strongly-built woman standing by the door of the church. She was wearing trousers, a faded blue woollen sweater and was bare-headed apart from a brightly-coloured scarf tying her thick, straw-coloured hair back into a pony tail. The only sign of her calling was a small cross of polished wood hanging from her neck on a silver chain. She embraced Cruz then stepped back, holding him at arms' length. "So what are you after?" she demanded, then catching sight of Coretta as she climbed rather unsteadily out of the car on her high heels, she exclaimed "Holy Mother what have you brought us this time?"

"Can we go inside Erica? Then I can explain" said Cruz, conscious of the band of curious children already clustering around them.

Cruz had known Erica Drexler for the best part of twenty years. The daughter of German immigrants, she had worked in the finance department of police headquarters, always with the ambition that one day the high-ups would recognise the need for female police officers and that she would be able to make the switch to the job she really wanted, enforcing the law out on the streets.

When the junta had overthrown the last civilian government, Erica had realised her hopes were futile and resigned. She had then sprung an even bigger surprise on her ex-colleagues by taking religious vows. But her new life was no cloistered existence: she had joined the Little Sisters of Santa Rosa, an order whose members lived their lives in the community. Largely by her own efforts she had raised the money to found the womens' refuge, built to serve the needs of the capital but just far enough away to provide some security against the more violent of her clients' partners.

Inside the building, which served not only as a church but also as community hall, school and cafeteria, Erica took Cruz aside, leaving Coretta standing uneasily, a shopping bag in each hand, staring at the brightly painted and rather gory mural of the Passion behind the altar.

"This is a refuge for desperate women who are too poor to have any other choice not a holiday home for your latest hot skirt!"

Cruz, forgoing the obvious response that Coretta was not wearing a skirt, hastened to assure Erica that the elegant piece of eye candy he had brought to her door was not what she seemed. "It's a case I'm working on" he explained half-truthfully. "A big one and Coretta's right in the thick of it. If you can just take her in for a week or so I would really appreciate it."

Erica eyed him stonily. "How much might it add up to, this appreciation?"

Cruz pulled out his wallet and slid out the five notes El Chico had given him. "How about five hundred dollars worth?"

"That, as Mr American Express man says, will do nicely. Now has Miss Sunday Supplement anything more practical to wear?"

Half an hour later Cruz said goodbye to Coretta who, having already changed back into her student gear, was sitting on a bench outside the church surrounded by an excited flock of children. They were listening to a story she was telling and appeared to be particularly fascinated by the blonde wig which she kept putting on and taking off as she impersonated different characters.

Driving back down the track alongside the foaming river, Cruz tried to remember a saying of his father's. How did it go? "The only thing that changes faster than the wind is a woman." He was finding it hard to reconcile the smiling girl he had left behind at the refuge with the steely, cold-eyed Coretta responsible for the lump on his temple. As for the wind, so far the day had been breathlessly calm, the air warmer and more humid than ever.

"Could be in for a storm" he muttered to himself as he jammed the Chevy's gearlever into second for the climb back up to the main road.

WEDNESDAY 5: *UNIVERSIDAD NACIONAL*

Salvador Arenas, librarian in charge of the University's manuscripts collection, led Cruz through a high-ceilinged reading room furnished with two long wooden desks at which several, mostly elderly, academics were studying bulky leather-bound volumes. At the far end of the room, Cruz followed Arenas through a glass-panelled door giving entrance to the librarian's office. The room was furnished with a huge polished wood desk that looked as though it had been inherited from the last Viceroy and several equally ample leather chairs. Portraits of what he assumed were past University dignitaries stared down at Cruz.

"Please sit down Inspector" Arenas, rotund and balding, with a drinker's nose, several chins and a stomach as ample as his furniture, seated himself behind his desk and indicated a facing chair for Cruz. "Were you by any chance a student here?"

Cruz shook his head. "Just the Police Academy Señor Arenas so excuse me if I'm a little ignorant about your procedures. Did you get me the list of everybody who has access to the secure store where you keep the more valuable documents?"

"Yes Inspector, I'll get it for you now." Arenas pressed a button on the side of his desk and a few moments later the door opened.

Arenas waved a hand at the newcomer. "My assistant Felipe Garcia" he told Cruz. "You have the list I asked for Felipe?"

Garcia was as slightly built as his boss was fat, with a head that seemed too large for his body. Although he didn't look more than thirty his dark curly hair had already noticeably receded from a forehead creased with worry lines. He stared nervously at Cruz through thick horn-rimmed glasses as he handed a sheet of paper to Arenas.

The librarian glanced at the sheet. "This is everybody who has access to the manuscripts store?

"Yes Señor Arenas, everybody." Garcia's voice had the high, nervous tone of somebody accused of a misdemeanour. "I assure you they're all most trustworthy people, I can't imagine that any of them..."

The librarian raised a hand to cut him off "That's for the Inspector to decide" he said as he passed the paper to Cruz.

Cruz scanned Garcia's list: there were five names including two women but one of the names made Cruz catch his breath.

"Marta Albañez, is she a literature student, early twenties, slight girl with short brown hair?

"That sounds like her" Arenas admitted. "Undergraduates aren't normally allowed into to the manuscripts store but her father is a Senior Lecturer in the Department of History and a close friend of Professor Bello. She was helping the Professor with some work he's trying to finish on sixteenth century viceregal documents. She's been in here quite regularly over the last two or three months."

"You also keep a record of when these people access the storeroom?"

"I have it right here" Arenas nodded. "I asked Garcia to bring it through earlier." He opened the right hand drawer of his desk, extracted a large leather bound ledger and turned to a page marked with a torn-off scrap of paper. He ran his finger down the page.

"Is Albañez listed?" Cruz queried.

Arenas nodded. "She first visited about three months back. Yes," he flipped the pages in a thick blue ledger, "Fourth September and she's been back eight times since then."

Cruz scratched his chin and wrote down the details on his own notepad.

"And you've lost six items in total?"

Arenas turned to Garcia "Felipe can confirm that. He's in charge of the manuscripts store on a day-to-day basis."

And if anyone has to carry a can for all this it'll be him, Cruz guessed.

Garcia's eyes blinked behind the lenses of his glasses. "Six manuscripts have gone missing from the collection, certainly."

"You mean there may be more?"

"We're almost sure it's only six."

"Almost?"

Garcia looked even more unhappy. "It's difficult to be certain, there's so much material and the catalogue is not always reliable."

"And two of the items disappeared **after** you realised that manuscripts had already gone missing?"

"Yes" Arenas intervened. "But one of them was still here two weeks ago. The professor himself examined it but when he came back last week to check a detail of the wording, it had disappeared."

"The other five names on this list. How long have they been working on the manuscripts?"

Arenas took back the list of names from Cruz. "Well, the Professor and Doctor Juarez have been using the library for years. Paula Echeverria and Jaime Guterriez are postgraduate students. Echeverria is in her third year and Guterriez in his second. They're both studying nineteenth century material, documents relating to different aspects of the independence movement."

"So not the most valuable stuff?"

Garcia broke in, temporarily forgetting his nervousness. "Inspector," he protested. "The nineteenth century papers are vital to understanding the formation of our national identity!"

"But in hard cash their value doesn't compare to the early colonial manuscripts?"

Arenas shook his head. "It's true that the sixteenth and seventeenth century manuscripts are worth much more. Some *Yanqui* collectors and even some of their universities are not as scrupulous as they should be about how they acquire material."

"And how much would they pay, these unscrupulous *Gringos*?"

Arenas shrugged. "Who can say? It's not an open market transaction but in US dollars, tens of thousands, maybe more. To us of course they're priceless, irreplaceable."

Cruz nodded sympathetically. "One more thing Señor Arenas. It seems that the manuscripts have been taken piecemeal. Why not take the six in one go?"

"That wouldn't be so easy Inspector. Some of them are quite bulky and they're all easily damaged. It was probably easier to slip them out individually. Also it might have required some time for the thief to identify the more valuable items."

"Probably smuggled out one by one then." Cruz folded the list of names and slipped it into his notebook.

"So Inspector, I take it from your questions that Señorita Albañez is your chief suspect?"

Cruz shook his head. "I'm sure you'll appreciate that I can't tell you anything at the moment."

"And if she comes back to the library?"

"Contact me immediately on this number." Cruz slid his card across the desk. "And thank you señores. That's all" he paused, "For the moment" he added. His eyes were on Garcia and he saw the assistant's expression of relief vanish as quickly as it had appeared.

WEDNESDAY 6: GOLDEN GATE BAR

As Cruz walked back to his car his mind ran on the possibility, even probability, that Marta Albañez was responsible for the manuscript thefts. It was hard to visualise the terrified girl Cruz had encountered at her house as someone who could steal a valuable manuscript then come back several more times to repeat the crime. But perhaps that was the reason she had been so scared when he identified himself as a policeman. Maybe she had assumed that the thefts from the library were what had brought him to her house, that he had been after her not Coretta!

Her behaviour and the period during which she'd had access to the manuscripts both pointed to her as the thief but if so, what was her motive? Judging by the size of the Albañez residence, her father must be comfortably off. A carefully planned series of thefts carried out over several months didn't seem to fit the idea of a crime resulting from some sudden impulse. Still, Cruz reassured himself, he now had a suspect and a good reason for a trip to the seaside. Tomorrow he would have to report to Delgado. Then he could make for *Costa Azul* and a chat with Senorita Albañez. After that Cruz had a hunch that another interview with Señor Garcia, this time on his own, would be productive.

Before getting into his car, Cruz took a look at his watch. Nearly six-o'clock, time to return to headquarters, drop off the Chevy and pick up his Peugeot. He fumbled in his pocket for his keys. As he did so felt a gun muzzle jab into the small of his back.

"*Mierda*, not again!" he muttered. There was a difference: this time it was a man's voice giving him orders.

"Walk slowly to the car over there and keep your hands out of your pockets." Caiman's voice, El Chico's bodyguard-cum-enforcer.

Cruz tried to keep his voice, level, "What's the reason for the drama Caiman? If El Chico wanted to see me you only needed to make a phone call."

"We tried phone calls. You never seem to be available. The big man's impatient, he wants to know what you've got on the girl."

"So far there's not much I can tell him" Cruz stalled.

The gun jabbed into him again, harder this time. "Can't, or won't? Take some good advice and stop playing games with us *puerco*."

Another of El Chico's *gorillas*, one Cruz didn't recognise, got out of the passenger seat of a large Mercedes saloon then opened the rear door on the same side. He had a shaved head, a broad, pock-marked face and although he was no taller than Cruz, looked as if he weighed a hundred kilos, most of it muscle.

He gestured to Cruz to get into the car then squeezed himself in afterwards, wedging Cruz against the opposite door. Caiman climbed into the driver's seat, pressed a switch then turned round to look at Cruz.

"The back doors are deadlocked so don't think of trying anything. Just sit there nice and quiet until we get to where we're going."

"Which is?" enquired Cruz.

"You'll find out." Caiman turned on the ignition. "We'll be there soon enough."

Cruz hunched back in his seat and tried to think. He had a lot to think about. Could the big man have got wind that Cruz had found Coretta but kept quiet about it? If so how would he react? Would he risk killing a cop? Cruz knew that his demise would not cause too much grief among his superiors. There had been a couple of previous cases, a uniform and a detective, their mutilated bodies had been found on a waste tip at *El Rincon*. The ELR took the blame for those deaths. The revolutionaries made a convenient scapegoat but few people believed the ELR were the real culprits.

Cruz needed to have a story ready good enough to convince the big man he had been working hard to find Coretta but that he'd had no luck so far. Coming up with something convincing wouldn't be easy with the *gorilla* squashing him against the side of the car and breathing chilli all over him.

By now they had arrived in the city centre and Cruz realised they were heading for the Golden Gate. The Mercedes slowed but the frontage of the bar was already jammed with vehicles. Caiman swore and drove on until he spotted a space and pulled into the kerb. He tripped the deadlock switch and the *gorilla* next to Cruz opened the door and clambered out before bending down to give Cruz the hard stare. "This is it *Puerco.*"

For a second Cruz wondered about making a run for it. No good. Caiman was already standing by the car, his hand tucked inside his jacket in familiar bodyguard style. Cruz took a deep breath and pushed himself along the seat towards the kerb. "Curse of the two reds" was his last thought before a searing flash of light blinded him and the Mercedes seemed to leap into the air. His head smacked violently against the back of the driver's seat and his world went black.

When Cruz opened his eyes there was a loud ringing in his ears and a stink of burning rubber in his nostrils. Terrified that the car might catch fire, he scrambled out through a gaping hole where the nearside rear door had been. As he stumbled onto the pavement he saw the *gorilla* lying on the pavement. He wasn't going to get up again: a chunk of flying debris had taken off the top of his skull and spattered most of its contents onto the paving stones.

Cruz retched and grabbed the roof of the car to stop himself from fainting. He became aware of a warm wetness on his chest. Looking down he saw that his shirt was spattered with blood. His head was bleeding and so, he realised, was his hand. At least he could just about stand up and move his arms and legs. Slowly, keeping one hand on the roof to steady himself, he edged round to the offside of the car. Another body was lying prone alongside the bonnet. When Cruz bent down he saw Caiman's face looking up at him, the lips drawn back in a snarl revealing the teeth filed to points that had given him his nickname, "Alligator."

Cruz couldn't see any wounds on the prone body but standing in the roadway Caiman would have caught the full blast of the explosion. Cruz peered through the pall of dust and smoke at what was left of the Golden Gate. The lower floor of the building had been completely wrecked and outside the remains of several cars burned fiercely. He shuddered at the realisation that if Caiman had found a parking space directly outside the entrance to the Gate, all three of them would have been blown to pieces.

A wave of dizziness hit Cruz and he sat down on the bonnet of the Mercedes. Then he felt a tug on his arm and looked up. A young policeman, his uniform covered in dust and spattered with blood was saying something to him but the ringing in his ears had been replaced by a loud hissing that sounded like a badly tuned radio. The youngster pointed at Cruz's blood-stained clothing. "Where are you hurt?" he mouthed slowly.

Cruz shook his head "I'm OK" he muttered and stood up, then followed the uniform down the street towards the remains of the Golden Gate. His hearing was beginning to recover and he thought he could detect the wail of sirens somewhere in the distance. In a few minutes the street would be jammed with ambulances and police vehicles but at the moment it was empty except for burning cars, scattered lumps of debris and bodies.

The young policeman suddenly halted then dropped to his knees next to what looked like a bundle of old clothes lying in the middle of the road. The bundle was partly hidden by a boldly-striped fragment of the canopy that had covered the Golden Gate's front entrance. The policeman pulled the debris aside then dropped it.

"His legs –they've been blown off" he whispered. Cruz peered at the bundle which he now recognised as a body then started to laugh. The policeman stared at him as Cruz bent down and slapped the casualty's cheek lightly with his hand.

"Wake up Nesto! Wake up! Somebody bust your trolley!" He started to laugh again then a wave of nausea hit him and he was forced to sit down in the road. His ears had started ringing again, louder than ever. He clutched his head in both hands to try and stop the noise but it was no good. Quite slowly he toppled sideways onto the tarmac and lay there. His cheeks felt wet and he wiped a hand across his face then stared at his fingers. They were wet too but it was tears, not blood.

THURSDAY 1: *CASA CRUZ*

"You're a lucky man *compadre* to have such a good nurse looking after you." Cruz stared drowsily at Tomas who had pulled up a chair next to his bed. Cruz's daughter Laura stood on the other side of the bed holding a tray with a jug of lemonade and a glass.

Laura ignored Tomas. "You have to drink as much as you can. The doctor said so" she told Cruz sternly. "And no alcohol, just lemonade. He said that as well."

Laura filled the glass and carefully placed the jug on the bedside table.

"Mama says you mustn't talk for too long" she warned her father. "You need to rest." With that parting shot she left them.

Cruz looked quizzically at his friend. "Nine years old and she's turning into her mother. Against two of them I haven't got a chance, they harass me in stereo. Now tell me the latest."

Tomas sat uneasily on the edge of his chair. Despite their long friendship, he was not a frequent visitor to Cruz's home. Felicia was always formally polite but still managed to make Tomas aware that he did not belong to the class of person she preferred to entertain.

"We've had confirmation that it was a bomb. It was in the boot of one of the cars parked outside the bar. They've found bits of a timer."

Cruz nodded. "How many casualties?"

"Six people inside the bar: the big man, two of his heavies, two more guys we think were customers and one of the staff. All dead."

Cruz remembered the waitress with the generous cleavage and the pleasant smile. He hoped she hadn't been on duty. "And outside?"

"Five more dead, including Caiman, another guy somebody recognised as El Chico muscle and three passers-by. Plus a dozen injured, including you."

"Cuts and bruises that's all."

Tomas shook his head. "Shock can be dangerous they say *amigo*. You should take a few days off, make sure you're over it properly before you come back in."

"Take time off with Felicia and Laura looking after me? I'd be climbing the walls. And I've got things to do. Tell me, how's Nesto?"

"They took him into the Sacred Heart for observation. I saw him last night and he was having the time of his life giving grief to the nuns. Turned out he'd hardly a scratch on him; much like you. Another case of the devil looking after his own."

Cruz grinned "If you say so *amigo*." He took a drink of lemonade, made a face then leaned over to open his bedside cabinet and pulled a hip flask out of the drawer. "Want some? It's vodka, no smell!" Tomas shook his head and watched as his friend poured a good measure into his glass, took a gulp then settled back against his pillows. "Any ideas about who planted the bomb?"

Tomas leaned forward. "Maybe, but how about you tell me first what you were doing outside the Golden Gate? This morning a security guard at the university rang in to report a suspicious vehicle left overnight in their car park. Turns out it was your pool car so how did you get back into town? Not to mention that the Golden Gate isn't exactly on the route from the university back to headquarters."

Cruz blew out his cheeks then took another drink. "Does Delgado know? About the car I mean."

"I don't think so but you'd better have a good story ready in case."

"Thanks for the warning. OK, I'd better tell you what happened."

When he'd heard Cruz out, Tomas shook his head. "The devil really is taking care of you my friend. If that bomb hadn't gone off I guess we'd have found you on the tip at *El Rincon* this morning, minus your *cojones*."

"That's what I was expecting" Cruz admitted. "But here I am and it's the big man who ends up on the slab, or at least he will do if they can find enough of him."

"That's going to mean more work for us when the dust settles. The *barrios* are buzzing like somebody kicked over a wasps' nest."

Cruz nodded. Whoever took out El Chico had set the scene for a vicious turf war. "So back to my question, what's the word on who took out Mr Big?"

Tomas pointed at the portable radio sitting on Cruz's bedside table. "You didn't listen this morning?"

"No. My head's still aching from yesterday. What did I miss?"

"There was a call to *Radio Nacional*. The ELR claimed responsibility. They used a standard codeword and said they were taking over the police's failed war on drugs."

"You believe it?"

"It's in every news bulletin and newspaper headline this morning."

"It must be true then." Cruz's tone suggested the opposite.

"So who do you think did it?"

Cruz spread his hands. "Plenty of people wanted the big man dead. It just doesn't sound to me like an ELR operation. They've always been careful to minimise civilian casualties. Whoever set this thing off didn't give a damn. Maybe they should start looking closer to home."

Tomas raised his eyebrows. "You mean Hector?"

"Yes, I do mean Hector, he stands to inherit the whole operation so long as he can keep the south side boys out of his territory."

"That's a big if. So why don't you put them in the frame for the big bang?"

"I do. They're on the list, along with El Chico's Colombian suppliers. Those Colombians might have decided to take over the retail end of the operation."

"That doesn't sound very likely. They get the thick end of the profits already and it could cause them a lot of grief if their other customers got spooked."

"Agreed. But there's at least one other possibility. How about if the Black Helmets planned to open a new front in their War on Drugs?"

Tomas's mouth rounded into an "O" of astonishment. "You're saying the army exploded a bomb in the middle of its own country's capital city?"

"I'm saying it's possible. Call it a plausible theory. They have the explosives and the expertise **and** a motive, even two motives."

"Two motives?"

"Sure. Number one they disrupt the drug trafficking in *Independencia* plus most of the coastal belt and number two they have a new stick to beat the ELR with, especially effective on any ELR sympathisers who object to seeing innocent civilians blown to bits."

"You better be careful who you share this theory of yours with."

Cruz grinned. "For the time being you and only you *compadre,* but remember what Coretta told us about those guys Diaz and Araya meeting up with Hector? We still can't be sure if they were really on the take or whether they were just trying to fool Hector into thinking they were bent. Either way it suggests the Black Helmets had an interest in getting rid of El Chico. If you can find out anything more about the bomb, I'd be interested. If it was plastic then I'd make the army number one suspect. Up to now the ELR have only ever used dynamite they stole from the mines. And check if forensics got anything on the detonator they used. Remember last year, that transformer station they blew up at *Las Hierbas* and the railway bridge at *Rio Negro*? The ELR used *Yanqui* detonators."

Tomas leaned back in his chair and gave Cruz a long stare before replying. "This still isn't your case you know. So why are you so interested?"

"I seem to be involved whether I want to be or not. First El Chico sends for me and gives me a load of bullshit about Coretta, then she threatens me with a hole in the head, then Marta Albañez turns up in the middle of the missing manuscripts case and finally I only escape from getting spread over the walls of the Golden Gate because Caiman couldn't find a fucking parking space!"

Cruz's voice had risen loud enough to be heard downstairs, provoking a shriek of protest from Felicia. Tomas whispered "Very convincing, but I don't buy it. It's the girl isn't it? That's why you're still so interested. So what have you done with her?"

Cruz shook his head. "Erica took her in. I'm hoping she can stay there until things cool down a little." Cruz hesitated, "There is one thing you could do for me. Can you let Adriana know what's happened? She's flying back from Caracas today and with eleven people dead this thing will have made the headlines there as well. She'll have been worried."

Tomas rolled his eyes towards the ceiling and Cruz leaned forward and patted his old partner's hand. "Don't worry about me. It's tough enough keeping two women happy. Why should I make things worse with three?"

As soon as Tomas had gone, Felicia came upstairs to tell Cruz that she was leaving to drive Laura to school. She was wearing a trouser suit that did nothing to flatter her plump shape and Cruz couldn't help making unfavourable mental comparisons with the figure cut by Coretta in the same kind of outfit. It hadn't helped that Felicia's hair was arranged in a style that looked as if it had been copied from something she'd seen on a Hollywood TV series. She bent over Cruz and kissed him lightly on the top of his head.

"I'm going on afterwards to Julietta's coffee morning but I'll be back by lunchtime. It's Rosa's day off today so you'll be on your own. Remember you're supposed to be resting. I've brought you up the morning paper but don't tire your eyes too much. *Ciao amor.*"

She was gone in a flurry of scent leaving Cruz staring at the headlines in *La Prensa Andina*. "Terrorists Strike in Capital: Many Dead." The story that followed pinned the blame for the bomb securely on the ELR and the editorial on page two mournfully recorded a new and bloody chapter in the Marxist/Anarchist campaign to promote violent revolution and the overthrow of stable government as instituted by the selfless and patriotic leaders of the *Junta Nacional*.

"Very neat" muttered Cruz who found it harder than ever to believe that the attack on the Golden Gate was the work of Coretta's friends in the ELR. Anybody who might expose what had really been going on was a potential threat to some very ruthless people. Coretta was in greater danger than ever.

THURSDAY 2: COASTAL FREEWAY

    The sun setting behind the coastal mountains blazed in Cruz's rearview mirror, at the same time casting a hazy golden glow on the whitewashed houses and eucalyptus groves of the flat valley farmland traversed by the *Carretera Pacifica*.
    Cruz was returning from a wasted trip to *Costa Azul*. That morning, after skimming *La Prensa's* account of the explosion at the Golden Gate, he'd decided that he couldn't face the frustration of a day lounging at home when so many questions were buzzing around in his head. He climbed out of bed, dressed and wrote Felicia a note telling her he had been called out on an urgent case and would be back that night. Then he'd made a couple of quick phone calls, one to the *Rio Blanco* refuge to check Coretta was safe and one to Delgado to let him know that he was following up an important lead on the manuscripts case.
    Cruz had timed his call to the *Comisario* to coincide with the senior officers' morning briefing, knowing he would be put through to his boss's secretary. That way he could leave a message without having to answer any awkward questions. Delgado might even be impressed at Cruz's dedication in ignoring his doctor's advice and coming straight back to work.
    As things turned out, Cruz might as well have spent the day in bed. When he got to *Costa Azul* he quickly discovered that the address given to him by Marta before he put her on the mail train didn't exist. A visit to the town's police station and a search through the local telephone directory also produced a nil result. There was no sign that anyone by the name of Albañez owned or rented a property in the town and a trawl of shops and hotels during the two hottest hours of the afternoon proved equally futile. By the time Cruz, tired, thirsty and suffering from a return of the ringing noise in his right ear had drawn his final blank, it was after four o'clock and time to head home.
    When he finally reached headquarters he found the lift out of action and wearily plodded up the stairs to his office. On his desk he found a note from Delgado demanding to know the details of the new lead he had on the manuscripts case. Thankfully the

Comisario had already left so instead Cruz rang Tomas's extension. He got no reply there either but had better luck when he called Adolf Messner, the overworked, cantankerous but always thorough German immigrant in charge of the police forensics laboratory. The lab had a backlog of cases that could result in reports not being finished for weeks. After listening to Messner's usual litany of complaints about antiquated equipment, shortage of chemicals and idle assistants, Cruz promised a bottle of the best whisky he could lay his hands on in return for priority on the Golden Gate explosion.

"Just make sure it's genuine Scotch" said Messner in his nasal German accent before conceding that he might have the report ready for Cruz by the following Monday.

Counting that as a result, Cruz finally rang *Rio Blanco* to make sure Coretta was still safe. He spoke to Erica who told him everything was fine. "She's a big hit with kids, I'm thinking of offering her a job as resident storyteller."

Cruz didn't mention that he planned to drive out to the refuge the next day. If Marta was mixed up in the manuscripts thefts her best friend would surely know about it. He reckoned he would get more out of Coretta if his visit was a surprise.

When he'd finished the call, Cruz glanced up at the mirror on the wall behind his desk. He had hung it so that he could check who was coming though the door behind him without having to turn round. His reflection looked as weary as he felt. "Time to go home" the face in the mirror told him. For once he took some good advice and left.

THURSDAY 3: GATO NEGRO

"Laura and I hardly see you these days" Felicia complained. Cruz was slumped in his favourite chair, his coffee cup resting on his lap, the saucer doubling as an ash tray. "And when you do get home I can hardly get a word out of you."

Cruz admitted to himself that his wife was right. That was not the same as admitting it to her. "It's nothing new, it's the job, you've always known it."

Felicia dropped the glossy magazine she had been flicking through onto the coffee table in front of her. "Yes I've always known it but in the old days you would make an effort. Now it seems like you invent every excuse you can think of to work late. And tonight when you do get back at a reasonable time you're too tired to even try and look interested when Laura shows you her schoolwork."

"I'm sorry. I should have done what you told me and stayed in bed. It's just this case I need to crack. There's pressure from the high-ups."

"And when are these high-ups going to do something for us? Alicia Martinez told me that Carmen Vasquez's husband has just got promoted. Chief Inspector Vasquez now and he's five years younger than you!"

Cruz knew how to play that one. He glared at Felicia. "Thanks very much, you really know how to make a man feel good about himself." He stood up, strode into the hallway and shrugged on his coat, ignoring Felicia's suddenly contrite expression. "I'm going out" he announced and before she could say any more he was through the door.

When he got to the *Gato Negro* he tried ringing Tomas again but there was still no answer. He bought himself a beer and sat down at his usual corner table. At this early hour the place was more than half empty. The doors were open to the warm night air and a Brazilian samba playing quietly over the loudspeaker behind the bar added to the peaceful atmosphere. It wasn't to last. As Cruz took his first swallow of cold beer a familiar figure appeared in the doorway, paused to take a look around, then caught sight of Cruz and strode over to his table.

"Amalio! Guessed I'd find you here. How goes it?"

Cruz would have been interested to know how Daley had tracked him down and even more interested in why. Instead of asking, he signalled to the waitress, the same girl who had witnessed his falling out with Tomas and asked the American what he wanted to drink.

"A Coke would be fine. Well *amigo*, you've had an exciting week."

Cruz admitted that he had, adding that with luck, the following week would be more boring.

Daley grinned. "You don't fool me buddy. The way I hear it, a quiet life is not your style."

Cruz fingered the plaster on his temple, one of his souvenirs from the Golden Gate blast. "And what way do you hear it Señor Daley?"

"Hey, call me Brad or I'll think I've offended you. It's just gossip around the office. They say you're a guy who likes to get things done: I respect that." Daley saw Cruz fumbling in his pocket and whipped out a pack of his own cigarettes. He offered the pack to Cruz, took one himself and lit both their cigarettes with his Zippo. Then instead of putting the pack back into his pocket he placed it upright on the table so that Cruz could read the label.

"This is your brand, right? Like it says in the ads you're a Marlboro' man, a cowboy. Don't take orders too well, like to work on your own. That's what they say Amalio."

Cruz had never been sure what to make of Daley, who he suspected played up his big, brash, rather dumb, Uncle Sam stereotype. He guessed that somewhere behind the bluff facade was an altogether more serious player. Cruz raised his glass and stared over the rim at the big *Yanqui*.

"They say a few things about you as well Brad."

Daley took out a handkerchief and wiped the back of his neck. "It's sure sticky again tonight. Feels like summer in

Mississippi." He waved a hand and called for another Coke and a beer for Cruz.

"So" Daley smiled, when the waitress had brought the drinks and retreated behind the bar again. "What do they say about me?"

Cruz took a long drink of his beer. "Well, for a start they say that the FBI is only interested in what goes on inside the USA and doesn't station liaison staff abroad. The rumour is that you work for another organisation with different initials."

Daley laughed. "Let's call it a useful cover story. It suits your bosses and my people as well. The Agency has gotten itself a reputation for direct action that isn't always helpful. I try to keep a low profile."

"That must be difficult for somebody your size Brad. Now why don't you tell me what you want."

Daley stubbed out his cigarette and met Cruz's stare.

"Well for a start I'd like to know what you were doing outside the Golden Gate yesterday. I've seen the report by the patrolman who was first on the scene. He says you were in the back of a car that two of El Chico's heavies had just got out of when the bomb went off."

Cruz's face must have told Daley he'd hit the target. He poured the rest of his Coke into a glass and took a drink without taking his eyes off Cruz. "Like I said that was for starters. I'm also very interested in a phone call made the night before from a house belonging to a Señor Albañez. The caller used what we're pretty sure was an alias but she, it was a she, said she had "captured" her word, a *"puerco"* also her word, who claimed to be a police Inspector and what should she do with him? Could that have been you Amalio?"

"So you had a phone tap on this Albañez house?"

Daley spread his hands wide. "Of course not. We don't tap phones in countries with friendly governments but I was allowed to see transcripts from a surveillance operation by your military police."

"I didn't realise you were so close to the Black Helmets."

"Naturally we cooperate with the legitimate security forces of allied countries."

"Naturally. And what makes you so interested in phone calls from the Albañez residence?"

"Odd things seem to happen there. Like police inspectors being kidnapped. That was you wasn't it Amalio?"

"So if I was kidnapped what am I doing here?"

Daley tapped his fingers on the rim of the table and stared at Cruz.

"OK, let me just assume for my own amusement it was you. Delgado tells me you're working on thefts of manuscripts from the University library. Was that why you were calling on Senorita Albañez? I happen to know her father is away so I guess it was the young lady you went to see?"

"I'm sorry Brad, but as Delgado no doubt told you, the manuscripts case is very sensitive. I can't possibly discuss any details without prior authorisation from the *Comisario.*"

Daley grinned. "Then I may just need to talk to him. How about the Golden Gate then? What were you doing in a car with two of El Chico's hard men? Don't tell me you nearly got yourself killed looking for manuscripts!"

Cruz took a drink then shrugged. "You know how it is, in our line of work you can't pick and choose who you have to deal with to get information."

Daley raised his eyebrows. "And you were aiming to get a lead from the big man himself? I have to hand it to you, you go right to the top!"

"Isn't that the best way? But you still haven't told me why you're so interested in my enquiries. I thought the Agency's priority was breaking up what's left of the ELR?"

Daley offered another cigarette to Cruz and when the Inspector shook his head took one himself, lit it and blew a haze of smoke towards the ceiling.

"Sure the ELR is a high priority but our life isn't that simple Amalio. We do have other targets."

"Right. I heard that your people suddenly got interested in cocaine trafficking. Is that one of your new targets?"

"Amalio the US Government has been working to suppress the illegal drug trade for decades. Nothing new about that."

"But what is new in our little republic is the military police stamping their big boots all over the drugs scene. Word is the generals have been told that if they don't show some results Uncle Sam is going to strike them off his birthday present list and that's why the Black Helmets are suddenly so busy. There's even a whisper they were the ones who blew up the Golden Gate."

Daley let out a belly laugh so loud it almost startled the waitress passing their table into dropping her tray of drinks. The laugh sounded genuine.

"Now you are kidding me *amigo!*"

Cruz smiled. "Well you know how these stories circulate."

Daley threw a couple of coins onto the table and pushed back his chair. "Nice talking to you Amalio but I got to be going." He pulled out his wallet and produced a small card which he flicked across the table. Cruz picked it up: it was blank except for a telephone number. "That's my unofficial contact number-they'll get a message to me anytime, not just office hours. I have a feeling you may need to call me before long but even if you don't I'll be in touch."

THURSDAY 4: PISO MONTEZ

Cruz didn't feel like heading directly home. Instead he drove to Adriana's flat, using a roundabout route to get there. Maybe it was paranoid but he couldn't shake off the suspicion that Daley or one of his CIA goons might be tailing him. If so he didn't spot them and when he drew up outside the familiar block of apartments he was relieved to see a light shining from Adriana's window. He'd been a little hurt that his mistress hadn't tried to get in touch. She should have got back on the midday flight from Caracas but there had been no message from her when he called into headquarters that evening. Maybe she had phoned, Cruz consoled himself, but then some halfwit had forgotten to pass the message on. Then he remembered that he'd asked Tomas to ring her and let her know about the bomb blast. She would think he was still convalescing at home: that must be why she hadn't rung him.

The lift was, as usual, out of order and Cruz had to climb the stairs before pressing Adriana's doorbell. Nothing happened and after waiting a while he tried again. He could hear music playing inside, but it took a third ring before the door opened slightly to reveal half of Adriana's face. She didn't look as pleased to see him as he'd hoped.

"Amalio! I wondered whoever it could be at this time. I'm getting ready for bed."

Cruz glanced at his watch. It was barely ten o'clock. He'd arrived later than this often enough and received a warmer welcome. "Are you going to let me in?"

Adriana shook her head. "No, it's late and I'm tired. You must be too after what Tomas told me you've been through. Call me tomorrow and we'll arrange something."

Before Cruz could reply, the rhythmic meringue music playing inside the flat suddenly increased in volume. "Hey *Adrianita* let's dance." A man's voice, a little slurred.

Cruz shoved at the door but the security chain stopped it opening further. He stepped back and kicked hard, aiming his foot near the edge of the door panel, as high as he could reach. There was a splintering noise as the chain gave way and the door swung open. Adriana shrieked in protest as Cruz shoved past her into the lounge.

"Who the hell are you?" demanded the man sitting on the sofa. He was wearing a dressing gown and it appeared, very little underneath. The lighting in the room was dim but Cruz recognised the balding, slightly paunchy figure he had seen a couple of times before, Adriana's boss, Enrico Guzman.

"Me?" Cruz answered. "I'm just Señor Tuesday afternoon."

"Amalio!" Adriana was tugging at his arm. "It's not what you think." The nightdress she was wearing gaped to show her breasts.

"Save your breath, you might need it later when fatgut here gets to work on you."

Guzman stood up a little unsteadily "How dare you! Do you know who you're talking to?"

"Yes, you must be the Thursday night screw."

"Get out before I throw you out!" Guzman lurched towards Cruz who stepped to one side and hit him hard in the stomach. The punch carried all the force of Cruz's anger and humiliation. The lawyer made a gurgling noise that sounded like the noise of water draining from a bathtub, doubled over and collapsed retching onto the carpet.

"I don't think he's going to be much good to you tonight" Cruz observed to Adriana, prodding his rival with a toecap.

"You animal!" Adriana screamed and dropped to her knees to cradle Guzman's head on her lap. He was still moaning and suddenly vomited noisily over Adriana's nightdress. She glared up at Cruz.

"Go! Get out or I'll call the..." she stopped as she realised what she was about to say.

"That might be difficult." Cruz laughed. "But at least you've got legal advice ready to hand if Senor Guzman can stop puking long enough to give you some! Don't worry, I'm going and I won't see you around."

Cruz clattered down the stairs past a couple of older women, neighbours attracted by the noise. "Is everything all right?" enquired one nervously.

"Nothing to worry about" Cruz assured them. "Just some poor fellow with a stomach upset. Everything's fine now." The odd thing, Cruz decided, as he drove home was that he'd been right. He didn't quite understand why but now it was all over, everything **was** fine.

FRIDAY 1: POLICE HEADQUARTERS

The morning meeting with Delgado had gone better than Cruz expected. He'd explained to the *Comisario* that he now had a suspect who had specialist knowledge of the most valuable material in the library, the opportunity to smuggle out the prize manuscripts and had suddenly disappeared after he had first interviewed her. He didn't mention Coretta by name but told his boss that he had a possible lead through one of the suspect's friends that he needed to follow up.

Delgado nodded. "We need to wrap this up as soon as we can. General Duarte has expressed personal interest in the case. As I remember, your sergeant is still incapacitated?"

"Yes sir. Broken leg, he's likely to be off for another few weeks."

The *Comisario* frowned. "Bloody fool, playing soccer at his age."

"Yes sir, I agree. But I have a replacement in mind if you'll sanction it."

"Let me guess: Caldera? You're sure he's up to this kind of case? It's not likely to end in a bar room shoot-out. I thought that was more his style."

"Well it's true he's a crack shot sir but he's also a good detective and if it turns out some respectable academics are mixed up in all this he can keep his mouth shut afterwards."

Cruz saw that he'd struck a chord. Delgado was interested only in the right kind of publicity. If someone close to the Junta was linked to the thefts then it would be important to keep the media well out of it. The generals kept a tight control on radio and television but there were still a few press journalists and editors willing to tweak the regime's tail when they got the chance.

"Caldera's in Clausen's team isn't he? OK you can have him."

"Thank you sir." Cruz was looking forward to giving the good news to Inspector Clausen, a young thruster whose ambition to propel himself up the promotion ladder was evident from the way he acted as cheer leader for Delgado at every departmental meeting.

"Just make sure you get me a result Cruz" Delgado replied, reverting to type. "And this time I want to be kept informed about what you're up to!"

"Of course sir. What our friend Señor Daley calls "a need to know basis"" he said in English, confident that the *Comisario* wouldn't pick up on the nuances of the phrase. He was wrong, Delgado leaned forward and fixed him with his steeliest glare.

"If you value your pension, don't make any mistake Cruz. I need to know **everything** that happens in this case and know it before you drop yourself, or more importantly me, in the shit. Understand?"

Cruz understood.

FRIDAY 2: ASILO RIO BLANCA

Erica looked more worried than Cruz had ever seen her. "Oh God I hope Coretta is safe. She told me you'd sent the young man who came to pick her up. He didn't look much like a policeman, he had long hair and a week's growth of beard but he told me he'd been working on an undercover operation."

They were standing outside the chapel at *Rio Blanco* surrounded by the usual throng of urchins attracted by any visitor to the refuge. "What time did they leave?" Cruz asked. Despite the fresh mountain air he felt a cold sweat on his back.

"He must have driven here in the dark. He arrived just after six and they were gone in less than half an hour. It all happened so quickly. I should have been more suspicious but Coretta seemed to know the young man, she'd obviously met him before and was happy to go with him." She was twisting the wooden cross on her neck round and round on its chain. "I shall never forgive myself if anything bad has happened to her."

Cruz was puzzled but at least it didn't seem as if the man who'd turned up with no warning and driven Coretta away was one of Hector's heavies. He put a hand on Erica's shoulder. "Don't blame yourself. You're not a jailor, there was nothing you could do if she wanted to leave. It was her choice. Now what would help is if you can tell me a bit more about what the guy looked like and the vehicle he was driving."

As Cruz was jotting down the details he felt a tug on his jacket. He looked down and saw a grubby face looking up at him, a girl about the same age as Laura, wearing a ragged poncho. "Hey señor, I know something about the lady you came for."

Cruz squatted down to bring his face on a level with the girl's. "You know something eh? And what's your name?"

The girl wiped her hand across her nose. "I'm Graciela and I know something but you have to pay me first."

"Graciela, that's a nice name. OK Graciela, but how do I know what your information is worth before I hear it?"

The girl grinned. "You have to trust me señor."

"OK, I'll tell you what I'll do." Cruz fumbled in his pockets and pulled out a couple of coins. "Look, here's ten pesetas on account. You can have that now." Cruz slipped a small copper coin into her open palm then held up a larger silver one. "And here's a hundred if I think you've earned it when I've heard what you've got to tell me."

Graciela frowned for a moment, then nodded. "I'll say it quietly, so the others can't hear" and bending forwards towards Cruz she whispered "the lady asked where they were going and the man said to *Las Espinas*."

Cruz leaned back and stared hard at Graciela. "You sure about this?"

"Yes señor. They were getting into the man's car and they didn't see me, I was hiding round the other side."

"And they didn't spot you when they drove off?"

"No señor, they sat talking in the man's car for a while and I crept away before they noticed me."

Cruz raised his eyebrows. "And just why were you hiding next to the car I wonder? You weren't thinking of stealing something from inside it?"

Graciela stared back at Cruz innocently. "Oh no señor, I'm not a thief."

"Yes she is!" squealed one of the girls in the ring of children surrounding them. "She stole some biscuits from the store last week."

"Daughter of a whore" screamed Graciela and dashed towards her accuser who ran off to hide behind the chapel. Graciela started off in pursuit, then remembered what Cruz was holding in his hand and hurried back towards him. "Can I have my hundred pesetas now señor?"

Cruz flipped the coin at her and she caught it in mid air with a whoop of delight and ran off, followed by the rest of the children. Cruz strolled over to Erica. "She told me they were heading for *Las Espinas*. Did you hear Coretta mention *Las Espinas* while she was here?"

Erica shook her head. "Why-ever would Coretta want to go there?"

Cruz shrugged. "I don't know but it's outside the territory of the guy who's after her. Maybe that's why she or whoever was with her, chose it. That's if Graciela isn't making the story up. What do you think?"

"I can't be sure but I think she's telling you the truth. She's not a bad girl, just a bit light-fingered."

"Well she's all we've got to go on at the moment. I'll head back now, the sooner we can follow this up the better. I'll call you as soon as I have any news."

As Cruz drove off down the rough track he could see Erica in his mirror, still standing in front of the chapel, her hand on her breast, twisting her cross backwards and forwards on its chain.

FRIDAY 3: GATO NEGRO

"I'm glad to see you two gentlemen are friends again." The waitress placed two beers carefully on the table in front of Cruz who returned her smile a little sheepishly.

"Thanks, we'll try to keep the glasses in one piece this time."

Tomàs took a drink and accepted Cruz's offer of a cigarette. He leaned forward keeping his voice low. "Listen, I know you're worried about the girl but there's no use jumping into a car and driving off to the *barrio*. It's a hundred to one we'd see nothing and a lot shorter odds that we'd get ourselves killed."

"What do you know about who runs things in *Las Espinas*?"

"It's like an island that *barrio*. The South Side guys don't control it. The place is run by a gang called *Los Pajaritos,* the Little Birds. God knows how they came by that name but the gang leader is a guy called Rocky Jara. I know a friend of Rocky's and he owes me. I can make contact, maybe get us protection in the *barrio*. That's what we need if we're going to keep a whole skin."

Cruz knew Tomàs was right. Without protection their only option would be to shoot their way into and out of the gang's territory and that would require a couple of hundred armed cops.

"OK if we get a message to this Jara guy what will his cooperation cost?

"That depends. If it does turn out to be the ELR that's picked her up then maybe they have some kind of operation in the *barrio,* a safe house at least, perhaps something more. If they have then I guess they'll have done a deal with the *Pajaritos*. From what I hear Jara's no *politico*. Any agreement between him and the ELR is going to be strictly commercial."

"Well you'd better make a call to your man. Then I want to make another couple of visits." Tomàs went over to the payphone by the bar to call his contact. When he came back, Cruz was already standing by the door. As they strolled across to his vehicle Cruz reminded Tomàs that if anyone in authority asked, their enquiries related purely to the manuscripts case. "The line is we're looking for Coretta because she's our link to Marta and Marta is prime suspect for the document thefts."

"I get it. Hey what happened to your car?"

"I took her up to *Rio Blanco* this morning and bust the front suspension on that dirt track. I just managed to crawl back to headquarters."

Cruz was back behind the wheel of the Chevette he had driven when he took Coretta up to the womens' refuge. They climbed in and Cruz started the engine and slammed the car into gear. "Damn thing drives like a tank" he complained.

"At least the air conditioning works" Tomàs grinned, waving his arm out of the passenger side window which seemed to be permanently stuck in the down position.

Cruz headed in the direction of *Sector Norte*. "So where exactly are we going?" Tomàs asked. "To visit a millionaire?"

"Could be" Cruz replied. "The guy who owns the place is a bent lawyer so he's probably a millionaire as well."

FRIDAY 4: CASA GONZALEZ

After that Cruz clammed up again and Tomàs knew better than to press for more details. He didn't have long to wait: soon Cruz turned off the main road then made a couple of lefts and rights to arrive in a broad avenue with large detached dwellings set back on each side of the road. They looked like more modern and luxurious versions of the house where Marta Albañez lived.

Cruz stopped the car half way along the road, opposite a residence with a red-tiled roof and an imposing pillared portico shading the front windows. "According to Coretta, this is the place where the party was held the night she stabbed Hector. It's owned by a Senor Raul Gonzalez, a legal shark who did the kind of work for El Chico that didn't involve blood on the carpet."

"Do you think he'll talk to us?" queried Tomas.

"He's out of the country. Apparently he took his wife and kids on vacation to Rio a couple of days after the party. My guess is it was a last-minute booking."

"So the place is empty?"

"Except for the servants. I talked to the uniform who works this patch. He told me Gonzalez has a couple of servants to look after the house, a husband and wife, plus a maid to do the fetching and carrying."

Tomas shook his head. "We're in the wrong job."

Cruz shrugged. "No my friend, we're in the right job, it's what they pay us that's wrong."

"So why are we here apart from admiring Senor Gonzalez's mansion?"

"I want to see how Coretta's story checks. So far we've got two stories, hers and El Chico's. Maybe one of the servants saw what happened, so let's talk to them."

As they walked up the gravelled drive Cruz pointed to a patio area running along the near side of the house. The edge of the paved area was dotted with mature shrubs separating the patio from the lawn and flower beds beyond. A garden table and set of chairs completed the scene. "That looks like the place where Hector and the others were sitting out."

Tomàs nodded. "And those shrubs are where Coretta said she was hiding."

Cruz rang the bell, a fancy two-tone affair. After a few moments they heard the sound of bolts being drawn back .

The door opened. "Sorry to keep you gentleman waiting." The man at the threshold was forty-something, lean-faced and wearing a short black jacket. He looked as if he, or his employer, had copied his outfit from a butler in an old-fashioned movie. The man's welcoming smile faded when Cruz showed his ID.

"You'll know what this is about" Cruz shouldered past him into the hallway. "The stabbing here last weekend. What's your name?"

"Reyes, Alberto Reyes."

"Well Señor Reyes, I need to interview you, your wife and the maid."

Reyes eyed Cruz warily. "But Inspector, this has been done already. The Military Police handled the case."

"Correction, they **were** handling it. Now I am. Are your wife and the maid both here?"

"They're upstairs Inspector, cleaning the bedrooms but Senor Gonzalez and his family are away, I'd like to call him before we answer any questions."

"I'm sure you would but you're not going to. Tomas, bring the two ladies downstairs. Now Señor Reyes, take me through to the kitchen."

The kitchen proved to be twice as big as the one in Cruz's house. At the far end and contrasting markedly with the gleaming modern appliances elsewhere, stood a big, old-fashioned, plank-topped table at which Cruz presumed the servants ate their meals. The kitchen itself occupied the rear corner of the house, one window facing the garden at the back of the property, the other looking out onto the patio area at the side.

Cruz got little out of Reyes or his wife. Reyes told him he had been on the front door all night greeting guests and keeping an eye out for gatecrashers. Maria Reyes, who was very obviously pregnant, had been serving drinks at a temporary bar set up at the far end of the main lounge from the kitchen but had felt tired and had gone to bed early. Both claimed to have seen nothing of what went on either outside on the patio or in the kitchen afterwards. The maid Carla, they told Cruz, had also been busy at the bar.

When Tomàs brought Carla through into the kitchen, Cruz, who was sitting at the big kitchen table gave a brief shake of the head to let his colleague know that neither Reyes nor his wife had given him anything useful.

Carla was short and thickset with the broad, almost mahogany-coloured face of a *mestiza* country girl. Cruz could see she was scared. "Please sit down and don't be frightened" he began in his good cop voice. "I just need you to tell me exactly what you saw the night Señor Torres was stabbed."

The girl nodded. She perched on the end of her chair her hands clasped in her lap. "So" Cruz continued, "what were you doing when the party started?"

"I was helping Señora Reyes set up the bar in the lounge, we used this kitchen table. It took four of us to carry it through."

"Four of you?"

"Yes sir, Señor Gonzalez helped. Señora Reyes has to be careful in her condition. The Señora gave me two tablecloths and together they were just big enough to cover the table. Then I helped set out the bottles and glasses and some trays of savouries and *dulces*."

"And then what?"

"By the time we'd finished setting out everything the first guests were arriving so I had to serve the drinks. Señora Reyes was meant to help me but she said she felt very tired and she went upstairs to lie down"

"Did you take the drinks round on a tray or just serve people at the bar?"

"At first I carried a tray around the room, then when it got crowded and people started to dance they had to come to the bar."

"You must have been busy with all those people. Did you come back into the kitchen for any reason?"

Carla dropped her eyes, Cruz could see her hands clenching tight.

"Maybe you ran out of glasses or ice?" Cruz persisted.

Carla shook her head in reply. Cruz decided to drop the good cop tone and try a bluff. "Listen" he rasped "You'd better understand this. I already have a statement from one of the guests who saw you leave the bar and carry a tray of dirty glasses towards the kitchen. And that was just before Señor Torres got knifed. If you don't tell us exactly what you saw I'm going to arrest you as an accessory to attempted murder!"

Carla's body began to shake and tears rolled down her cheeks. "It's not true!" she blurted. "I wasn't carrying any glasses sir. Whoever said I was, they were lying."

"But you did go back to the kitchen? Another witness has told us that the girl who stabbed Señor Torres picked up a knife someone had been using to cut bread. That someone was you wasn't it? Come on! Do you want me to arrest you? Do you want to spend tonight in a police cell? I warn you it's not a pleasant place for a nice girl like you."

Carla sobbed louder than ever. "Look" Cruz softened his tone. "I don't want to turn you into a criminal but if you won't talk to me I'll have no choice."

The girl wriggled and twisted as if she was struggling to break free from invisible ropes tying her to the chair. "Señor I'm scared if I talk to you I'll lose my job. I have two children, my mother looks after them. What will happen to us without my *salario*?"

"It'll be even worse for them if you go to gaol Carla. Just tell me what you know and nothing bad will happen to you."

Carla wiped her eyes with the back of her hand. "Señor Reyes was on the door then he came over to me and told me he was feeling hungry. With all the rushing around to get everything ready neither of us had had a chance to eat. He said he would look after the bar while I went to the kitchen and got something for us. That's when I saw the girl."

"Was this her?" Cruz slipped Coretta's photo from his wallet and showed it to Carla.

"Yes sir." She whispered. "That's the girl I saw."

"You saw her dancing earlier?"

Carla shook her head. "No sir. She was out there." Carla pointed to the window overlooking the patio.

"You mean she was in the garden?"

"Yes sir, she was sitting on the patio."

Cruz jumped up and stared out of the window. "You mean she was sitting there at that table?"

"Yes sir, with Senor Torres and two other men. I was standing at the worktop just where you are now. I was slicing bread and that's when I saw her."

"What were they doing?"

"Doing sir? Like I said they were sitting at the table."

Cruz came back to the table and sat down again, next to Carla. He felt like shouting at the girl but knew that wouldn't help. "Now Carla, this is very important. I mean what exactly were they doing? Were they drinking, or laughing and joking or what?"

"No sir, they were just talking. They all had their heads together like this." The girl leaned towards Cruz until her broad nose was almost touching his cheek. "They didn't seem like they were at a party at all."

"How do you mean Carla?"

"I mean they looked very serious sir. And the two men I didn't know, they weren't in uniform but still they looked like policemen, or soldiers, maybe. Anyway I finished slicing the bread and some tomatoes then I went over to the fridge. I knew we had some *chorizo* in there, it was already sliced up from the day before. I put it on two plates with the bread and tomatoes then put them on a tray and I was carrying it down the corridor to the lounge when the young lady pushed past me and ran into the kitchen. She nearly knocked the tray out of my hands and one of the plates fell on the floor."

"So what happened next?"

"Well sir, I got down on my knees to clean up the mess and that's when Señor Torres came running down the corridor. He nearly knocked me flat but I just managed to get out of his way."

Cruz put a hand on the girl's shoulder. "That's good Carla, you're doing very well so far. Now, can you remember what happened next?"

Cruz's reversion to good cop produced a few more tears. "Sir it all happened so fast. The girl screamed, then I heard Señor Torres give a yell and the girl came running past me out of the kitchen. She had my kitchen knife in her hand and she shoved me out of the way. I saw I had blood on my apron, from her hand where she pushed me."

"And where did she go after that?

"I don't know sir, I think she must have run out the front door. She dropped the knife in the corridor and it was all bloody and I was screaming and people pushed past me into the kitchen and they were yelling and shouting too and soon after that the police came, the other police sir, the Black Helmets and they took Señor Torres away."

"Did they question you?" "

"No sir, Señor Gonzalez, he told me to go and change my apron and not to tell the police anything or I might be in big trouble if they thought I had something to do with what happened to Señor Torres."

Carla's face crumpled and her shoulders started to shake again. "And now I have told you" she wailed.

FRIDAY 5: CASA ALBAÑEZ

Cruz rummaged around on the parcel shelf "These *maldito* pool cars! Nobody ever cleans them out!" At last he located his pack of Marlboro' and passed it to his partner. "Light me one will you."

Tomàs lit a cigarette and gave it to Cruz before extracting a cheroot from his own top pocket. Cruz wound down his window as Tomàs lit the cheroot and blew out a cloud of blue smoke.

"What do they put in those things, cabbage leaves?"

"Calm yourself boss. This is prime Colombian leaf, better for you than those little *Yanqui* sticks you choke yourself with."

Cruz shook his head. "Prime Colombian! That's something you sniff not smoke *amigo*!"

Tomàs grinned. "How about we change the subject. Where next?"

"To the Albañez place. I couldn't find any trace of Marta in *Costa Azul*. If she did go there she might have come straight back. If she didn't, there's a chance her father's home by now. Maybe he can tell us who persuaded his little girl to steal those manuscripts. I can't believe it was her own idea."

"And if nobody's there?"

"Well if the place is empty we can just have a damn good root around. Who knows what we'll turn up?"

Cruz pulled up the Chevette in the same place he'd parked last time, a few metres past the entrance gate to the driveway. There was little to see from the outside. The drive was empty, the front door firmly closed and the downstairs blinds were drawn.

"Somebody's been here since Tuesday night." Cruz observed. "Marta's car has gone. It was parked outside when we left. You know your way round the back so I'll take the front door. If nobody answers I'll come round to you and we'll break a window."

Tomas hurried round the side of the house and Cruz strolled up to the front door. He checked the door was locked then pressed hard on the bell and for good measure gave the heavy iron door knocker three loud raps. There was no response so he rang and knocked again with the same result. "Three for luck" he muttered to himself and tried once more. The place remained quiet as a tomb.

Cruz shrugged then walked around the side of the house until he caught sight of his partner under a shallow veranda at the rear. "This is where I got in last time" said Tomàs pointing to a half-glazed door. When he tried the handle, it turned and the door swung open. Cruz pulled out his revolver and stepped inside, Tomàs following. He advanced down a narrow corridor leading to a spacious if rather old-fashioned kitchen. A plate and knife lay on the table and a mug stood alongside them. Cruz picked up the mug: it contained something resembling penicillin floating on the remains of what once might have been coffee.

"Looks like these have been here a while" he whispered to Tomàs and led the way down another corridor which brought them to the hallway Cruz remembered from his last visit to the house. On their left was the lounge where Coretta had jumped him. The door was half open and when he cautiously pushed it further he saw that the room was as empty as the kitchen. Cruz pointed to the ceiling with his gun and headed for the wide staircase which led up from the hallway.

Halfway up the stairs, Cruz felt a tug on his arm from Tomàs. Cruz turned and saw Tomàs sniff, then wrinkle his nose. Almost at the same time Cruz caught the smell and knew what they were going to find.

The first body was sprawled on the landing, a young man in his early twenties with shoulder length hair, wearing jeans, a windcheater and trainers. He wore round, wire framed glasses, one lens of which had been smashed by the bullet that had gone through his eye. Another shot had been responsible for the red stain that had seeped through the front of his jacket. Cruz folded a handkerchief over his nose then bent down to get a closer look. "Shot from close range, probably a two-two." He placed a hand on the corpse's shoulder, then under its armpit. The corpse was cold but the limbs had lost most of the rigidity of rigor mortis. "My guess is the boy's been dead at least a couple of days."

He felt for the inside pocket of the windcheater and pulled out a bloodstained wallet. The contents seemed to be intact. He extracted an identity card from the wallet. "Alejandro Pujol" he read aloud. "Residence given as here in the capital."

Tomàs nodded. "Wasn't Alejandro the name of Marta's boyfriend?"

"It was" Cruz agreed. "So did he come here to pick up something or to meet up with her?"

They found the answer to Cruz's question in the bathroom. Marta Albañez was lying on the floor, her head almost hidden under the handbasin. She was naked from the waist up and her hair looked as if it had been soaked and had then dried in unruly spikes. There was a small bullet wound at the base of her skull with a halo of soot marking around the wound. "Looks like she had her head shoved in the basin before she was shot" said Tomàs. "Trying to get her to talk I guess."

Cruz nodded. He was used to dead bodies but this was different from the usual gang murder or random domestic killing. He took a deep breath and tried not to imagine the girl's last moments. He couldn't believe that Marta would have held out very long. He remembered her frightened eyes and the terror she had about guns. He hoped she'd told her killer what he wanted to know quickly. He knelt down beside the girl. The body was as cold as Alejandro's and Cruz was able to bend the elbow with little effort. "Killed about the same time, probably the same gun."

Marta's bedroom was easy enough to identify from the pink colour scheme and the fluffy animals sitting on the bed. Stuffed between the bed and the bedside cabinet was a handbag. Inside it, among a jumble of cosmetics, handkerchiefs, combs and pens, Cruz found Marta's ID card and a notecase containing five thousand pesetas and nearly three hundred U.S. dollars.

"They weren't interested in this then" said Tomas. "Looks like a professional job."

Cruz nodded agreement. "I'll go along with that. I'm betting this was down to Hector or even El Chico. These two could have been killed before the Golden Gate bomb."

Tomas nodded. "They wanted to know where Coretta was?"

"That's my guess. And Marta didn't know. She only knew I was trying to find somewhere safe for Coretta to stay the night."

"Which is why El Chico had you picked up on Wednesday night."

Cruz picked up a photograph from the dressing table. It showed Marta and Alejandro smiling at the camera. "I should be grateful to whoever planted that bomb."

Tomas walked across to stare at the photo. "So you put her on a train to Costa Azul on Tuesday night to hide out there until the heat was off then she comes back here, probably on Wednesday and gets herself shot. Why?"

Cruz carefully replaced the photo on the dressing table. "I'm guessing, but maybe Alejandro turned up here looking for Marta. El Chico's guys were watching the place and grabbed him. They made him call her and ask her to come back here. Whatever story Alejandro told her she must have believed him and that was that. She walked straight into a trap."

The smell from the corridor had permeated the bedroom and Cruz was desperate for some fresh air. "OK, it's time to call this in. And somebody will need to try and reach Marta's father. We'll just have to hope he's in radio contact with civilisation. You'd better start knocking doors. Somebody might just have seen something."

"Sure boss." Tomas paused on his way to the door. "You need to be careful. El Chico may be history but you're unfinished business for Hector."

Cruz shrugged. There was something else on his mind: the stolen manuscripts. Could it be that Marta's murder was somehow linked to that other piece of unfinished business?

Delgado was not best pleased to get Cruz's call on his home phone and on a Friday night. "I have guests" was his response to the Inspector's initial greeting "This had better be important." His tone changed when Cruz told him about the murders. "Doctor Albañez's daughter? And he's away you say? You've arranged for a forensic examination of the house? Good. Make sure they know I'll be taking a personal interest in this. And another thing, I want this kept out of the press, at least until we're sure why the girl was killed. You'd better come over here tomorrow morning and brief me on what you've got. Now I have to get back to my guests. Eight o'clock sharp, in my office."

"Yes sir" replied Cruz. "Hope you have a hangover" he added, after the line had gone dead.

SATURDAY 1: POLICE HEADQUARTERS

Instead it was Cruz whose head was throbbing when he reached the *Comisario's* office nearly ten minutes late. Not that he deserved to be suffering, at least in his own estimation. The previous night he had been a model of marital fidelity. Other members of the *Policia Nacional* Central Detective Squad had followed the usual Friday night routine, working their way round the less respectable city centre bars before ending up in a strip club and for those still capable, the not-so-exclusive hotel on *Libertad* whose girls made a speciality of satisfying the needs of the plainclothes unit.

Not Cruz; he'd spent the evening at home, first seeing Laura to bed and then sharing a bottle of wine and most of a bottle of *pisco* with Felicia. Cruz had decided it was time to make a fresh effort on the domestic front and when, after he had achieved a slightly unsteady ascent of the stairs, Felicia had appeared in the door of their bedroom wearing the low-cut silk nightdress that he'd always liked, it felt very much the right decision.

Cruz didn't recollect too much detail after that. The shock had come this morning when the bedside alarm hit him like someone prodding at his inner ear with a needle.

"So, what's your next move?" queried Delgado after listening to Cruz's account of what he had found at the Albañez house.

"Sir I have a lead on Marta Albañez's best friend, a Coretta Sanchez-Mendoza. She's linked to the ELR and we've had a whisper she could be hiding out in a safe house in *Las Espinas*. I've got a feeling that she can tell us a lot about why Marta Albañez was killed and whether her murder was linked to the stolen manuscripts."

"*Las Espinas?* That's a tough nut. If we go in there, it'll mean a big operation, I'll need sanction from the General."

"Sir, I think Caldera and I can get in there without making waves. He has a contact in the *barrio* who can arrange things."

"Arrange things? I don't like making deals with gangs."

"Not precisely a deal sir" said Cruz, while thinking that was exactly what it was.

"What you haven't explained to me yet is why a simple case of document theft ends up with the murder of a girl from one of the most respectable families in *Independencia*. Doctor Albañez is a distinguished archaeologist, a very eminent member of the faculty. His wife came from a well-known family in the south, they own one of the biggest *estancias* in *Austral* province and her father was a senator back in the fifties. What can their daughter possibly have to do with some low-life stealing manuscripts to sell on the black market?"

Cruz might have pointed out that none of the people with access to the historic manuscripts section of the university library could be accurately described as low life but he didn't want to start a discussion, he wanted to get out of Delgado's office without being forbidden to enter *Las Espinas*. After that he could buy himself a cup of black coffee and get together with Tomàs.

Half an hour later he'd ticked off two of his three priorities. Tomàs was the unfinished business. He hadn't answered his phone either in the squad room or at home and nobody at headquarters admitted to having seen him. Cruz had left his usual cryptic note on his colleague's desk then made for the *Gato Negro*. He'd just started on his second cup of coffee and was feeling a little more like a functioning member of the human race when Tomàs showed up, sat down opposite Cruz and called to the waitress to bring him an expresso.

"We're on boss. My contact has talked to Rocky Jara. Rocky says maybe he can help but he wants to see us first. I told my man I'd get back to him."

"So Señor Jara might be able to assist the *Policia Nacional*. That's very public-spirited of him. In exchange for what?"

"We'll find out when we talk to him."

"Your contact. Does he have a name?"

"He's called Luis. That's the only name I have. He's usually reliable."

"And Rocky Jara, he knows Luis is an informant?"

"Not so much an informant boss. More a communication channel."

"In the old days that was a job for a priest. You remember old Father Robles?"

"Sure but that wouldn't work with Rocky Jara, he's a Protestant."

"An *Evangelico!*" Cruz guffawed. "Running a *barrio* gang like the Little Birds? Holy Jesus, now I've heard everything!"

Tomàs grinned. "Don't let Rocky hear you swear. He doesn't like bad language."

"I see, he just likes pushing drugs and bumping off anyone who thinks *Las Espinas* isn't his personal territory. And anyway what's with this "Rocky" thing?"

Tomàs drained his coffee and pushed back his chair. "He's a fan of those *Yanqui* films, you know, that fighter Rocky, comes from nowhere, ends up champion of the world. You can see the appeal for a guy from the *barrio*. Anyway it's time we move. Luis doesn't like to wait too long. He's always a little edgy. He thinks hanging around in one place makes him too much of a target."

Cruz stood up. "Sounds like your friend Luis has a few enemies."

Tomàs tossed a note onto the table. "In the *barrio,* everyone has enemies."

SATURDAY 2: BARRIO LAS ESPINAS

On the way they made a detour to Tomàs's apartment to change their clothes. "If we're going to move around in *Las Espinas* we need to blend in." He told Cruz. "You don't see too many suits and panama hats in that place."

As he spoke, Tomàs was stripping off his jacket and trousers and replacing them with a pair of frayed jeans, a faded T-shirt and a battered black leather jacket. He hadn't forgotten Cruz who was handed a pair of surfer-style shorts, a stained T-shirt bearing the slogan "Washington Redskins," a studded denim top with the sleeves cut off and a pair of dirty looking trainers. "Sorry about the shorts boss" apologised Tomàs, seeing the look on Cruz's face. "I didn't have time to get my hands on a pair of trousers your size."

Cruz shook his head. "I am **not** going to *Las Espinas* or anywhere else wearing those damn things. I'll rub some dirt into the knees of these trousers and they'll pass for *barrio* fashion."

Tomàs looked doubtful but when his colleague came back from the yard, he conceded that Cruz looked suitably grubby. "Pity you shaved this morning boss" he added, rubbing his own stubble. "Smooth cheeks aren't too plentiful where we're going." Cruz, whose hands were still grimy, massaged his face with his dirty fingers then went through into Tomàs's tiny kitchen and glanced at the mirror hanging above the sink. "Shit, I look ugly enough to scare myself."

"You'll do boss" Tomàs agreed. "Just remember, no swearing when we meet Rocky!"

Visitors to *Las Espinas* didn't arrive in the *barrio* by car if they wanted to stay unobtrusive. Cruz couldn't remember the last time he'd travelled on a *micro*. He and Tomàs were sharing standing room in the gangway with a densely packed scrum of other passengers. Every time the driver stood on the brakes, the fat woman behind Cruz who was carrying a heavily-loaded plastic bag in each hand, used him as a crash barrier, then glared at him as if he'd tried to interfere with her.

Cruz clung desperately to the length of nylon rope which stood in for a hanging strap and silently prayed for the journey to end. He was trying to see through the dirt-encrusted window opposite him to check how far they'd come, when he felt himself jabbed in the ribs.

"Hey, you in dreamland? Twenty pesetas, or forty if you're paying for your *amigo* as well." Before Cruz could fumble in his pocket, Tomàs handed over a couple of coins to the boy collecting fares. He stowed them in the leather bag strapped to his waist before shoving past Cruz towards the rear of the bus.

"Nearly there boss" said Tomàs. "I can see the turn-around ahead." Pushed, trodden on and barged into a dozen times, Cruz felt like he'd been in a bar room brawl. He heaved a sigh of relief as peering over the shoulders of the passengers in front of him, he caught sight of the turn-around marking the end of the road. Beyond that he could make out the jumble of shacks and alleyways that comprised *Las Espinas*.

The *micro* driver, who throughout the trip had alternated between flattening the accelerator and then the brake pedal against the floor, careered up to the turn-around then jammed on the brakes. The fat woman slammed into Cruz one more time and at last he was able to stagger after Tomàs towards the exit. As he reached the opening, from which the door had been removed as an un-necessary inconvenience, Cruz put out a hand to touch the gaudily-coloured *San Cristofero* mascot swinging from the rear view mirror.

"You work that guy pretty hard" he remarked to the driver who glanced at him and raised a finger. "Your mother, *Puerco*" was all he said before pulling a newspaper out of his pocket and starting in on the racing results. Cruz grabbed the driver's shirt collar and yanked him backwards.

"Not here, boss!" Tomàs pulled his friend off the bus and Cruz followed him down an alleyway between two rows of huts constructed from a mixture of corrugated iron and plastic sheeting.

He could only hope that the natives of *Las Espinas* wouldn't be as quick at penetrating his disguise as the bus driver.

Fortunately the alley was so crowded nobody had time or space to look too closely at Cruz or Tomàs. It had rained during the night, reducing the dirt track between the shacks to ankle deep mud and Cruz struggled to keep his feet as he followed Tomàs past a succession of stalls selling empanadas, hot dogs and other less identifiable delicacies. As he plodded through the mire, sniffing the bewildering mixture of cooking smells mingled with the ever-present stink of rotting garbage and open sewers, Cruz was transported back to his days as a young cop working the *barrios*. That was before the drug gangs had become the only law in places like *Las Espinas*.

At the end of the row of stalls, Tomàs halted at an intersection. The alley they were following climbed steeply up the almost precipitous hillside ahead, another ran at right angles parallel to the foot of the slope. Where the two alleys crossed was a small piece of ground in the middle of which stood a rusting electricity pylon.

Cruz stared up at the pylon, a monument to the ambitions of the civilian government overthrown by the current military regime. *Las Espinas* had been chosen as the first *barrio* to receive the blessing of electricity but the scheme had got only as far as erecting a line of pylons. Phase Two of the project, installing the power cables, never happened. The funding had run out, or more likely had been diverted into the pockets of the officials and contractors responsible for completing the work. Pylons located where they were easily accessible by vehicle had been speedily dismantled by thieves and sold for scrap but the one in front of Tomàs and Cruz had somehow survived. It now served as a convenient and unmistakable meeting point in the *barrio*'s maze of alleys and passageways.

"There's Luis" muttered Tomàs as a hunched figure with a pock-marked face and unkempt shoulder-length hair, emerged from a side alley to their right and strolled towards them. Luis stopped to light a dimp produced from behind his ear then nodded to Tomàs before turning onto the steep track up the hillside. Tomàs followed him, Cruz at his heels and they saw Luis disappear into a hut. Tomàs pushed aside the plastic sheet that stood in for a door and the two men entered the shack.

When their eyes had adjusted to the gloomy interior, they saw Luis sitting at a table constructed out of rough planks resting on a couple of packing cases. A large woman wearing an outsize T-shirt she'd pulled up to enable a baby to get at her ample breast, was half-lying, half-sitting in a hammock slung between two of the shack's roof beams.

"Hey woman!" called Luis, "Fetch us a drink."

"Get 'em yourself" was the response. "Can't you see I'm busy you lazy bastard!"

Muttering under his breath, Luis got to his feet and disappeared behind a plaited straw mat which curtained off the rear of the hut. He emerged a moment later and inviting his visitors to sit down, he placed a bottle and three tin mugs onto the table and poured three generous measures. Cruz picked up his mug and sniffed.

"Hey, don't worry, that's good stuff" said Luis. "You only go blind if you drink the whole bottle!" He laughed and put out his hand to take the cigarette Cruz offered. Cruz was hoping that the liquor was powerful enough to disinfect his mug. He took a cautious sip of his drink and felt the fiery liquid sandpapering his throat. Luis chuckled at the expression on Cruz's face.

"Takes a little getting used to eh? But it does the trick!"

"Not for you it doesn't!" There was a sudden howl and Cruz turned round to see the woman in the hammock ease her complaining infant off one nipple before she offered the other and peace was restored. Settling down again she nodded towards Luis. "Half a bottle of that stuff and he's good for nothing. I should know!"

Her partner rolled his eyes at Cruz and took another swig of firewater. Cruz nodded to Tomàs who dropped his cigarette onto the dirt floor and scrunched it under his foot. "Business, Luis" he said. "Did you arrange things with Rocky?"

"Sure. He'll see you at his house. It's not far from here but it's a climb."

"Up on the hill top, right?" queried Tomàs.

"Right, Rocky don't like anybody overlooking him. He's the king of *Las Espinas*."

"When do we get to see him?" Cruz interjected.

"He said midday. Either of you gentlemen got a watch?"

"See, he has to ask you the time!" It was the woman again. "The dumb prick lost his watch in a dice game last night."

Tomàs checked his wrist. "Nearly eleven-thirty. We should be moving."

The woman levered herself up in the hammock, provoking another squawk of protest from her child. "You guys greasing Luis for taking you to see Rocky?" Her eyes flicked from Cruz to Tomàs. "Sure you are. Give me the money. If he gets his hands on it I won't see a penny. C'mon, hand it over."

Cruz glanced at Luis, who gave a defeated shrug. He passed a ten dollar bill to the woman.

"Thanks Señor and make sure he comes back in one piece. He's not much but he's all me and the baby have got."

The climb up the hillside soon left Cruz wheezing for breath. The slope was so steep that the houses on either side of the track looked as if they were built on top of one another. In contrast to the crowded alleys down below, there were many fewer people about. Cruz guessed that nobody tackled this ascent unless they had to.

Tomàs appeared unaffected by the climb, "He must keep himself in better shape than I do" Cruz said to himself enviously. Luis, although carrying less weight than Cruz, was finding the ascent even more of a struggle. Three-quarters of the way up the hill, he halted "I got to take a rest."

"Yeah" said Tomàs "You should take a rest from bad liquor and too much dope."

Luis grinned. "You want to take away two of my three pleasures in life." Cruz didn't bother asking him what the third was, he could guess. In any case he was too busy staring at the view. The whole of *Las Espinas* was spread out below them. It looked like an anthill somebody had kicked over and then trodden on, except that this anthill was a couple of kilometres wide and almost as deep.

Cruz wondered how many thousands, no tens of thousands, were crammed into the crazy jumble of shacks and shelters clambering up the slope towards them? When he'd been a young patrolman the police had kept order of a kind in the slum districts of *Independencia*, a crude and brutal order maybe but over the last twenty years the *barrios* had exploded in size and population and the biggest had long passed out of even the roughest rule of any law except street justice. Cruz felt a sudden surge of despair that a place like *Las Espinas* could ever be rescued from the tentacles of poverty, disease and crime. And who even cared? Certainly not the junta or its comfortable middle class supporters who would no sooner dream of visiting *Las Espinas* that they would book themselves a day trip to Hell's gate.

Tomàs, called Cruz back to the business in hand. "Better get going boss." A little way further up the track, Luis branched off to their right along a narrow path running across the slope. Just above them a low rocky escarpment marked the crown of the hill and ahead Cruz saw yet another ramshackle construction of rough timber and rusty corrugated iron. Bigger than its neighbours, it was dug into the hillside so that it had two storeys at the front and only one at the rear. A wooden veranda at first floor level gave a view out across the *barrio* below.

The path Luis was following led to a wooden gate topped with razor wire. The gate was unguarded and there was no other sign of life inside the fence. Luis reached for a rope hanging down by the side of the gate and pulled vigorously. The rope was attached to a brass bell suspended from a pole which gave a loud clang at each pull.

"Come on in. The gate's not locked." The voice startled Cruz, seeming to come from nowhere until he noticed a small speaker attached to the gatepost.

Luis pushed open the gate. "He keeps dogs in here. They should be shut up but don't hang around." Cruz hurried after Luis towards a rough plank door in the nearest wall of the shack. He glanced nervously left and right but all remained quiet until his knock was answered by a furious barking from somewhere inside.

The door was opened by a skinny-looking teenage boy, head shaven except for a tuft like a cock's tail sticking up at the back. "Rocky's brother" Luis hissed in Cruz's ear, as the boy, his face expressionless, announced "Rocky's on the veranda. You two cops can come in." He pointed a finger at Luis. "You, wait outside."

Cruz could tell Luis was less than thrilled at the prospect. "Don't worry" said the boy to their guide as Cruz and Tomàs stepped through the doorway "There's not enough meat on you to interest the dogs."

SATURDAY 3: *CASA JARA*

Rocky Jara was sitting on the veranda in a big, old fashioned armchair. Beside him a pair of binoculars lay on a low table next to a chunky leather-bound book. Cruz wondered who had carried the chair up the precipitous path they had just climbed. Maybe it had been a toughening-up exercise for Rocky's gang members.

At first glance, the head of the *Pajaritos* looked to Cruz like any number of young men he might walk past in the street without a second glance. He had a broad, thin-lipped face with a slightly flattened nose, hair almost short enough to be called a crew cut and was wearing jeans with a tight white T-shirt that displayed his muscles to advantage. Rocky reminded Cruz of an off-duty policeman or soldier more than the *jefe* of one of *Independencia's* most powerful gangs.

The gang-leader looked the two scruffy cops up and down. "I see you got yourselves dressed up especially to meet me. Which one of you is Cruz?"

Tomàs pointed to Cruz. Rocky nodded. "So you must be Caldera then. Before we get down to business why not take a look behind you."

Cruz, sensing Rocky's proprietorial pride in the view, didn't tell him that he'd already stopped to admire it on the way up. And to be fair it repaid a second look. Below the veranda the ground fell away almost sheer, except that Cruz couldn't see any actual ground, just a crazy jumble of roofs climbing up towards them. A few were painted in bright reds, blues and yellows but most had simply faded to the orange-brown colour of rust. The smell of wood smoke drifted up towards them, mingled with the reek of kerosene stoves and whiff of sewage.

"You must feel a bit like God up here" said Cruz, momentarily forgetting Rocky's religious sentiments.

"No man who has read this can feel like God, although every one of us has a little piece of the Lord inside him." replied Rocky, laying his palm on the book next to his elbow.

"I'm sorry. I didn't mean to offend you" Cruz answered hastily, "it's just such a magnificent view."

Rocky raised a hand in gracious acceptance of the apology. "So, Inspector Cruz, why did you want to see me?"

Cruz explained about their search for Coretta and his guess that she might be holed up in an ELR safe house somewhere in the *barrio*.

Rocky leaned forward in his chair and stared hard at Cruz. "And you thought if the ELR were here I would know about it?" Cruz nodded. "Well, you're right. I do know about their safe house and I can find out easily enough who's in there now, but why should I tell you?"

"We're trying to solve a murder" Cruz replied. "And we think the girl's in big danger, even here in the *barrio*."

Rocky's eyes remained fixed on Cruz. "Inspector, I promise you that the only danger in this *barrio* comes from me." Suddenly his voice had gone colder, harder.

Cruz held his stare. "It's possible the Black Helmets are mixed up in this case. What if they decided to come looking for this girl?"

Rocky shook his head. "You think those guys are going to try anything here, you're wrong. Sure I know that all of a sudden they're busting dealers right and left. There's even word going round that they took out El Chico. But coming here? They're not that stupid." He grabbed Cruz's arm and led him to the corner of the veranda from where the gate they had come through earlier was visible.

"See! No watchtowers, no guards, nothing except a fence and a couple of guard dogs. Know why that is? Because my bodyguards are everywhere, the people who live down there in those shacks, **they** look out for me. The first sign of trouble I'm gone from here and lost down in those alleyways. The army guys, they could spend a year looking and they wouldn't get a sniff."

Cruz nodded. "So you stay safe as long as you don't leave the *barrio*."

"Sure and why should I want to leave? That was El Chico's big mistake. He buys himself a mansion in a fancy neighbourhood, drives around the city in a limo, mixes with big shots, that way they get to him. Not me, I stick with my own people. They want a loan, they want a job, they want a problem fixed, they come to me. I look after them, they look after me."

Cruz smiled. "They want another kind of fix they come to you as well."

Rocky smiled back, unperturbed. "Sure, that's how I make my living." He laid a hand on his Bible. "Know something? The Holy Book condemns drunkenness, lusting after women, blasphemy but it don't say nothing about heroin, or cocaine or dope. El Chico ran liquor dens and whorehouses but I don't. Nothing I do goes against what's in here."

"So what about the guys you fall out with?" Tomas asked. "They seem to have a habit of turning up dead and not from old age."

"I saw a film once" said Rocky. "Some cops visited a bar where a hoodlum was drinking and encouraged him to boast about a murder he'd committed. One of them had a microphone hidden under his shirt and the tape got him convicted. You wouldn't be working anything on the same line would you?"

Cruz heard the warning bell in his head loud and clear. He stood and lifted up his T-shirt. "Tomàs!" His colleague stood up as well and repeated the performance. "We're not here to try anything stupid" Cruz assured Rocky. "We're just hoping for a little cooperation."

Rocky laughed. "*Puercos* asking me for help, that's good. You'd better explain to me why I should help you."

Cruz had the feeling that he should have worked all this out a little better before he and Tomàs set off for *Las Espinas.*

"These ELR guys. You're happy to have them running a safe house on your patch?"

"Why not? They don't cause me trouble and they pay me a little commission to make sure I don't cause them any. And they hate the Black Helmets even more than I do. My enemy's enemy equals my friend, right?"

Cruz tried another tack. "OK then, is there anything we can do for you?"

Rocky leaned back in his chair so that he could reach a small electric bell-push fastened to the wall of the shack just behind him. He pressed the button. "I thought you'd never get round to asking." The skinny youth reappeared in the doorway. "Jorge, fetch us three bottles of Coke."

The youth nodded and disappeared into the house. Rocky said nothing until Jorge returned a few moments later bringing the bottles, already opened. Rocky took a swig from his and then wiped his mouth. "Jorge and me, we got another brother: Rodrigo. He's in the middle, four years younger than me. A few months back he got careless moving some stuff. The south side boys set him up and he was arrested. He got a ten year sentence, he'll serve five at least and they've put him in *Puente Alto*. It's a shithole, I want him moved. That place on the coast, *Bahia Blanca*, near *Costa Azul*, it's warmer there, they say the food's better. Is that something you can do for me?"

Cruz played for time by taking a swallow from his bottle. It was ice-cold. How did Rocky manage that with no mains power? Ice box or generator?

"What exactly was he carrying?"

"A suitcase full of H. Like I said, he got careless."

"I'll see what can be done but I'll need to make some calls."

"Make them and when you're done, come back to me."

SATURDAY 4: *BAR CONDORITO*

Electric power may not have made it as far as *Las Espinas* but at least someone had managed to connect a phone line. Luis took them to a bar next to the bus turn-round that had a payphone, Jorge accompanying them to report back to his brother on the success or otherwise of the negotiations. When they entered the *Bar Condorito* Cruz saw that a customer was already using the phone. Jorge reached over the caller's shoulder and pressed down on the receiver. The man turned with a snarl to see who had cut him off, then recognised Jorge and backed away.

The other patrons of the *Condorito* also shifted themselves further from the table where Jorge, Tomàs and Luis sat down while Cruz tried to contact Delgado. He prayed his boss wasn't out playing golf, walking the dog or indulging in any other activity that might keep a police *comisario* out of earshot of his home telephone on a Saturday afternoon.

He was in luck, but there was a long silence after Cruz had explained what Rocky wanted. Finally Delgado spoke. "You expect me to go to the General and ask for Jara's brother to get special treatment? Are you crazy?"

"Remember what you said sir. Normally it would take a military operation to get us into *Las Espinas*. This way just me and Caldera can do the business. No fuss."

"I called the General this morning about the Albañez murder. Such as well-connected family, it's bound to be a high profile case. He asked me if there was a political dimension. Is there?"

"I'm not sure. It certainly looked like a professional job. Whoever did it could have been looking for the other girl. That's why we need to find her quickly."

"And that means me telephoning the General on a Saturday?"

"Just like I had to ring you sir" Cruz couldn't stop himself from saying.

Another silence long enough for Cruz to worry he was going to run out of change. "I'll make the call. Just be sure you get me a result on this one."

"A result that makes you look good" thought Cruz while his mouth was saying something more diplomatic.

Delgado agreed that if he was successful, he would ensure Rodrigo Jara called the payphone number at four o'clock to let Jorge know that he was being transferred from *Puente Alto*. Cruz's watch told him it was just past one. The timing was tight but if the General could be persuaded to make a decision, it was feasible.

Cruz explained the situation to Jorge and the boy left them to report back to Rocky, first warning the bar owner that the two strangers were under Rocky's personal protection. Cruz, anxious to talk things over with Tomas, slipped Luis another ten dollar bill and told him to make himself scarce.

Once they were alone, Cruz went over to the bar and ordered a couple of beers.

"You got anything to eat?" Cruz's stomach was telling him that it was already past noon.

"My wife just made *empanadas*. They're beef, very tasty, her speciality. For you señores, on the house."

Cruz decided that his resolution to lay off the calories could be postponed. A few minutes later he and Tomas were sharing a large plateful of pasties, washed down by bottles of cold beer. Once they had cleared the plate, they sat back in their chairs. Tomas produced a packet of his pungent cigars but Cruz shook his head and lit a cigarette. He winked at Tomas.

"It's not a bad life in the *barrio* compadre!"

"Not if the big boss is your friend" Tomas replied. "Mind you, this place could do with a facelift."

Cruz glanced around the walls, rusty tin sheets braced by a few lengths of rough planking, and bare of decoration except for a few faded posters of naked beauties, their charms partly obscured by obscene additions scrawled onto their anatomies.

"I don't recall you were so fussy in the old days. Maybe some woman has been trying to civilise you?"

Tomas, who always remained cagey about his own love life, grinned and changed the subject.

"Do you think Delgado can pull this off boss? I mean getting Rodrigo out of Puente Alto."

"That depends on how hard he's prepared to push. If the General goes along with it, then it'll happen."

"But in less than three hours? What about the paperwork? When I did escort duty a couple of times I needed a briefcase just to carry all the forms we had to sign in triplicate!"

Cruz drained his glass and signalled for two more bottles. "That was in the bad old days before the army took charge. Now it doesn't need anything more than a telex from somebody with the right number of stars on his shoulder. "The Nation United In Action!"" he added, quoting one of the Junta's favourite slogans.

Tomàs gave a disbelieving grunt and poured more beer into his glass. Then he leaned towards Cruz and said quietly "Boss, don't look round too quick but there's a youngish guy just come in. He's at the bar having a beer but he's been taking a peep at us between swallows."

Cruz gently eased himself around in his seat until he had a view of the bar and the man leaning against it. His baggy jeans and dirty white T-shirt looked like typical *barrio* attire and the fact that he hadn't shaved in a week helped him to blend in with the bar's other patrons, but his face didn't fit in so well. His high forehead, narrow cheekbones and longish chin gave him a very European look, contrasting with the broad, flat *indio* faces around him.

Cruz raised his glass and called "*Salud* amigo. How goes it?" The newcomer muttered a reply that Cruz didn't catch, quickly finished his drink and hurried out the door.

"Was it something I said?" queried Cruz. "Or did he just not like the look of us?"

"I guess he's got an urgent appointment" Tomàs replied. "The question is, who with?"

An hour and two more bottles of beer later, Tomàs decided he needed to take a leak. The *Condorito's* sanitary arrangements were basic in the extreme. Patrons went outside, entered the tiny alleyway separating the bar from the shack next door and pissed against whichever wall took their fancy. Judging by the smell wafting from the rear of the building, anyone needing more than a piss simply walked round the back.

Tomàs was refastening his flies when he became aware that the anonymous-looking man who had entered the alley just after him was pointing a gun at his stomach. At the same moment a voice from behind told him to face the wall and put his hands on the back of his head. When he did so he was quickly frisked and his wallet extracted from the pocket of his jeans. He had no gun to lose because Luis had warned him to leave his automatic at home. Rocky was not in the habit of receiving armed visitors.

"If this is a mugging you better know I'm here to meet Rocky Jara and when he finds out what's happened he's going to come looking for you."

"Shut your mouth!" A gun muzzle jabbed his spine to encourage him towards the rear of the shack. When he rounded the back corner of the bar he found himself in a narrow space that looked and smelt like the bottom of a latrine. The gun prodded against his neck. Tomàs took a deep breath, realising he might not have many more to take. He glanced up at the strip of blue sky between the shacks. "Jesus, what a place to die" he muttered to nobody but himself.

When, ten minutes later, Tomàs had not reappeared, Cruz began to get worried. He went over to the bar. "If Jorge shows up, I'll be just outside."

The afternoon was now well advanced and although the opposite wall was lit by bright sunlight, most of the narrow street was in shade. Cruz strolled to the corner of the building and peered round it: no sign of Tomàs. He walked across to the other corner. The stink confirmed that this was what passed for the bar's facilities but the alley was empty.

Trying to ignore the smell, Cruz called Tomàs's name. Receiving no reply he entered the alley. When he reached the far end he stopped and peered cautiously round the corner. As he did so, he heard a noise from behind him. Before he could turn round, a sack was jammed over his head and pulled down over his shoulders. A hug like a bear held him immobile as a rope was wrapped around him and pulled so tight that his arms felt like they were being welded to his sides.

"Move!" the voice demanded and Cruz was yanked forward. Unprepared he stumbled, lost his balance and unable to save himself, fell sideways, cracking his skull against something hard then slumping to his hands and knees in the wet filth of the alleyway.

SATURDAY 5: ELR HIDEOUT, *LAS ESPINAS*

"Get up and keep moving *puerco!*" Cruz got up and kept moving. He had little choice as the rope securing his arms dragged him forwards. Cruz concentrated on trying to stay on his feet but soon lost his balance. This time somebody grabbed him before he fell and kept a hand on his shoulder to steady him. At intervals his captors halted and spun him around so that he soon lost all sense of direction. He felt dizzy and nauseous and was desperate not to vomit the mixture of beer and empanada in his stomach inside the bag.

Eventually they halted once more, then Cruz felt himself being pulled and shoved up a short ladder. The light penetrating the sacking suddenly dimmed and a door slammed behind him. A moment later Cruz's bonds were loosened and the sacking was yanked off his head. Cruz rubbed his bruised arms to try and restore circulation. When his eyes had adjusted to the gloom he saw that he had been brought into a room with plank walls and floor, a tin roof and one small window covered by a grimy piece of plastic sheeting.

In front of Cruz stood a youngish bearded man wearing a pair of horn-rimmed spectacles and dressed in what looked like a dark-coloured boiler suit. His captor nodded and the detective heard a chair leg scrape on the floor as a meaty hand on his shoulder pushed him effortlessly down onto the seat and held him there.

Whoever was behind him felt inside his back pocket, extracted his wallet and threw it to the student type standing in front of Cruz. The hand came off his shoulder and Cruz half turned to see a squat figure almost as wide as the door behind him, a man with a black spade beard and greasy hair pulled back into a pony tail. The two things that caught Cruz's attention were the malevolent glare he was directing at the cop and the length of what looked like rubber hosepipe in his right hand.

"That's Ernesto" said the spectacled student type. "You can call me Fidel. Not our real names of course. You are, in case you haven't already guessed, a prisoner of the ELR, Inspector Cruz. You see I know your name even without checking in this wallet."

Cruz stared back at Fidel and didn't say anything.

"In a little while we'll ask you some questions. I'd advise you to answer them truthfully. Ernesto will help me with your interrogation and I should warn you that he dislikes cops. In fact he hates your guts and sometimes his feelings get the better of him."

"What's happened to my partner?" Cruz broke in. "Did you bring him here?"

"Detective Caldera? Yes he's here. In fact I can show him to you. Ernesto!"

Cruz felt the vice-like grip on his arms again as he was dragged to his feet and shoved towards a door in the wall. Fidel opened the door, revealing another room in the middle of which Tomas was sitting slumped in a chair. His hands were tied behind him and his face was bruised and covered with blood oozing from a wound in his scalp.

When Cruz called his name Tomas barely moved his head in response before Fidel closed the door. "Your friend was a little slow to cooperate but we were able to change his mind eventually. He gave us some very useful information which we would like you to corroborate. We'll leave you alone for a little while to think about your options. Tie him up Ernesto."

Cruz's arms were seized, tied together and bound to the chair back. Then Ernesto latched a shutter into position to block the window and the two ELR men left, locking the door behind them. Cruz was left alone in the dark to contemplate what was going to happen to him next.

To take his mind off the sick feeling in his stomach Cruz tried to guess who had tipped off the ELR. There were two likely candidates: Jorge and Luis. Cruz prayed it was Luis. If the culprit was Jorge then the Jara brothers were playing some kind of double game and he and Tomàs could expect no help from them. That would leave only Delgado and Cruz found it hard to convince himself that the *Comisario* would back a full scale invasion of the *barrio* just to rescue his most troublesome subordinate. He had gloomily concluded that Rocky was their best hope when he heard a bolt slide in the door behind him.

"Amalio, are you in there?"

Cruz jolted upright as if he had been prodded by a live electric wire. It was the first time she had used his given name. He heard a fumbling in the dark, then one of the window shutters was released and light flooded into the room. Coretta knelt in front of him and raised a bottle to his lips.

Cruz hadn't realised how thirsty he was until he tasted the cold water on his tongue. He took a long drink then asked Coretta to untie the rope binding his hands. "I need to see to Tomàs, they beat him up pretty badly. Then we have to get out of here."

Coretta shook her head. "It's too risky. Fidel could be back any minute and there are guards on the door."

Cruz nodded towards the window. "What about that? We could get through there."

"That just looks out onto a yard, you'd need to climb a three metre fence to reach the street."

Cruz swore: from the glimpse he'd had of his partner he was in no condition to climb fences. "Take a look at Tomàs, will you? Make sure he's breathing OK."

Coretta stood listening for a moment then apparently satisfied that all was quiet, she opened the door to the room Tomàs was held in and disappeared inside. To Cruz's frayed nerves it seemed as if she was in there for an eternity. When she came back she laid a hand on Cruz's shoulder. "I don't think he's badly hurt, just bruises and a cut on his head. He's conscious and he drank a little water."

Cruz leaned back in his chair and stared at Coretta. "If he is OK it's no thanks to your ELR friends. Maybe you can tell me whose side you're on in all of this?"

Coretta squatted down in front of Cruz. "I don't really want to be on anybody's side. I'm here because Fidel brought me. He'd found out that I'd been taken to Rio Blanco and he knew Hector had a contract out on me. He said this was the safest place to hide out but he didn't give me a choice."

"Does he know you've been working for the Black Helmets?"

Coretta shook her head. "If they find out about that they could kill me!"

Cruz kept his eyes fixed on the girl. He still wasn't sure what was going on inside her head. "Don't worry, I'm not going to tell them. But listen, if you're really not part of Fidel's little game then prove it to me. Can you get word to Rocky Jara? I don't think he was in on what's happened to us and if he wasn't then he's not going to be happy about it. Maybe he can get us out of here."

Coretta nodded. "I'll try. I've got to go now. If I get a chance I'll come back later." She leaned forward and touched a cool palm to Cruz's cheek. *"Ciao puercito"* she whispered in his ear, then quickly replaced the shutter and was gone, leaving him in darkness.

Cruz wriggled and twisted in his chair but his bonds were too tight to shift and as he struggled, the rough rope chafed his wrists painfully. After a couple of minutes he gave up, leaned back into his chair and tried to think. He had no way of knowing if Coretta's story was true, whether she had effectively been abducted from Rio Blanco by Fidel or whether she had gone willingly back to her old ELR *compañeros.* For all he knew, their brief tete a tete had been merely an attempt to soften him up before Fidel and Ernesto tried tougher tactics. Could Coretta get word to Jara and if so, would it turn out that Rocky had approved his kidnap? Cruz didn't think so but like everything else, he couldn't be sure about that either.

The questions kept beating around inside his skull like demented bats until, to keep them at bay, he decided to try and get to Tomàs. By now his eyes were better accustomed to what little light leaked past the shutter and he managed to drag his chair over against the door and depress the latch using his forehead. Fortunately for Cruz, the door opened inwards and he was able to use his feet to push it open without making too much noise.

"Tomàs, it's me. Can you talk?" He called softly into the darkness.

"Hey boss" came the reply in something between a whisper and a groan. "I'm OK, just a little sore. I'll live, unless they got something else in mind for us."

Cruz dragged himself towards the sound of Tomàs's voice until his foot bumped into the leg of his *compadre's* chair.

"How are you boss? They beat you up as well?"

"Not yet, they must be saving me for dessert. Listen, I asked Coretta to get word to Rocky. Maybe he can get us out of here."

"Maybe, if he's on the level and if Coretta is too. In the meantime we got one more trick. Those dummies didn't take my trainers off me. There's a blade in the right heel. Maybe you could reach it."

Cruz shook his head, forgetting the gesture was invisible to Tomas. "If Rocky doesn't show it may be time to turn kamikaze. Keep the blade safe till then *amigo.*"

"OK, let's hope we get another chance to use it."

"Let's hope we don't have to." With an effort Cruz managed to turn his chair to face the way he'd come. "I'm going back now. Try and shut the door behind me."

Cruz slowly dragged himself back through the doorway. The legs of his chair seemed to make a lot of noise as they were scraped across the floor but nobody burst in to find out what was going on. Behind him he heard the door slam as Tomàs gave it a kick but still there was no sign that the guards were paying them any attention.

He sat in the semi-darkness, wondering whether he should have taken a chance and tried to reach Tomàs's blade. Every so often, encouraged by the beer he had drunk earlier, he started to doze but whenever he sagged in his chair, the rope securing his wrists tightened painfully and jerked him awake again.

After what felt like several hours of purgatory, he heard a bolt rattle, followed by a creak as the door opened. A torch was shone into his face. "Time for our little chat *puerco."* Fidel's voice.

"And don't forget Ernesto gets impatient very quickly if you don't answer my questions."

Cruz tried to turn away from the blinding light but Ernesto grabbed his head from behind and twisted it back to face the torch beam.

"Let's start with your full name and rank." Cruz answered. "Good, Inspector. Now, which division do you work in?" Cruz his eyes screwed tight against the glare, told him that as well. No point doing otherwise, Fidel almost certainly knew anyway.

"Now, maybe you can tell us what an Inspector from Criminal Investigations is doing in *Las Espinas* with just one *agente* for company. This is a pig-free zone Inspector. We think it shows a lack of respect for just two of you to walk around, not even carrying a firearm. The least we would expect if cops decide to come calling is a couple of hundred headbangers from the riot squad and a battalion of Black Helmets in reserve. So exactly what were you up to?"

Cruz decided to stick to the facts as much as he could, even though his story might sound a little far-fetched. "I was following a lead on a criminal case." Cruz heard a grunt of disbelief from behind him and tensed in the expectation of a blow but none came.

"Careful, Inspector. Ernesto didn't like that answer much, he's getting restive."

"Like it or not, it happens to be true. I needed to speak to a girl we heard was holed up he.."

Before he could say any more, several unpleasant things happened to Cruz at almost the same time. First something hard hit him just above his ear, knocking him and the chair clean over. The side of his head smacked against the floor and he blacked out, to be roused by a deafening noise and flashes of light which at first seemed to be happening inside his skull. Finally, a heavy weight fell across his chest, pinning him down so that he could hardly breathe. He tried to call out but managed little more than a groan until the weight was suddenly lifted off him and a voice that wasn't Fidel asked him if he was able to stand.

Before Cruz's head cleared sufficiently for him to answer, he was grabbed under the arms and hauled to his feet. He staggered, tripped over a body lying on the floor and almost fell over again before somebody shoved a chair seat against the back of his knees.

"Sit down" the voice commanded and this time he recognised the speaker. It was Rocky Jara. Cruz gratefully subsided onto the chair. He closed his eyes for a moment and when he opened them, saw Fidel standing against the wall, his hands on top of his head and the muzzle of an M-16 prodding him in the belly. The rifle was held by a stocky, shaven-headed individual in jeans and what resembled an army camouflage jacket.

"My *compadre"* Cruz mumbled. "He's through there. Is he OK?"

Rocky Jara came from behind Cruz and stepped over the body on the floor to reach the door. Like his companion he was carrying an automatic rifle. He nodded towards Fidel "Keep an eye on him Pico. If he makes a move, blow him through the wall." Pico glared at Fidel as if there was nothing that would give him greater pleasure.

When Jara came back into the room he nodded to Cruz. "Your buddy should be OK when he's cleaned up a little." He walked slowly over to Fidel and stood in front of him. "These guys were here under my protection. Did you know that?" he said softly.

"I…I.. no, they said something but we didn't, aagh!" the grunt of pain was in response to Rocky ramming the muzzle of his gun into Fidel's gut. Fidel bent double groaning until Rocky seized him by the hair and pulled him upright. "Listen you lanky piece of shit." He still spoke softly, almost confidentially. "I let you stay here, in my *barrio,* just as long as you don't cause me any trouble. That was the deal and that means you don't mess with **anybody** without talking to me first. Do something like this again and you'll get the same as this vulture meat." He turned and kicked Ernesto's body which lay sprawled on the floor, leaking blood.

"Jorge!" this time Rocky was loud and his shout brought his brother hurrying to join them. "Search the place, collect all the weapons and bring them up to the house." He turned to Fidel.

"From now on, no guns! We see you carrying and I'll burn this place down with you in it. You got that?" Fidel nodded: Cruz could see that he got it all right.

SATURDAY 6: *HOSPITAL BOLIVAR*

A couple of hours later Cruz was sitting in a corridor painted in the sickly green colour typical of hospital corridors the world over. This particular one happened to be in the military hospital which ministered to the needs of the armed forces and the police. Cruz was waiting for Tomàs to emerge from the cubicle where he was being patched up. While he waited he tried to figure out what, if anything, he had learned at the cost of another bang on the head and a beaten-up partner. What he hadn't achieved was to question Coretta about what had really led to her falling out with Hector and provoked her flight to the ELR safe house.

Safe from the cops maybe, he thought wryly, but not from Rocky Jara. Fidel and the rest of his gang would have to tread very carefully from now on. What Cruz had confirmed from his trip to *Las Espinas* was that the ELR was not about to take over the *barrios,* much less pose a real threat to the *junta.* If Rocky had believed the ELR was as powerful as the Government liked to pretend, he would have been a lot more careful about how he dealt with Fidel. After scaring the shit out of the young revolutionary, Rocky had turned to Cruz.

"As the Holy Book says Inspector, *An eye for an eye.* He beat up your friend pretty bad, now he's all yours." Then he'd handed Cruz a pistol. "The chamber's empty but you won't need bullets to teach this guy a lesson." By this time Fidel, slumped against the wall, was shaking like a man with hypothermia. Jorge, who had just come back into the room, pointed at Fidel's trousers and laughed "Hey look, he's pissed himself and nobody hardly touched him yet!"

Cruz had held the gun gently to the side of Fidel's face as if measuring him for a pistol whipping. Fear seemed to have stripped years off Fidel, he looked less like a revolutionary than a terrified adolescent. Cruz shook his head and gave the gun back to Rocky. "I don't need this" he'd said then stepped forward and knee'd Fidel hard in the groin. Fidel collapsed on the floor retching. Cruz had given him another kick then left him lying and gone to tend to Tomàs.

Fidel had got off lightly compared to what would happen to Luis when Rocky found him. Fidel had confirmed Cruz's suspicions that Luis had been the one who alerted the ELR to the presence of two cops in the *barrio*. It had been a dumb thing to do but maybe Luis was desperate to earn a few more dollars. He must have been to think word wouldn't get back to Rocky. For the moment he'd vanished but Cruz wouldn't give a five peseta piece for his chances of seeing another sunrise when Rocky laid hands on him.

Which brought him back to Coretta. There had been no trace of her when Jorge and the others searched the ELR house. Two young girls they'd found on the premises along with half a dozen of Fidel's comrades, had claimed they'd never seen Coretta before she'd turned up with Fidel the previous day. When Cruz had asked Rocky if it was Coretta who had warned him about the kidnapping, Rocky had told him that it was the bartender at the *Condorito* who had passed the word that his two customers had suddenly disappeared. Rocky had worked out the rest himself.

Fidel had sworn that he had no idea how Coretta had vanished into thin air and given the state he was in, Cruz had been inclined to believe him. The two ELR men who had been guarding the front entrance to the house until Rocky's men jumped them had stuck to their story that Coretta hadn't got out that way. The only other possibility was the rear yard. Before he left, Cruz had taken a look at the fence she would have had to climb over. He discovered a blanket folded double then draped over the top wire, as good evidence as he was likely to find that it had been Coretta's escape route.

At least Rocky's brother had made the call to say that he was on his way to the coast so Rocky owed Cruz a favour and his men were scouring the *barrio* in search of Coretta. She wouldn't find it easy to disguise herself well enough to avoid notice among the shacks and alleyways of *Las Espinas*. "Don't worry" Rocky had told him. "We'll find her."

Cruz, anxious to get Tomàs to hospital, had no choice but to settle for that. He was wondering whether Rocky's men might have already tracked down Coretta when a severe-looking middle-aged woman in the uniform of an army nurse came up to him and said that he would be able to see Tomàs. As he followed her along the corridor she warned him that it could only be a brief visit. "The cuts and bruises on his face are superficial but he's had a blow on the back of the head and the doctor is concerned about concussion. He'll be kept in at least until tomorrow for observation. In the meantime he's not to be upset in any way."

"Don't worry, I'm not here to interrogate him" Cruz grinned but got no smile in response as the nurse led him to a side ward containing just a single bed. Tomàs's face was red and swollen. A large purple bruise on his left cheekbone and dressings on his forehead and chin did nothing to improve his appearance. Cruz looked down at him.

"Your turn to be the patient this time *compadre*. How are you feeling?"

Tomàs tried to shake his head and winced. "Not too good boss." He mumbled. "I got a stinking headache and I'm seeing double."

"Too bad your nurse isn't better looking. One of her is more than enough. Just take things easy and we'll soon be enjoying a beer together in the *Gato Negro*."

"Sure boss. I'll be OK after a night's rest."

"You'd better be. How am I going to stay out of trouble without you to take care of me?"

"Just be careful. I'm not the only one who can't see straight on this one and we both know why."

Cruz didn't argue. He had a suspicion that Tomàs was right.

As Cruz was passing the hospital reception desk on his way out, he remembered that he hadn't contacted Delgado to update him on what had happened in *Las Espinas*. It was late but Delgado had been insistent that he wanted to be kept in the picture so Cruz drew a deep breath and rang his home number. To his relief all he got was an answerphone. He left a message saying that he would ring again in the morning.

Cruz replaced the receiver then called the front desk at police headquarters. He'd told Rocky to ring the same number if he had any information about Coretta. He was lucky, the desk sergeant was Nuñez, an old buddy from his uniform days, who had not only taken a call for Cruz but made a note of it.

"Your guy said that the girl you're interested in took a *micro* from *Las Espinas* into town. The conductor remembered her because she was such a looker. He thinks she got off at the University stop. That bus goes right past the main entrance to the campus. The other reason he remembered her, she'd no money to pay the fare. He said that if she hadn't been such a doll he would have thrown her off. And now just for my peace of mind, please tell me this is a genuine case you're working Inspector, you're not just expanding your harem?"

"Thanks Enrique and now please fuck a long way off." Cruz, cut the call before the sergeant could think of a comeback then glanced at his watch and dialled his home number. If Coretta was broke and scared she would maybe try to hole up for the night somewhere on the University campus. If she had, there was a chance he might be able to find her. At least he had to try.

"Hello *amor*. It's me. Sorry I couldn't call you before. I'm at the hospital, no not me, Tomàs. No he's not badly hurt. Listen, I won't be back until very late, maybe not till morning. I know, kiss Laura for me. Yes I'll be careful. I have to go now. You too."

SATURDAY 7: *UNIVERSIDAD NACIONAL*

One advantage of visiting the hospital was that whatever the hour, there was always a line of taxis outside the main entrance. Cruz told his driver to head for the University then sank gratefully onto the back seat of the venerable Ford that had been at the front of the rank. He had no real plan for what to do. He realised he knew little about what went on at the University at this time on a Saturday night. He'd never entered the campus except in daytime and on police business. Was it possible that a concert or some other event might still be in progress? If so he would have to hope he wouldn't attract too much attention in his grubby *barrio* outfit.

He needn't have worried. When the taxi drew up outside the main gates of the campus all was dark and quiet. Then as Cruz got out he realised that Coretta wasn't the only one with no money for fares. The small roll of bills he had taken to *Las Espinas* had disappeared when he was kidnapped. He didn't even have his Police ID which he'd left behind, along with his gun, at Tomas's apartment.

"I'm sorry *amigo* I can't pay you, I'm a Police..." The rest of Cruz's explanation was lost in a volley of obscenities from the *taxista*.

"I shoulda known better picking up a piece of lowlife *mierda* like you." The driver pushed open his door almost flattening Cruz and jumped out with surprising agility for a man of his bulk. In his right hand he held a blackjack and from the look on his face he was keen to use it.

Cruz tried reason first. "Listen, I'm not bullshitting. I'm a policeman and if you do anything stupid you're going to find yourself in big..." At this point Cruz realised the *taxista* wasn't paying attention. He ducked just in time to avoid a blow meant for the side of his head and kicked his opponent's shin, wishing he was wearing good old-fashioned police boots rather than trainers. The *taxista* grunted and made to grab Cruz by the hair but before he could get a grip, Cruz hit him as hard as he could in his impressive gut. The man bent over almost double and Cruz chopped him on the back of the neck. His opponent dropped the blackjack and sank to his knees on the pavement.

Cruz bent down to speak into his ear. "Just be grateful you didn't smack me with this." He jabbed the driver in the face with the blackjack then threw it high over the University gate into the darkness. "You see I really am a cop. If you want your fare, come down to *Pepe* on Monday morning and collect it. Now piss off before I take your number and have my pals in traffic give you some real grief!"

The *taxista* muttered something inaudible but Cruz didn't bother asking him to repeat it. He had a new distraction. Someone was shining a light at him from the other side of the gates. "Hey you!" The voice was coming from a dark figure holding a torch. "What's all the noise about?"

Cruz heard the taxi behind him grind into gear then drive away. He walked up to the gate and as he got closer could see that the torch carrier was wearing a peaked cap. "You security?" he asked. The figure nodded. "Open the gate please." With no identification and looking pretty much like a tramp, Cruz knew he was going to have to rely on confidence and an authoritative manner.

"Come on, open up. I'm Inspector Cruz, *Policia Nacional.* Do I have to ring your boss and have your arse kicked from here to *Costa Azul?* Get a move on, this is urgent!"

The guard stared at Cruz. He was breathing as heavily as if he'd just sprinted a hundred metres and Cruz could smell the liquor on his breath. There was a long pause, then the torch wavered as the guard groped in a pocket for his bunch of keys. "Take it easy boss" he muttered. "I'm just doing my job." After a brief struggle he managed to fit the right key in the lock and swung open the gate. "You'll have to sign in, it's the rule, see. Anybody coming onto the campus after eight o'clock has got to sign the book."

Cruz followed the guard into a small wooden hut standing to the left of a paved walkway. The path led towards an imposing four-storied building fronted by a stone pillared colonnade which Cruz recognised as the University senate house. The hut was a lot less impressive. It had just enough room for a single chair and a battered desk on which sat a telephone, a large open ledger and a half-empty bottle of *pisco*. It didn't appear that the guard took the trouble to bring a glass. After more scratching around and heavy breathing he produced a pen and Cruz wrote his name and official address on the first blank line of the ledger. He gave a cursory glance at the names above his own. Even if she was here he could hardly expect Coretta to have signed in but according to the book there had been no late visitors for over a week.

He handed the guard's pen back to him and summoned up a smile. "Thanks *amigo*. Now tell me your name."

The guard coughed nervously and reached for the *pisco*. Cruz quickly grabbed the bottle and held it behind his back. "You can have this when you've answered a few questions. First, your name?"

"Echavez, Francisco Echavez. Now can I have my bottle señor?"

"You call me Inspector and no you can't, not yet. Second question: what time did you start your shift?"

Echavez was starting to sweat. He looked to Cruz like a real alcoholic rather than someone who took a drink to fight the tedium of his job. "Eight o'clock Inspector, I work eight to eight."

"Has anyone come onto the campus since you started your shift?"

Echavez licked his lips. "Nobody's come through the gate tonight sir."

"What about other ways of getting onto the campus?"

Echavez shrugged "Well there's a few holes in the fence. It's those *maldito* students, they're always making short cuts the lazy bastards. And the cleaners are just as bad. I reckon some of them are nicking stuff out of the stores. As soon as the fence gets mended somebody breaks it down again."

"So people and gear could get in and out of the campus and you'd be none the wiser? Makes me wonder what's the point of you being here."

"I do my best sir, but there's only one of me and that fence is more than a kilometre long."

Cruz nodded and tried a more sympathetic tone. "OK, just a couple more questions and you can have your bottle back. You said nobody's come in tonight. What about unusual comings and goings on other nights recently, particularly after dark?"

Echavez shook his head, rather too quickly for Cruz's liking.

"C'mon think about it? Anything at all? Over the last few months even?"

"No Inspector, nothing, not a thing!"

"The ELR had an organisation on this campus didn't they? Is it still active?"

"No sir. The Black Helmets occupied the whole University for a week after the riots last year. They arrested a whole bunch of people, staff and students. The ELR got wiped out I guess."

"So who is it's been slipping you bottles of booze to keep your mouth shut about what you see on the night shift?"

It wasn't entirely a shot in the dark. The bottle Cruz was holding wasn't the kind of cheap rotgut a drunk on security guard's wages would buy to keep himself happy. It was a quality brand, the kind Felicia would buy to mix *pisco* sours when she invited friends round for a drink.

"Who told you that? I swear I never..."

Cruz cut Echavez's denials off short. He held the bottle up in front of the guard's face.

"Francisco, you have a choice. You tell me what's been going on here or I smash this bottle right now, then tomorrow morning I ring your boss and tell him exactly what you've been up to."

Beads of sweat were running down Echavez's temples and the hand he stretched out towards his bottle was shaking. Cruz whipped it away from his grasping fingers. "This is your last chance Francisco. Talk!"

The guard slumped down into the chair, his head in his hands. "OK boss, but you better make sure you get all those guys or I'm going to be vulture meat."

Cruz put the *pisco* bottle on the table, well out of Echavez's reach and leaned against the wall of the hut. "All what guys?"

"The ELR. Like I said, the Black Helmets came in last year and arrested a load of their people, not just the leaders but anybody with a face they didn't like."

"So how come the ELR are still active?"

"I guess it's like killing cockroaches, you fumigate, sweep out loads of dead bugs, think you got 'em all but there's always a few you miss and in a coupla months they're back again."

Cruz's eye fell on a crumpled pack of cigarettes and a book of matches sitting on the table. He realised he was desperate for a smoke, filched a cigarette and lit it. It was a cheap local brand and the smoke rasped the back of his throat but he was grateful for the nicotine. He pushed the pack towards Echavez who shook his head. There was only one thing he wanted and it came in a bottle.

"So Francisco, who did the Black Helmets miss?"

"Not many, but there's a few I seen coming and going after dark."

"Staff? Students?"

"Mostly students, but one or two staff as well. Give me a drink Inspector, a drink for Christ's sake."

"Give me some names first Francisco, names I can check out."

Echavez shook his head. "Those students, I don't know their names. How would I know them among thousands?"

"But if they came in late they should have signed their names in your book."

"You know it wasn't like that Inspector. When they had a late meeting I would get a bottle to look the other way."

"So, here's your bottle less than half drunk. That means there's a meeting on tonight?"

"A guy brought me that just after I came on shift. Told me to keep an eye out, somebody would be coming in after him, a woman."

"And this guy. You knew him?"

Echavez rubbed a grimy hand across his eyes and sighed. "I don't know his name. I think he works in the library."

"The library!" Cruz couldn't hold back an exclamation. "What does he look like?"

Echavez's glance wavered from Cruz's face back towards the bottle. "He's a small guy with curly black hair and he wears thick glasses. Does that earn me a drink?"

Cruz shoved the bottle towards the guard who seized it and took a long pull. Cruz waited until Echavez came up for breath then snatched the bottle and put it back on the table. "So how did this mysterious guy leave? On foot or by car?"

Echavez looked puzzled. "He walked of course, back to the library maybe."

"The library? You mean he's still here on the campus?"

"Sure he is."

"And the girl, did she turn up?"

"Yes she came through not long afterwards. Maybe a little after nine o'clock."

"Did you get a look at her?"

Echavez grinned. "Not enough, it was dark but she's a nice-looking *chica*. I'd have liked to see more of her."

"What was she wearing?"

"Just a T-shirt and jeans and a scarf over her head."

"And they're both still on the campus?"

Echavez nodded. "So far as I know, unless they went through the fence someplace."

"You see anybody else tonight?"

The guard shook his head. "No but they don't always come through the main gate. Like I said there's other places you can get through easy enough."

Cruz handed his bottle back to the Echavez then leaned across the table and picked up the telephone. "This give me an outside line?"

"No sir, it just connects through to the bursar's office."

"So how do you call for help if there's an emergency during your shift?"

Echavez pointed to a red button on the wall above the desk. "That's the alarm sir, it rings through to the local police station."

"Does it work?"

Echavez shrugged. "I think so sir, I never tried it."

Cruz stared at the button. If he pressed it either nothing would happen or if the system worked, a cop car would come racing up to the gates, no doubt with lights flashing and sirens blaring. Enough to wake up even a half-asleep ELR lookout.

"Listen carefully my friend." Cruz pointed to the clock on the wall. It showed twenty minutes past midnight. "I'm going to check out that library building. If I don't come back by one o'clock, press that button. You understand? One o'clock. Have you got a gun?"

Echavez shook his head. "No sir, just that." He pointed to a truncheon hanging by its strap on the wall.

Cruz lifted it off its hook and tested its weight: it was heavy enough to make an effective weapon. "Give me your torch." Echavez handed it over.

"Now just to help you stay awake, I'm going to take this bottle with me. You'll get it again when I come back." Echavez didn't look too happy about that but Cruz ignored his protests and made him repeat his instructions. "One o'clock sir, I press the button."

Cruz tossed the pack of cigarettes back onto the table. "Here, have a smoke, take your mind off your thirst. And don't forget the alarm."

SATURDAY 8: *BIBLIOTECA DE LA UNIVERSIDAD NACIONAL*

Cruz deposited Echavez's bottle under a bush behind the guard hut then set off in search of the library. Things looked different in the dark but after a couple of wrong turns, Cruz found his way to the building he'd visited to interview the librarian Arenas and his assistant Garcia about the manuscript thefts. Unsurprisingly the place was in darkness and when Cruz made his way cautiously up the steps to the main door it was firmly shut. He decided to look for a less obvious entrance and headed for the rear of the building. When he got there he found himself in a narrow space separating the library from the adjacent building, a modern block several storeys high.

It was pitch dark in the alleyway and Cruz stopped to turn on his torch. As he was fiddling with the switch, he saw a narrow strip of light high on the wall above him. The light was coming through a chink in the shutters of an upper window in the library block and shining on the opposite wall. Cruz moved slowly down the alley, careful to keep his torch pointing downwards, until he came to a rear entrance to the building.

This door was also closed but when he tried the handle it opened with what seemed to Cruz a horribly loud, grating sound. He hid behind the half-open door and waited to see if anyone had heard. After he'd counted slowly to thirty and nothing had happened, he slipped through the doorway. It was completely black inside the building but when Cruz shone his torch ahead he saw that he was in luck: a staircase led directly to the upper floor. Cruz started up the stairs, trying to tread as lightly as possible but unable to prevent the bare wood creaking at each step.

When he reached a narrow landing, Cruz stopped to listen again. In front of him was another door. It was closed but a faint glow shone through a fanlight and coming from the other side of the woodwork was a low, rumbling sound that he couldn't identify. He gently tried the old-fashioned brass doorknob. It turned sweetly enough and Cruz pushed the door open a few centimetres then froze as he caught sight of a pair of feet in the beam of his torch.

He stood motionless, still holding the door handle, not daring to breath.

The feet didn't move and after a few seconds Cruz switched off his torch. When his eyes had adjusted he could make out a figure sitting slumped in a chair a metre or so inside the doorway. The dim radiance he'd seen through the fanlight was coming down a narrow corridor which made a ninety-degree left turn shielding him from the source of the light. The rumbling noise he'd heard was the steady snoring of whoever was in the chair. Cautiously Cruz took a closer look and recognised Garcia the librarian's mop of curly hair.

Cruz slipped off his trainers, placed them behind the door, then pushed it open enough to slip through. Garcia didn't stir as Cruz crept past him in bare feet . When he reached the bend, he peered warily round the corner. The corridor ran on for some distance, doors leading off on either side. Like the first one, each had a small fanlight above it. Through one of these, about half way along, a light was shining.

Cruz took a deep breath and moved as quietly as he knew how towards the lighted room. As he drew closer he could hear the murmer of people talking. He put an ear to the door and the voice speaking was instantly recognisable."It's no good. I tried to talk to him on the phone but he thinks it was us who bombed the Golden Gate." Coretta sounded weary.

"Screw him anyway. We just go back to Plan A." A man's voice, educated, a little edgy, a young man's voice, a student maybe, wondered Cruz. If so, he sounded like a harder case than Fidel.

"Maybe that would have worked if the bomb had taken him out but it didn't." Another male voice, deeper, older.

"Did he say anything else?" the younger voice again.

Coretta answered. "He just told me he wanted me dead and he would arrange that very soon."

"He's all mouth and no *cojones.* If it wasn't for El Chico he'd have been a nobody."

The older voice. "We need Hector in on this deal. Once he's had time to think about it he'll see reason. I'll talk to him later. What about the equipment? Did you get what you needed?"

"We got it. It's set up in the old storage shed behind the science block."

"And what about the cash?"

Coretta broke in. "It's fixed. How about you?"

"I have it. Fifty/fifty like we said. And my guys on the frontier are all set. I just need to make a phone call. You've got the cash with you?"

"We'll get it to you very soon. "The younger voice again.

"You said you'd already got the money." The older man's tone was harder now.

"We just need to make a contact." Coretta's voice. "We'll have it tomorrow."

"You'd better, or it won't just be Hector who's looking for you."

"Don't worry, she'll have it." The younger male sounded sure of himself. "So when does the stuff arrive?"

"Three days after I've seen your cash. In full. Bring it to the same place as last time, $250,000 U.S. or the deal's off."

Cruz heard chairs scrape on the floor. He glanced at his watch. Five to one! If Echavez hadn't fallen asleep he would sound the alarm on the hour and if the system worked all hell would break loose soon after that.

Cruz cursed himself for setting such an early deadline but it was too late to do anything about that now. All he could do was retreat and try to follow the conspirators. He crept back down the corridor and took a quick glance round the corner, hoping that Garcia would still be asleep. No luck, the guy was not only awake, he was on his feet and smoking a cigarette. Cruz ducked back out of sight and tried to think what to do. Another glance at his watch, less than a minute to go. He felt a rush of adrenalin, the light was dim and Garcia wouldn't be expecting an intruder to approach him from inside the building. Cruz stood up straight and sauntered round the corner, telling himself not to hurry.

Garcia was standing with his back to Cruz and didn't hear him coming until he was more than half way down the corridor. When he finally turned round Cruz called out "Hey Felipe we're nearly finished in there. Coretta asked me to let you know..." Thrown by the use of his name, Garcia hesitated and Cruz hit him hard just above the ear with Echavez's truncheon. With a groan Garcia slumped to his knees. Cruz hit him again and he pitched onto his face and lay motionless.

Cruz stowed the truncheon in his pocket then stopped to listen. He wasn't sure if a bell was ringing somewhere on the floor below or whether that was just his imagination. Quickly he frisked Garcia and found he was unarmed. He grabbed the librarian's ankles and dragged him towards the nearest door in the corridor. It was locked. Cruz cursed and tried the next one. This time the door swung open. He hurriedly pulled the body through, closed the door and ran towards the stairs.

Cruz grabbed his trainers and slipped them back on. Now he could definitely hear an alarm and not just the bell but footsteps behind him. Cruz sprinted down the stairs and out into the night. With no time to think he turned right and reached the next corner just as the others dashed out of the building. A shout of "Felipe!" Coretta's voice. "They think I'm Garcia" Cruz realised and kept running, searching for somewhere he could hide. He reached a grassed area by the side of the Senate House and dodged to his left where a stand of laurel bushes gave good cover. He just had time to crouch in the shadows before he saw three dark figures sprinting towards him. He would have to rely on bluff. Flicking on Echavez's torch he yelled. "Police! Halt or I fire!"

In the beam of the torch Cruz saw two men, one short and stocky with a military style crew cut, the second a younger man with a stubble beard and longer hair. Behind them, Cruz caught a glimpse of Coretta, a little way behind the others. She froze in the light but the crewcutted figure in front of her rolled sideways into darkness and a moment later Cruz heard the crack of a weapon. A bullet fanned his ear and whipped through the leaves beside his head. Cruz flicked off his torch and threw himself to the ground as the gunman loosed a volley of shots.

"Move!" a voice shouted and he heard his quarry running past him. Cruz got to his feet and followed the runners. He rounded the corner of the building and as he did so he caught sight of the flashing lights of a patrol car pulling onto the pavement opposite the Campus gates.

The three in front of him had seen the car before he did and turned away from the Senate House before disappearing into the cover of a line of trees growing alongside an ornate wrought iron fence that marked the boundary of the campus. Cruz ran towards the fence then ducked behind a tree as someone fired at him again out of the darkness. Ahead he heard a voice calling out urgently, then silence. Cautiously he moved forward, using the tree trunks to give himself as much cover as possible. A little way on he came to a bend in the fence where it angled away from the road and wrought iron gave way to steel posts and barbed wire. Just past the bend he came to a hole in the fence where the middle wire had been cut and looped back round a post.

Cruz risked switching his torch quickly on and off and caught a glimpse of a well-trodden path leading through the gap in the fence. He ducked under the top strand of wire and followed the path which led him around the rear of an apartment block to reach a paved road. Looking to his right, Cruz saw a patrol car's flashing light and realised that this was the same road that ran along the frontage of the campus. Fifty metres to his left was what looked like an army jeep parked by the roadside. The engine was running and as he watched it suddenly pulled out and accelerated away: he'd lost them.

Cruz cursed then jogged back up the road towards the university gates where the patrol car was still parked. When he reached the gates he found a traffic cop leaning against the driver's door smoking a cigarette. He knew Cruz by sight and jerked to attention when he realised who it was sprinting out of the darkness. "My partner's checking out the buildings with the night watchman Inspector."

Cruz had been too far off to see the identification plate on the jeep. The only leads he had left were the lookout Garcia and what he'd overhead about the conspirators using the science block storage shed. Telling the patrolman to stay put, Cruz hurried back towards the library building. On the way he saw no sign of Echavez or the other cop but when he reached the rear door of the library it was still wide open and the light inside the entrance hall had been switched on.

Cruz made his way back up the stairs and as he reached the top he heard voices. He called out and a few moments later Echavez came down the corridor with the second patrolman. "We couldn't find nobody..." he began just as Cruz kicked the second door and it swung open to reveal Felipe sitting propped against the wall and holding his head.

"His name's Garcia, cuff him and take him out to the car, I'll be with you in a minute" Cruz told the startled cop. "You come along with me" he ordered Echavez and led the way back towards the room where he had overheard Coretta and the others.

Once inside he saw the place was used as a bookstore. He squeezed between rows of bookcases to the far end of the room where he found a long wooden table on which piles of books were stacked. Three chairs were drawn up around one end of the table where enough space had been cleared, Cruz guessed, to spread out papers and maps. If he was right, the conspirators had taken their documents with them. The only things left on the table were three empty bottles of Coke. Cruz looked around until he found an empty plastic bag in a waste bin. He carefully dropped the bottles into the bag, trying to avoid smudging any prints. Then he turned to Echavez and told him to lead the way to the storage shed.

Cruz followed the guard past a newish looking four storey building. A plaque beside the front door read *"Departmentos de Quimica y Biologia."* Echavez turned down a passageway to reach the rear of the block. Separated from the main building by a stretch of grass was a smaller flat-roofed structure.

"This is the old chemical store señor. It's not been used since the new building was finished a couple of years back."

Cruz shone his torch at the building. The front door had a large notice fixed to it. It showed a skull and crossbones underneath which was written *"Entrada Prohibido."*

Cruz turned to the guard. "Have you got a key?"

Echavez nodded. He fumbled in his pocket, pulled out a large key ring and began trying one after another. None of them worked. He scratched his head and stared accusingly at the door. "I don't understand, the key's got to be on this ring. Maybe the lock's jammed."

Cruz shone his torch on the lock: it looked brand new and there were scratch marks in the wood around the barrel. "The lock's been changed" he announced. He grabbed the door handle and yanked as hard as he could but the door didn't budge. He looked down at the trainers he was wearing, shook his head then turned to Echavez.

"You're wearing nice big boots. Kick that door in."

"Señor it's damaging University prop…"

Cruz grabbed him by the lapels if his jacket. "Do it or you'll be the one getting the kicking!"

Echavez did as he was told. On his fourth attempt there was a splintering noise and the door sagged open. Cruz shone his torch into the darkness. He saw a pull switch dangling from the ceiling, grabbed at it and after a moment's delay a pair of fluorescent tubes flickered into life.

The pallid glow from the tubes revealed racks of steel shelving lining the walls of the store. They were loaded with rows of bottles and jars. It looked as though more shelving units had once occupied the whole room but at the far end empty units had been piled on top of each other to clear an area which was now filled by several folding tables. They had been pushed together to form a spacious worktop which was almost covered by an array of large glass tanks looking, to Cruz's eyes, like empty tropical fish aquaria. In front of them was an array of flasks, plastic tubing and gas burners. Chemistry hadn't been Cruz's strongest subject but the set-up looked a lot more impressive than anything he'd seen in his school laboratory.

Next to the table sat half a dozen large plastic buckets fitted with lids. The whole store reeked of chemicals and dominating the rest was an odour that reminded Cruz of something familiar. What the hell was it? Cruz turned to Echavez who was standing nervously in the doorway. "Keep that door wide open" he told him "And for the love of God don't light a cigarette."

Cruz walked over to the nearest rack of shelving and peered at a row of dark brown glass bottles. The labels read in English "Potassium Permanganate." On the bottom rack were several large glass containers, the size of the straw-wrapped flagons used to sell cheap wine in. Cruz caught a whiff of acid and dimly remembered that the formula HCL stamped on the glass was hydrochloric acid. He went over to the table and the odour of something both penetrating and familiar grew stronger. Then it came back to him –Felicia's nail varnish remover –acetone. That was the smell coming from two unlabelled glass carboys stowed under one of the tables loaded with laboratory equipment.

Cruz stared at the complicated arrangement of tubes and flasks then noticed three or four cloth-wrapped packages sitting on a shelf at the far side of the table. He squeezed his way past the worktop and picked up one of them. It was tightly wrapped in coarse cotton cloth, bound with twine and weighed at least a couple of kilos. He called out to Echavez "Got a knife?"

"Yes señor, right here."Anxious to please, the guard scurried over to Cruz and handed him a battered-looking penknife. Cruz cut the twine on the parcel he was holding and unwrapped it. Inside was a light brown substance the consistency of marzipan, something he'd first come across during his time on *barrio* patrol duty: *basa,* the coca paste that was mixed with cheap tobacco and smoked by slum dwellers who couldn't afford purer forms of cocaine. It was also, Cruz knew, the half way house to producing high grade coke and he was willing to bet that the fancy array of chemical equipment sitting on the table next to him was intended to do just that.

"Señor!" Echavez who had wandered across to the far side of the storeroom beckoned Cruz over to him. "I never seen a thing like this before." He pointed to a rectangular white metal box sitting on a wheeled trolley. It had a glass door in the front and thanks to his wife, Cruz knew what it was. Felicia had shown him a picture of something that looked identical in one of her glossy magazines. "It's a microwave oven" he told the guard. "The latest thing *Yanqui* housewives cook dinner in. So what's an oven doing in here?"

Cruz opened the door, sniffed inside and smelt nothing. "Not cooking dinner" he muttered, more to himself than Echavez. He shone Echavez's torch into the interior of the shiny box: it looked immaculate. Then he drew his finger along the base of the oven and licked it. He felt a bitterness on his tongue and a spreading numbness. Once more he scraped his finger along the bottom of the oven and this time examined the result by torchlight. Fine white grains of powder were sticking to his fingertip. Now he knew for sure the nature of the deal Coretta was involved in. He looked up at Echavez who was staring at him with a puzzled expression.

"I'll stay here and look after this. You go and fetch one of the cops at the gate and tell him it's a Code 2, you got that? Code 2!" Echavez hurried away repeating the message to himself as he went. Cruz hoped that giving the patrolmen a Code 2 "major incident in progress" warning would produce some rapid action. He wasn't disappointed. He'd barely stepped outside the storeroom to get a breath of clean air when he heard the sound of an overweight traffic cop gasping for breath as he ran faster than he'd done since his recruit training. When he saw Cruz standing with his hands in his pockets staring up at the stars, he ground to a halt. All around was dark and utterly peaceful.

He stared at Cruz then holstered his gun. "Where are the bad guys Inspector?"

Cruz stared right back at him and shrugged. "You have to ask? Everywhere my friend: in this city the bad guys are everywhere."

SATURDAY 9: *CASA CRUZ*

Cruz thought that sounded like a good line but his words were drowned by the sirens of several more police vehicles responding to the Code 2 emergency. A sergeant Cruz knew clambered out of one of the cars. The detective pulled him to one side and instructed him to make sure no-one entered the chemical store or the library storeroom until the forensics team arrived. Once he had arranged for the site to be kept secure he climbed into the front seat of the car in which Garcia sat handcuffed to one of the uniforms.

As they sat off back to headquarters Cruz turned to look at Garcia. Hunched on the rear seat alongside the burly patrolman he looked like a lost kid being returned to his parents. "How's your head Felipe?" Cruz queried.

Garcia winced then closed his eyes as if trying to make Cruz and the other cops disappear. "Answer the Inspector!" barked the cop sitting next to him and the librarian almost jumped out of his seat.

"It hurts" he replied eventually in little more than a whisper.

"Speak up you prick!" the cop shouted.

"Don't hassle the poor guy" Cruz broke in. "He's going to do a lot of talking to me later, aren't you Felipe?" By then Cruz had decided that the talking would be done much later, after he'd had the chance of some sleep. In any case a night in solitary should soften up Garcia nicely.

Back at *Pepe*, Cruz saw his prisoner booked into a cell then commandeered the patrol car again to take him home. When he reached his front door Cruz swore as he remembered he'd left his keys at Tomas's place. He tried the handle and to his relief found the door was unlocked. He didn't feel like waking Felicia and answering her inevitable questions. He slipped off his trainers and padded through into the kitchen, stripped and did his best to wash off the day's filth at the sink before tying a towel round his middle, filling a glass with water and heading for the drinks cabinet in the lounge.

Although he was tired his head was buzzing and he knew he wouldn't be able to sleep until he'd sat down with a whisky and thought things through. Cruz poured himself a double, added the same amount of water and slumped into his favourite armchair. He took a drink and leaned back against the headrest.

"Literature and drama" he muttered to himself: Coretta's university course. Given her acting abilities she should have gained top marks in her second subject. Far from being blackmailed into spying on Hector she had been involved in trying to set up some kind of three-way operation involving El Chico's organisation, the ELR and the military cops, or at least some bent officers from the Black Helmets. The production facility at the university laboratory had shown Cruz how such an operation might work: the Black Helmets smuggling in blocks of coca paste, the ELR processing the paste into high grade snow and Hector responsible for distribution.

Cruz wondered whether the scheme had been El Chico's idea. He doubted it: the drug baron had an efficient operation already running and if the Colombians found out about the proposed new arrangements they wouldn't be very happy about it. When Colombian *drogistas* weren't happy, things tended to get nasty very quickly. Maybe it was their bomb that made such a mess of El Chico and incidentally saved Cruz's life? Whoever planted it, a dozen people were dead if you included scared little Marta Albañez and her boyfriend.

Scared maybe, but more determined than he had guessed. It was pretty clear that in collusion with Garcia she had been responsible for the theft of the university manuscripts. Coretta's voice in the library "We're just waiting for the payment to come through. You'll have it tomorrow." The Black Helmets had insisted that the ELR pay half the cost of the smuggled coca blocks and where else could the ELR have laid their hands on $250,000? Most of their members were dead or in jail and Cruz recalled that their last attempt at raising funds by a bank raid in *Sector Norte* had been a disaster. Their getaway car had been intercepted after a tipoff and all four ELR volunteers in the vehicle had been shot dead.

The stealthy removal of valuable items from the university library's manuscripts department must have seemed a much safer option than more traditional ways of bankrolling the cocaine operation. Sadly it had cost Marta her life to find out that there were no safe options when you got involved in drug trafficking. Which led Cruz to the question of what had happened to the $250,000 that Marta's manuscript thefts had raised? Had whoever shot her got their hands on the money? Or was it still hidden somewhere in the *Casa Albañez*.

Inevitably Cruz's thoughts kept sliding back towards Coretta. First of all to the two brief times they'd been alone together: at Adriana's flat and during the drive up to Rio Blanco. It was during those couple of short hours that he'd fallen for her. "A liar but a charming liar" he murmured to himself, a charming liar in deep trouble, with Hector and the cops on her tail and no $250,000 to placate the Black Helmets.

Where was she now? He flinched from the thought that Coretta could at that precise moment, be under interrogation at the Officers' School. He felt a cold sweat break out on his neck: there was no way he could let this case go. Not until he knew for certain what had happened to her.

As he finished his drink a light flicked on in the hall and Felicia appeared in the doorway. "I heard you come in, are you coming up now?" She sounded querulous and as tired as he felt. As if she'd been lying awake waiting for him to come home. She'd done that often enough through the years, Cruz remembered with a twinge of guilt. He wanted to tell her to leave him alone: instead he just nodded and followed her wearily up the stairs to bed.

SUNDAY 1: POLICE HEADQUARTERS

Cruz opened his eyes and glanced at his watch. Nearly six o'clock. Felicia didn't stir as he slid back the bedclothes, opened the wardrobe door as quietly as he could and took out the clothes he needed. He carried them downstairs, had a quick wash at the kitchen sink and got dressed. He didn't want a conversation about why he was going out at this time on a Sunday morning and when he phoned for a taxi he asked the driver to wait at the end of the road. First of all he had to get to Tomàs's flat to collect his wallet, ID, gun and the clothes he'd left there. Once that was taken care of he could head for Pepe and a conversation with Felipe Garcia.

Cruz switched on the kettle and while he was waiting hunted in the cupboard under the stairs for the bag Felicia kept her purse in. He was in luck: she must have called in at the bank yesterday. The purse contained ten crisp new hundred peseta notes. Cruz helped himself to half the money and while he was drinking his coffee scrawled his wife a note. telling her he'd been called in to interrogate a suspect.

He emerged from the house just in time to see his taxi turn the corner and pull into the kerb. He got into the cab, gave Tomàs's address and sat back hoping that Señora Robles, the widow who rented half of her house to Tomàs, hadn't gone to early morning mass.

He needn't have worried. She was in and recognised Cruz when he rang her bell to explain what had happened to her tenant. "Poor Señor Caldera" she lamented. "I hope you shoot those *desgraciados* when you catch them. Honest people can't sleep at night with those thugs around!"

Cruz reassured her that one of her tenant's attackers was already dead and the other in custody then told her he needed to collect some clean clothes for Tomàs. The senora, still protesting about the state of the world, handed him a spare key to his *compadre's* rooms. Cruz quickly retrieved his possessions and to avoid any further delay slipped the key under the widow's door before hurrying back out to his waiting taxi.

When he arrived at headquarters he waved his ID at Nuñez who was on the desk and sprinted for the beckoning open door of the lift. The sergeant called after him but fearing a message from Delgado that he was in no mood to receive, he pretended he hadn't heard and pressed the lift button. Up in his office he put a call through to the *Hospital Bolivar* and was told Tomàs appeared to be recovering well but wouldn't be discharged until after he had been checked again by a consultant sometime in the afternoon.

Cruz put down the phone and as he did so his eye caught a brown envelope half hidden under a pile of Newspapers featuring the Golden Gate bombing which someone had dropped on his desk. The envelope had the red sticker identifying it as a forensics lab report. Cruz lit a cigarette then used a pencil to slit open the envelope. Inside the envelope was a note which Cruz recognised as the handwriting of Adolf Messner, the forensics lab technician.

The note was brief and to the point. "Tomàs said you wanted what we've got on the bomb. Not a lot so far. Explosive was plastic, probably Semtex (Czecho-Slovak manufactured). Detonator, pencil-type, I'm still working on exact model . That's it to date. Final report with you Monday. Looking forward to a bottle of the usual. A.M."

Cruz crumpled the note and dropped it into his waste bin. East European explosive and a type of fuse developed for covert operations not commercial use. Neither suggested to him an operation carried out by the surviving remnants of the ELR. He turned his mind to Felipe Garcia. If he could get the librarian to talk, Garcia should be able to fill the gaps in what Cruz knew about the connection between the ELR, the Black Helmets and Hector Torres. Cruz stubbed out his cigarette then rummaged for a note pad in his desk drawer. As he did so there was a knock on his door. It was Nuñez, the desk sergeant Cruz had spoken to on the phone the night before.

"I've just come off shift" he announced. "There's something you should know."

Cruz waved him in and Nuñez closed the door behind him.

"Sit down" Cruz invited." Now, what's on your mind?"

Nuñez sat down and wiped his forehead with the back of his hand. "I tried to tell you earlier but you were too quick into that lift. It's Garcia, that little runt you brought in last night. He's dead, suicide."

"Shit!" Cruz stood up but with no space to pace around he had to sit down again. "What the hell happened?"

Nuñez shuffled in his chair. "You asked us to keep him in solitary. We took his belt and shoelaces but he managed to tear up his shirt. He tied the strips together and hung himself from the bars of his cell."

Cruz swore again, it hadn't occurred to him that Garcia would be so terrified of interrogation that he would kill himself. Maybe he'd realised that it was the only way he would be able to keep his mouth shut but now Cruz had no idea where to turn for his next lead. Still there was no point in taking out his frustration on the sergeant, who at least had come to break the bad news in person.

"These things happen Carlos, just go home and get yourself a good day's sleep."

When Nuñez got up to leave, Cruz followed him to the end of the corridor and bought himself a coffee from the machine. It was the same muddy colour as usual but Cruz hoped it had at least a trace of caffeine in it. He carried the plastic cup back to his desk, took a sip, grimaced and lit another cigarette. For a long minute he stared at the blank concrete wall that comprised the view from his office window, then he shifted his gaze to the telephone. He knew he had to make a call but he didn't know where that call was going to take him: he would be stepping into the unknown.

SUNDAY 2: *BAR GATO NEGRO*

Cruz wondered whether he should have chosen a less obvious venue for the meeting. It was too late now. At least the familiarity of his surroundings made him feel a little more comfortable. He took a pull at his beer and as he put down his glass he heard the door swing. He looked up and saw Brad Daley glance round the bar before spotting Cruz sitting in the corner. He strode across and trusted his considerable bulk to one of the *Gato Negro's* tubular steel chairs.

"Amalio, good to see you again!" he picked up the bottle in front of him, "Say, you got me a Coke. That's what I call service!" He pulled out a pack of Marlboro' extracted a couple, offered one to Cruz and leaned forward.

"So what have you got Amalio? This is the first time you've called me so I'm expecting something good. Now you'll tell me you have a spare ticket for the soccer game tonight, right?" Daley laughed, flicked his lighter at Cruz's cigarette, then lit his own. He took a swig of Coke and gave Cruz a quizzical glance.

Cruz leaned forward and parked his cigarette in the ashtray. "It would save us both time Brad if you told me how much you know about the case I've been working on."

"Now which case might that be exactly?" Daley smiled. "The stolen manuscripts case you're officially assigned to or the one involving the beautiful Señorita Coretta Sanchez Mendoza alias Corazon Silva Moran alias Miss ELR pinup of 1985? Not to mention the mystery of the big bang at the Golden Gate. Seems like you were rather closely mixed up in that as well."

"A little too close for comfort. I didn't realise I was important enough to occupy so much of your attention. "

"You mix with such interesting people Amalio, it's hard to ignore you."

"Well here are a couple more for you to think about. A Colonel Diaz and a Captain Araya, both Black Helmets. What can you tell me about them?

Daley leaned back in his chair and gave Cruz a hard stare. For the moment his usual affability had vanished. "First you better tell me why you want to know."

"Because it looks like they've decided to go freelance and they seem to be mixed up in this case of mine right up to their shiny epaulettes."

"How do you mean they've gone freelance?" Daley' eyes hadn't left Cruz's face.

Cruz shrugged. "Maybe freelance is the wrong word. Let's say they've set up a cooperative venture with a couple of unlikely partners."

"And who might these unlikely partners be?"

"How about the ELR and Hector Torres?"

Daley' raised his eyebrows then shook his head very slowly. "Unlikely partners is right! So what's your evidence?"

Cruz ran through what he'd got: Coretta's original story, as modified by the maid Carla, about the meeting at the Gonzalez party and what he'd heard himself when he eavesdropped on the conspirators at the university library. "I'm pretty sure the third guy in on that meeting was Captain Araya and that he was the one who shot at me when I tried to stop them escaping. From what both Coretta and the maid told me he's acting for Diaz."

"That prick!" Daley hissed, the strain of keeping his voice down turning his usually ruddy complexion almost purple. "Diaz spent six months in the States last year at Uncle Sam's expense training in anti-insurgency warfare and all the time the bastard was planning this."

"We don't know who came up with the original idea. It may have been the ELR, they're obviously desperate for money."

"Sure I can see what's in it for them, and maybe for Diaz if all he's interested in is making himself very rich. But why did El Chico get involved? He had a nice efficient operation going with the Colombians. Why risk upsetting them, especially when the profits are going to be split three ways?"

Cruz shook his head. "I don't think El Chico was involved. I think this was Hector's play. Suppose he was getting impatient, daddy not having a high enough opinion of his talents, keeping him on a tight rein? So he decides to try a little private enterprise. Maybe he was dumb enough to think he could keep it secret from El Chico, at least until everything was up and running. Then for some reason, there was a major falling-out between Hector and Coretta at the Gonzalez party."

"And El Chico asked you to find the girl."

A cold finger touched Cruz's heart. He thought about a denial but there didn't seem to be any point.

"You knew about that?"

"Sure Amalio, but don't worry, I haven't told Delgado, or anyone else in the department."

"And I don't suppose you'll tell me how you know?"

Daley grinned, his affability clearly in recovery.

"Just like you *amigo*, I protect my sources."

Cruz knew that one day Daley would use his knowledge but there was nothing he could do about it. Meanwhile the American was pulling a sheaf of photographs from the inside pocket of his jacket. "This other guy, the younger one you overheard in the library. Could he have been one of these?" He fanned the photos, standard size mugshots, across the table in front of Cruz.

Cruz took his time. There were ten photos in the set, all showing young men, some light skinned, some dark, some with shoulder length hair, others with short-cropped prison cuts. The fourth photo was the face he had seen in the beam of his torch the previous night, lean-faced, about thirty, with cropped hair and stubbled cheeks. To make sure, Cruz looked at the whole set then went through them again, although he hardly needed to. It was definitely number four. He pointed to the photo. "That's him."

Daley raised his eyebrows, gathered up the rest of the photos and pushed the fourth one towards Cruz. "You're sure? Absolutely sure?"

Cruz nodded. "I'm certain."

"I hate to press you but you've no doubt at all?"

Cruz was irritated at the American's persistence. "I had the guy full in the beam of my torch. He was less than ten metres away. Do you think I'm blind?"

"Cool it Amalio" Daley turned over the photo. There was no name on the back, just a number. "I'm sure you're eyesight's fine. It's just that this guy is an ex-university student called Salas, Roberto Salas and he's supposed to be locked up in *Puente Alto*. He was captured a few months back when the Black Helmets raided an ELR hideout in the mountains."

Cruz shook his head. "Well I can tell you he wasn't in *Puente Alto* last night. He was back on campus. You said he was a student. You don't happen to know what he was studying?"

Daley looked thoughtful. "As it happens, I do. Not politics or sociology like most of the ELR recruits. He was a Masters student, first degree in chemistry."

Cruz tapped the photo with his finger. "Then I think we have a story on this one. First the theory, then judging by the setup I found last night, he's started on the practical."

Daley picked up the photo and returned it to his pocket. "It hangs together all right. I'll check out my contacts. Find out if this guy Salas has been released."

Cruz nodded. "The other thing we need to know is where Araya took Salas and the girl last night. Remember they drove away together from the campus in a military jeep. If Araya blamed the others for their meeting being busted they could have had a falling out, especially if he thought they'd compromised the drugs operation. He could have taken them to the Officers School and you know what that means. Can you check on that?"

Cruz hadn't quite managed to keep his voice level. Daley signalled the waitress for more drinks and as they waited he gave the Inspector a sly glance. "Amalio, I sometimes get this feeling about where you're coming from. It's all about the girl, right?"

Cruz shook his head. "No it isn't but she's a big part of this case. Now answer my question Brad" he said quickly, hoping to move Daley on. "You must have contacts in the Black Helmets. Can you find out whether Araya brought in anybody for interrogation last night?"

Daley picked up his bottle of Coke and drained it. "I guess I can, assuming he did it officially but from what you tell me we can't be sure about that. He couldn't risk anybody knowing that he'd nearly been arrested alongside two ELR terrorists. Not unless he's got enough pull in the military to cover the whole thing up."

"I appreciate that, but it's the first thing we need to know, whether Coretta and Salas are banged up in the Officers' School. If not then I can start checking out other possibilities."

Daley stubbed out his cigarette. "If you do track them down somewhere else I want to know about it. Agreed?"

"Agreed" Cruz replied and accepted the meaty hand extended to him. Daley's grip almost crushed his fingers as they shook.

"Right, that's a deal" said Daley, "Now how about a real drink to celebrate?"

SUNDAY 3: *HOSPITAL BOLIVAR*

A couple of hours later Cruz parked outside the main entrance to the *Hospital Bolivar*. With difficulty he had managed to restrain himself to two *piscos* during the session with Daley. He had a feeling he would need a clear head to cope with what was left of his weekend.

Tomas was waiting in the reception area. His right cheek was badly swollen and the same eye was little more than a slit but he told his partner that apart from the state of his face, he had suffered nothing worse than bruised ribs. "What's next boss?" he asked Cruz. "Are we working or playing?"

Cruz shook his head. "What's next is I drive you home. Plenty of rest and no hard liquor for you *compadre*. Law enforcement will just have to do without you for a couple of days."

As he led Tomas towards his car, Cruz heard an odd squealing noise behind him. He turned and was surprised to see Nesto the beggar propelling what looked like a rebuild of the cart he been sitting in when he'd miraculously escaped injury at the time the Golden Gate bomb exploded.

"Nesto! What in hell's name are you doing here?"

"Hey Inspector, this is my new pitch. Don't know why I didn't try it before. People are either worried about being sick or grateful they got cured. Either way they feel generous when they see poor old Nesto. And I owe it to you Inspector. You got me taken here in that shiny ambulance. If it wasn't for you they'd have left me lying in the street!"

Cruz grinned. "You must have been my good deed for the day *amigo*." He dropped a couple of coins in the tin cup nailed to the front of Nesto's cart.

Nesto raised a hand in salute then gestured to Cruz to bend down. "I heard something might interest you Inspector." He whispered. "About Hector, son of the late lamented you-know-who."

"What about him?" Cruz stared down at Nesto wondering, not for the first time who he'd inherited his bright blue eyes from. The rest of his face looked pure *Indio*.

"He's putting the word round about a good looking university student he wants to talk to real bad. A lady called Coretta, or maybe Corazon, seems like she's got two names. Usually a bad sign that but Hector he very much wants to see her, even if she don't want to see him. You maybe got an interest in her too Inspector, a pretty girl like her?"

"Does everybody in this city know my business?" Cruz asked himself irritably while maintaining a smile and dropping a couple of extra coins in Nesto's cup.

Cruz knew that Tomas had overheard the exchange and as they climbed into the Chevette he glanced across at his partner. "Just don't say a word about pretty girls."

Tomas tried a grin, then winced at the pain of his bruised face. "As if. I got enough smacks in the mouth yesterday. Just tell me what happened after you came to see me in the hospital."

Cruz blasted his horn at a *taxista* trying to overtake him on the inside. "Maybe nothing happened. Maybe I just went home and had a quiet night in front of the TV."

"Yeah and maybe *El Presidente* called round and you watched the football together. No, something happened, I can tell."

"Holy Mother!" exclaimed Cruz. "I'm just glad I'm not married to you, you're worse than Felicia!" He eased back on the accelerator and as the Chevette rattled its way through the back streets of the old quarter, he brought his partner up to date on what had happened at *Las Espinas* and later at the University campus.

When Cruz told his Tomas what he'd overheard at the meeting in the library storeroom, his *compadre* gave a low whistle. "Hector, the ELR and the Black Helmets? Who would believe that!"

Cruz nodded. "Not me if I hadn't heard it with my own ears."

"Three sworn enemies getting into bed with each other. How long do you think it'll last?"

Cruz shook his head. "Not long: in fact I guess this little love match is already starting to fall apart. The ELR end of this operation is in deep shit. Now Marta Albañez is dead it looks like Salas and Coretta won't be able to come up with the money they were due to hand over to Araya today. What's more Salas's nice little cocaine factory in the chemicals store got blown so they can't deliver even if they did manage to lay their hands on $250,000."

"Which isn't good news for Coretta" Tomas observed in a carefully neutral voice.

"Not good news at all" Cruz agreed, trying to ignore the nagging anxiety in his stomach.

SUNDAY 4: *PISO CALDERA*

When they arrived at his apartment, Tomas's first concern was to get safely inside his front door before his landlady Señora Robles spotted him. "If she saw the state of my face she'd have hysterics" he explained to Cruz.

Cruz was busy searching for a bottle opener in what passed for Tomas's kitchen. "You need a woman in here my friend, this place looks like a rubbish tip."

Tomas sat down with a sigh in one of the two chairs that still possessed all four of their legs. "Sure" he replied. "You'll have to lend me one of yours. Hey look." He pointed to his answering machine. It sat alongside the telephone on an upturned packing crate used as a table. The green light on the machine was winking. "Shall I?"

Cruz nodded. Tomas picked up the phone, listened then replaced the receiver. "Two calls" he announced. "Delgado wants to speak to you. He's tried your home number and guessed you might be here."

"How did he seem? Happy? Sad?"

"You need to ask? He sounded as though his blood pressure was off the scale. "

"You think he might really have a heart attack or are you just trying to cheer me up? Who was the second call?"

"That was your Gringo friend Mister Daley. He also wants you to call him, on the number he gave you."

Cruz jumped out of his seat and hurried over to the phone. Daley picked up on the third ring.

"Amalio listen, two things you should know. First, I'm as sure as I can be that nobody was brought into the Officers' School for interrogation last night."

Cruz's felt the stress that had been building inside him evaporate. "What was the other thing?"

"Not good news. A squad of Black Helmets rolled up at the University this morning and took away all the laboratory equipment and the other stuff you found in the science block storeroom."

"Blood of Christ! All of it? They would have needed a truck!"

"Correction, two trucks. That's what they brought, plus a warrant signed by the Minister of Interior. They told your sergeant guarding the place that the gear was needed as evidence in an ongoing investigation."

"Any lead on where they took the stuff?" Cruz asked hopefully.

"Nothing yet. All I can tell you is that it didn't go into the Officers' School."

"That's something I suppose. They couldn't have taken it there unless the whole organisation was bent. I'll put the word round, check if anybody noticed military trucks in a place you wouldn't expect to see them."

"Sure and I'll keep trying my end. Stay in touch."

Daley rang off. Cruz replaced the receiver then picked it up again but stood looking out of Tomas's grimy back window without dialling. He was watching a mockingbird pecking at a grub it was attempting to extract from a crack between the cobbles in the yard. It didn't seem to be having much success but Cruz was impressed by the way it kept on trying.

Tomas's voice broke into his thoughts. "Are you going to ring Delgado boss or just stare at that bird all day?"

Cruz knew that if he called the *Comisario* he would almost certainly be pulled off the case. Delgado would want one of his special protégés, Clausen or somebody like him, someone more reliable and more controllable than Cruz to lead the investigation. If, Cruz thought sourly, the Generals are even willing to sanction an investigation that might spray a load of shit onto some shiny military reputations. He put the receiver back on its cradle and turned to look at Tomas.

"I never got Delgado's message. I dropped you off outside and drove off. I didn't tell you where I was going. You went straight to your bedroom had a lie down and dozed off. When you woke up you came through here, saw your machine blinking and picked up

Delgado's message. You rang him straight away. That'll happen in exactly one hour."

Tomas nodded. "Are you going to tell me where you're going?"

Cruz smiled at his *compadre*. "Do you really want to know? Happy ignorance might be more comfortable."

Tomas shook his head. "No it wouldn't. I'd just spend the rest of the day wondering where the hell you'd got into trouble this time."

Cruz dug into his pocket for his car eyes. "I'm not planning to get into trouble, but you're right, I would feel safer if somebody knew where I was. The first place I'm heading is the Albañez house."

Tomas raised his eyebrows. "The Albañez house. Why there?"

"Delgado's managed to keep Marta's murder out of the papers but if Coretta and Salas are still free agents they'll have realised by now that something's wrong. They're desperate for that $250,000 and they'll be looking for her and the money. Her father's house is the obvious place to start."

SUNDAY 5: *CASA ALBAÑEZ*

Cruz parked at the far end of the avenue leading to the Albañez residence. He wasn't sure who might be on the premises and didn't want to give warning of his approach. There was an outside chance that Marta's father, who at the earliest wouldn't have got news of her death until yesterday, might have got a flight back from a jungle airstrip. Cruz fervently hoped he hadn't made it yet: he didn't feel up to dealing with a grieving parent. He needn't have worried: when he reached the gate the only sign of life was a bored looking uniform sitting on the front door step, smoking a cigarette.

When he saw Cruz coming up the drive the young *guardia* jumped to his feet and flattened the butt of his cigarette under his boot. Cruz didn't recognise the youngster and flashed his warrant card.

"Anybody else been here today?"

The *guardia* had leapt to attention when he saw Cruz's card. "No Inspector, just me. To keep snoopers away sir."

Cruz nodded, assuming that Marta's death would have been reported in the morning papers.

"I'm just going into the house to check out a couple of things. Any idea when Doctor Albañez is due back?"

"No sir. I just know I'm here until six o'clock, then somebody else takes over."

"Good, let me know if anybody turns up."

Cruz was bothered by an irrational anxiety that Delgado would suddenly pop up from behind one of Doctor Albañez's rose bushes. He told himself not to be stupid, the *Comisario* wasn't that clairvoyant. He pushed open the front door and entered the hallway. The house felt pleasantly cool but he could smell the familiar hospital odour that seemed to linger in any place visited by the body handlers from the police morgue.

Cruz walked through once more into the lounge where Coretta and Marta had held him at gunpoint and stopped dead. The place had been ransacked, chairs overturned, cushions slashed. The drawers of a huge, old fashioned chest had been pulled out and their contents tipped onto the floor. Cruz made his way through into the kitchen and saw that the same thing had happened there. Cupboards hung open and drawers had been emptied. He ran quickly upstairs and found more evidence of a hasty but thorough search. Had the searchers found what they were looking for?

Cruz hurried downstairs and grabbed the shoulder of the *guardia*. "You said nobody had been here this morning. Are you sure of that?"

The startled youngster took a pace back and stammered. "None of our people sir. Just a couple of cleaners who told me they'd been asked to tidy up the place before Doctor Albañez came back."

"Cleaners! What did they look like?"

By now the *guardia* was looking terrified. "A man and a woman sir, both quite young. The woman had a headscarf on so I couldn't see much of her face. The guy had short hair, like he'd been in the army. They were dressed in overalls sir, like you'd expect and they had a note saying they were employed by the Doctor and authorised to enter the house to clean it while he was away. They had their own key."

Cruz hand was still gripping the *guardia's* shoulder. "Were they carrying anything when they went in?"

"No sir. They told me their cleaning stuff was already in the house."

"And when they came out?"

"No sir, they came out empty-handed."

Cruz's eyes bored into those of the *guardia*. "You are totally sure of that?"

"Yes sir"

"And which way did they go?"

"They told me they were heading for *Rinconada* Inspector. They said they could catch a *micro* at the end of this road."

"How long ago was this?"

"A couple of hours sir, I guess."

Long gone, thought Cruz, wherever they were headed. *Rinconada* was a barrio on the west side of the capital which was a plausible place for domestic staff to live but the fact that they'd mentioned it to the Guardia meant it was a blind. It was also pretty obvious that they knew Marta was dead but suspected that she might have hidden what they were looking for somewhere inside the house. It didn't look as though they'd found anything. It was just possible $250,000 might have been concealed inside two pairs of overalls but it would have been easier to use a bag to carry the bills if they had found Marta's stash.

Cruz left the young policeman to sweat outside and re-entered the house. Feeling thirsty he went into the kitchen to get a glass of water. As he turned the tap on he saw a note pad lying on the worktop next to the sink. He was fairly sure it hadn't been there the last time he'd been in the house. He picked it up and walked over to the window. At first glance the pad was blank but he could make out impressions of letters and numbers. He walked through into the lounge and angling the pad under the bulb of a table lamp, he was able to read what had been written on the previous page: *EC 12.30 CA 14.15.*

Cruz ripped another page off the pad and wrote down the cryptic message. He stared at it trying to work out possible alternative meanings before deciding that the answer was almost certainly the obvious one. Train times, *EC* an abbreviation of *Estacion Central* and *CA* standing for *Costa Azul.* He walked over to the far corner of the lounge where a phone sat on a small polished wood table and dialled the front desk at *Pepe.* "This is Inspector Cruz and it's urgent. Check out the train times from Central Station to *Costa Azul.* I want to know if there was a train leaving at 12.30 today, due in at 14.15. Yes I'll hold."

As Cruz stood with the receiver in his hand, his glance fell on a framed photo hanging on the wall. It showed a middle-aged couple sitting in deck chairs in a garden. Kneeling in front of them was a young girl maybe thirteen or fourteen years old, unmistakably Marta. Behind the group was the corner of a single storey white-painted villa and beyond a low wooden fence, what looked like a promenade with the sea in the background.

Cruz stared hard at the photo and recognised the ornate iron posts of the street lamps running along the promenade. "*Costa Azul!*" he exclaimed. "Yes Inspector" said the voice in his ear. "There's a train leaves at 12.30 on Sundays for *Costa Azul*, arrives at 14.15." Cruz glanced at his watch. If Coretta and Salas were on that train they should have arrived more than an hour ago. "Good, thanks for that. Now one more thing, get me the number of the police barracks in *Costa.*"

After Cruz had been given the number, he spent some time ferreting through the papers left strewn on the floor in front of a large roll top desk. The desk occupied most of the space in a small side room off the main lounge. Doctor Albañez obviously used it as an office. Eventually he found an out-of-date identity card for the Doctor giving his mother's maiden name and a teaching certificate awarded to his wife under her maiden name. Next he rang the *Costa Azul* police and persuaded a sleepy sounding *guardia* to rouse himself and check out the addresses of properties owned by a Doctor or Señor, or possibly Señora, Aravena or Rosetti.

As he waited for the call back Cruz mentally kicked himself for not checking out the names before his last fruitless visit to the coast. He'd found no trace of any property owned or rented by an Albañez although Marta had told him she was going to stay at her parents' house when he put her on the train less than a week ago. He'd assumed she'd been lying but he could have been wrong if the house was simply registered under another name. Cruz went back into the kitchen to retrieve his glass of water and as he took a drink the phone rang. The *guardia* still sounded half asleep but he'd done as Cruz asked.

"There's a house on *Calle Pacifica* Inspector. Number 21, registered to a Señora Rosetti."

"Calle Pacifica, where exactly is that?"

"It's the name of the street running along the seafront sir."

Cruz took a deep breath and tried to think clearly. The last thing he wanted was the local cops charging round to *Calle Pacifica* and alerting Coretta and Salas, maybe even provoking a shoot-out. On the other hand if they waited until he got there it might mean the fugitives had time to find what they wanted then get clean away.

"Put me through to your duty commander right away."

Cruz pictured an unknown *teniente,* collar unbuttoned, feet on desk, snoozing through another lazy Sunday afternoon. Luckily he was wrong, the imaginary *teniente* turned out to be a youngish and keen-sounding sergeant. "The commander's off sick sir, I'm in charge for this shift. Is there anything we can do for you?"

Cruz told the sergeant as little as he could, merely saying that a pair of suspects in a drugs case might be holed up in the property on *Calle Pacifica.*

"Do you want us to send a car round to take a look at the place Inspector?"

"Yes but no flashing lights. Use an unmarked car and don't approach the house. Just keep it under surveillance. If anybody leaves get their number plate but don't try to tail them."

Cruz knew that two old ELR hands like Coretta and Salas would almost certainly spot any hamfisted attempt by the local force to follow them. He checked his watch again. Almost four o'clock. If he left straight away he should just make it in daylight. "I'll be there in ninety minutes" he told the *guardia,* slammed down the receiver and ran all the way back to his car.

SUNDAY 6: *COSTA AZUL*

The police barracks in *Costa Azul* was a single story concrete-block rectangle, which Cruz was confident would take the prize for ugliest building in town. Its appearance wasn't improved by a faded coat of whitewash and the blue paint peeling off its window shutters and front gates. Sergeant Ibarrez was waiting outside when Cruz drove up to the gates. His immaculate uniform and smart salute were worthy of a guard commander at *Pepe* and he seemed every bit as keen as he'd sounded on the phone. "I've got Officer Toro parked up at the near end of *Calle Pacifica*. I've given him a radio. Our sets aren't secure so I told him only to call in if anybody enters or leaves the house. So far it seems to be quiet."

Cruz nodded. Thank God he'd had the luck to find a policeman with brains in a place like *Costa Azul*. "Well done sergeant. I'm going down there now and I'll get Toro to radio in if we need any help."

Ibarrez was looking at him curiously. "I was surprised to see you arrive on your own Inspector. I was expecting back-up if you're planning to go into the house."

Cruz tried a reassuring smile. "We're not ready to make arrests yet sergeant. And as it happens my partner's been injured."

Mentioning Tomas made Cruz realise how much he was missing his *compadre's* presence.

"Well if anything does go wrong Toro's reliable and a good shot."

"Let's hope he doesn't need to prove that. Now, how do I find the place?"

It turned out that *Calle Pacifica* was on the northern edge of the town, fronting the narrow strip of sand and shingle that formed the beach. As Cruz drove along the promenade, the Pacific was living up to its name, gentle waves sparkling in the rays of the setting sun. He tried to imagine living in one of the neat little houses with a sea view, sitting on the veranda every evening to watch the sun go down.

"You'd be bored out of your skull" he told himself as he stopped in a side street that intersected with *Pacifica*. He got out of the Chevette and walked until he caught site of a car parked on the beach side of the street with the driver still in it, apparently reading a paper. He rapped on the side window.

"Are you Toro?"

The burly young man at the wheel nodded. Cruz strolled round to the passenger side, climbed in and introduced himself. "Any action since you got here?"

Toro shook his head. "Nothing sir. Are you sure your guys are in there?"

Cruz shrugged ""Probably, although one of them is a girl." He asked Toro which house was Number 21 and the officer pointed to a property a little way down the road. It looked almost identical to the other houses on the street, modern constructions built as retirement homes or holiday getaways, single storey with a veranda running along the front and a tiny garden. Fronting the garden was a low fence that matched the one Cruz had seen in the photograph at the Albañez house.

"So what do we do now sir?"

"If everything stays quiet we wait until it gets dark then we'll take a closer look."

Cruz settled himself back in his seat. The car was a Dodge, bigger and more comfortable than his Chevette. He felt in his pockets and drew out his pack of Marlboro'. Empty: he looked across at Toro. "Got a cigarette?"

"Sorry sir, I don't smoke."

Just my luck Cruz thought, crumpling his empty pack and throwing it onto the back seat. He reached down and fiddled with the knobs on the car radio. All he managed to produce was an angry hiss.

"Afraid that doesn't work Inspector, the aerial got broken off last week and it still hasn't been fixed."

"*Puta!*" Cruz switched off the noise. "What do you do to pass the time then Toro?"

Toro picked up a paperback book off his lap. Cruz glanced at the title "An Introduction to the Criminal Law of the Republic" and raised his eyebrows.

"I'm sitting my sergeants' exam next week" Toro explained.

"Glad to hear it" Cruz replied. "I wouldn't like to think you were reading it for entertainment."

Toro grinned. "No sir, I'm not that desperate."

Half an hour later Cruz was searching through his pockets again, hoping to find a stray cigarette that had escaped from its packet when Toro exclaimed "Sir, look!"

Cruz peered through the windscreen: a figure had emerged from the front door of Number 21, a man wearing a baseball cap. The peak obscured the upper part of his face but Cruz was confident it was Roberto Salas, the man he'd identified in Brad Daley's photograph. After quickly glancing left and right the figure set off briskly down the street heading away from where the two policemen were parked.

"Do I follow him?" asked Toro.

Cruz shook his head. Salas was not carrying anything and there was no sign of Coretta. Cruz was betting that Salas would be coming back.

"No, we wait" he said, trying to sound confident. Ten minutes later, just as Cruz's belief in his judgement was beginning to wane, a car appeared round the corner at the far end of *Pacifica*, drove rapidly towards them and halted outside Number 21. Its horn beeped once and almost immediately Coretta appeared at the front door. She ran down the path carrying a large briefcase and climbed quickly into the passenger seat.

Cruz fumbled in his pocket, produced the keys to his Chevette and dropped them in Toro's lap. "As soon as they're past, get out and I'll follow them. I'm parked in the next side street. They'd recognise my car so take it to your barracks and we'll swop back later."

As Salas drove towards them Toro lifted his newspaper to cover his face and Cruz slid down in his seat until he was invisible from a passing car. He heard Salas drive past and sat up quickly to catch the registration before their quarry vanished at the end of the street. Then he opened the car door. "Come on! Get moving or I'll lose them!"

Toro didn't shift. "Can't I come with you sir? I'd like to see this thing through."

Cruz hesitated. Toro seemed bright enough and could be very useful backup but Cruz suspected his quarry was heading back to the capital and God knew where they might end up. "Borrowing" an officer without authorisation could get him into even deeper trouble. Not just him either.

"Not possible. This investigation could make a load of shit fly and some of it would stick to you. If you want to make sergeant you'd better get out now!"

Toro clambered out of the car and Cruz wriggled across into the driver's seat. He pressed the button to lower the passenger side window then fumbled in his wallet and found the card that Daley had given him. He scribbled the telephone number from the card onto a piece of paper and handed it to Toro. "One more thing you can do for me. Ring this number. A gringo will answer it but he speaks Spanish. Tell him I'm following our two ELR suspects. They're travelling in a small blue Renault, registration BE74893, probably stolen and I think they're heading back to *Independencia*. Tell him I think they've picked up the dollars and they'll be heading for a meet. No idea where that will be. You got all that?"

Toro repeated the message back then saluted. Cruz executed a rapid three point turn and drove off leaving the young officer standing on the pavement. The Renault had long since disappeared round the corner at the end of the street but Cruz was confident it was heading back towards the capital. The gathering darkness might make it harder to spot his quarry but would also make it more difficult for them to realise they were being followed.

Cruz's first objective was to get himself onto the Pacific Freeway. That proved harder than he expected. He missed a turn somewhere and found himself in a maze of back streets before he finally emerged onto a road he recognised: the main route down to the fishing harbour. A couple of hundred metres further on he was relieved to see the *Carreterra Pacifica* sign marking the junction onto the main road.

    The Highway was quiet at this hour and what little traffic was moving was mostly headed for the coast. After fiddling around on the dashboard, Cruz managed to switch on his headlights and was able to put his foot down. He glanced at his watch, a quarter to eight and already almost pitch dark. As the road began its long climb over the coastal mountains his lights illuminated the ghostly, contorted shapes of the dry scrub that lined the verges. Occasionally the yellow or green glow of a pair of eyes was caught in the beam, goat or wild dog or, for all he knew, some bigger and more dangerous night hunter.

    After half an hour the only eastbound vehicles Cruz had passed were a pair of lorries grinding their way uphill, laden with fish for the capital. At last he rounded a hairpin and reached the end of the climb. A roadside *taverna* marked the summit and he glanced regretfully at the lighted entrance as he drove past, wishing he could risk stopping to buy cigarettes.

    It wasn't just nicotine Cruz needed. His stomach was rumbling and he realised he hadn't eaten anything all day. He rummaged around in the side pockets of the Dodge then tried the glove compartment and struck lucky. A chocolate bar and a screw top drink bottle: Toro's emergency supplies. Steering precariously with one hand he managed to unscrew the bottle top and took a cautious drink. As he might have guessed: orange squash. At least the chocolate tasted good but after he'd finished the bar he was still ravenous and he needed a cigarette more than ever.

SUNDAY 7: *CARRETARRA PACIFICA*

Despite Cruz's hunger he was starting to feel drowsy: he wound down the two front windows of the car and took in some deep breaths of cool night air. As he did so he saw two red dots in the distance, the rear lights of a car. Was it the Renault? To be sure he would have to get a lot closer. He floored the accelerator and rapidly closed on the other vehicle until he was near enough to be certain. If he stayed behind the other car after closing so fast, it would look suspicious so he pulled out to overtake. Once he was past the Renault he kept going for a couple of kilometres until he reached a side road. A small copse grew in the angle between the two roads and he pulled over into the deeper shadow of the trees and switched off his lights.

Cruz sat in the darkness, listening to the ticking of his engine as it cooled and the chirping of cicadas from the undergrowth beside the car. Less than a minute passed before he saw a flash of headlights then heard the high-pitched complaint of an engine being pushed to its limits. Cruz quickly pulled out quickly but this time he kept back as far as he dared without losing sight of his quarry's rear lights.

As he drove, Cruz tried to guess where Salas and Coretta might be headed. If his guess was right and they'd picked up the $250,000 and had arranged with Diaz to hand over the money, where would they meet up? Would they risk the University campus again? Surely not, but what were the alternatives? Coretta's contacts had all been blown and the Albañez residence was under police guard. Would Hector be involved? It didn't sound likely from what Cruz had overheard but if he'd pulled out of the deal how would the remaining partners cope without a distribution network? He decided there was no point in trying to think too far ahead: all he could do was to hang on to the car in front and hope that Toro had got his message through to Daley.

Cruz reached the final hairpin before the long stretch of dead-straight road that led across the central plain towards the capital. He touched his brakes and as he did so he caught the Renault in his headlights. It was parked just off the highway on a dirt track that joined the *Carreterra* almost at the apex of the bend. Before could react, the darkness ahead exploded in flashes of gunfire, his windscreen shattered and he heard the bang of a bursting tyre.

    Cruz felt the Dodge lurch sickeningly. The steering wheel tried to wrench itself free from his hands and as he struggled to hold on, the car slewed sideways, slid off the carriageway and slammed broadside into a tree trunk. Cruz, who'd shut his eyes before the moment of impact, opened them again and took a long, deep breath. His shoulder was hurting but he quickly forgot about the pain when he glanced in his rear view mirror and saw the Renault reversing back onto the road. Moments later, it was heading towards him. Frantically he pulled at the door handle. The door was jammed shut so he twisted in his seat and kicked until it gave way and he half-climbed, half-tumbled out of the car, dazzled by the headlights of the oncoming vehicle. He groped for his gun, only to find that it was no longer in his pocket.

    The Renault slowed as it drew alongside the crumpled Dodge. Cruz crawled further back behind the cover of the tree. He heard voices: Salas saying something he didn't catch then Coretta, calling sharply "No! Leave it!" Salas laughed and the Renault accelerated away into the night.

    Cruz slowly got to his feet. He took a few paces to see if he could still walk and found that apart from his shoulder, bruised where he had slammed against the door, he seemed to be uninjured. He stuck his head inside the car and found a torch in the glove box. Switching it on, he took a look round and saw that the Dodge was going nowhere without some major surgery. The nearside front tyre had been shredded, the windscreen had gone except for a jagged fringe of glass and water trickling from the punctured radiator was forming a pool under the front bumper.

    Cruz swore. The fugitives had been more alert than he'd bargained for. Maybe they had identified the Dodge as an unmarked police car when Toro was watching the bungalow on *Calle Pacifica*. If so they'd have realised they were being tailed as soon as Cruz overtook them, if not before. He didn't know whether Salas had meant to kill him but from the fugitives' point of view it hardly mattered now that he was stranded miles from anywhere. Cruz shone the torch around inside the car until he saw his gun nestling in the corner of the driver's footwell. He pocketed the weapon then walked slowly back onto the carriageway.

The fish lorry hadn't seemed too keen to stop. In fact the driver had almost run Cruz over as he stood in the road waving his torch. He wound down his window and swore rapidly and eloquently at Cruz who pulled himself up into the cab and produced his police identification. The confirmation that his unexpected passenger was a cop didn't seem to cheer the driver up: he muttered more obscenities under his breath as slammed the truck into gear.

"What's your name *amigo?*" Cruz demanded.

"Pablo" the trucker grunted. "Pablo Cinchon." Cinchon was leathery-skinned and bald with a week's stubble on his chin. He looked as if he might have been a fisherman before taking up the marginally less dangerous occupation of driving a truck on the *Carreterra*. It was obvious he hadn't left his old life far behind. Both he and the truck smelled impressively of fish.

"Cheer up Pablito" Cruz told him. "I'm not going to inspect your load or check your tyres. All I need is a lift to the city."

Cinchon didn't bother to reply, he just dug a crumpled pack of cigarettes out of his shirt pocket, stuck one in his face and lit it before dropping his box of matches onto the dashboard.

Cruz picked up the box then leaned across and plucked the pack from Cinchon's pocket. He helped himself to a cigarette, lit it and took a long drag. The strong tobacco made his head swim but it tasted good. He leaned back in his seat and tried to ignore the roar of the truck's engine and the stink of fish. He had the same problem as before to think about. Where would the drug meet take place? He'd ruled out the University but what had Araya said during the campus meeting Cruz had spied on? Suddenly his memory clicked into gear. *Bring it to the same place as last time.*

"That's it!" Cruz exclaimed and grinned at the scowling Cinchon. He pulled out his wallet and extracted a bill. "Get me to the city centre in an hour and this is all yours. Ten *Yanqui* dollars. Can you make that?" Cinchon spat out of the cab window then nodded. He pressed his foot down on the accelerator until the whole cab shook. The noise and vibration gave Cruz the feeling that he was sitting inside a cement mixer. He folded his wallet and was about to restow it into his pocket when another thought struck him. He unzipped the small compartment where he kept Brad Daley's emergency contact card. He had one more call to make.

SUNDAY 8: *CASA GONZALEZ*

"We're here señor." Cruz, who'd nodded off during the short trip from the city centre shook himself awake and climbed out of the cab. At least this time he could pay the fare: he didn't feel up to another brawl with an irate *taxista*.

Once the cab had driven off, Cruz tried to get his bearings by the feeble light of a couple of street lamps. Ahead of him he could see a road junction and he knew that the front entrance gate to the lawyer Gonzalez's house was no more than a hundred metres round the corner from the intersection. That had been where Hector, Coretta and the Black Helmets had met up at the start of all this business. If Cruz had guessed correctly and *the same place* meant exactly that, Coretta and Salas could be there at that moment meeting the two renegade Black Helmets officers to hand over the $250,000 they collected in *Costa Azul*.

When Cruz had rung Brad Daley from the noisy city centre bar where Cinchon had dropped him off, the *Yanqui* had told him that within the last half hour there had been a report of a Renault abandoned and set on fire in a western suburb of the city.

"Looks like they've switched cars. So don't bother looking for a Renault when you get to the Gonzalez house. I'll be there with you as soon as I can collect enough backup." Cruz had told him he couldn't risk waiting: the conspirators might finish their business and be gone before Daley and his men could arrive.

"OK Amalio, but take care. You've no idea how many people are in there."

Cruz had checked his watch. "I'll expect you by eleven o'clock."

"Right. Now, we need a way to let you know we're in position without warning the bad guys..."

Standing on the pavement in the deserted street Cruz could only hope that what he'd agreed with Daley would work out. He took his gun out of his pocket, checked the magazine, clicked on the safety and slipped the weapon into the waist band of his trousers. Then he took a deep breath and walked on until he reached the driveway of the large villa adjoining the Gonzalez property.

The place was in darkness and Cruz decided to take a chance. He slipped through the entrance, moving cautiously until his eyes adjusted to the gloom. Beyond an expanse of grass dotted with small trees he could make out a high hedge which, when he reached it, proved to be a thick belt of laurel. He worked his way along the hedge until he came to place where a gap between two bushes gave him enough space to wriggle through into the garden next door.

Gonzalez's house was directly ahead, separated from him by what looked like an ornamental rose garden. Two of the upstairs rooms were illuminated but the lower part of the building was dark. Cruz realised that he was on the opposite side of the house from the patio where Coretta, Hector and the Black Helmets had held the meeting that ended in a fight between the two cousins.

He crept onwards, keeping close to the hedge until he reached a stone wall. He followed the wall which Cruz guessed marked the rear boundary of the property. He was now looking at the back of the house and saw a light shining in the kitchen where he'd interviewed Carla the maid. More light was coming from beyond the corner of the house: the area where the patio was located. Would he be lucky enough to find the conspirators meeting outside again?

Cruz inched carefully forward crouching as low as he could until a dark shape suddenly loomed up in front of him. He reached for his pistol but before he could draw, a gun muzzle, hard and cold on his neck, froze him. "Stay quiet and keep your hands still" a voice hissed in his ear. The figure in front of him came closer, revealing that it was also holding a gun.

A hand swiftly patted him down and extracted the pistol from his waistband. "Turn yourself round and head back the way you came. No tricks *puerco* or you're dead meat. Move!"

Hector Torres leaned back in his chair and stared at Cruz who stared back, hoping that his face wasn't revealing how scared he felt. Now that Cruz had a better view of him than at their first meeting in the Golden Gate Bar, he could see that Hector, who must still be in his twenties, was already putting on weight. Not the muscle slowly turning to flab that was his father's problem. Hector didn't look as if he'd ever had that much muscle. With his slicked-back hair, pinched nose and rosebud lips he still reminded Cruz of a bandleader or a compère on one of the TV quiz shows Felicia liked to watch. Then Cruz saw that that although he looked nothing like El Chico, his eyes had the same black, opaque stare as his father's.

"Well Inspector" Hector clasped his hands under his chin in an oddly schoolmasterly gesture, as if he was about to test Cruz with a difficult question but instead of asking him what was the capital of Indonesia or the square root of seventeen plus thirty-two he just slowly shook his head. "You've been giving me some problems this past week."

Cruz kept his mouth shut.

"You were supposed to find a girl and let us know where she was. Instead it seems you kept her all to yourself. That upset my father very much. Luckily for you he passed away before he could tell you exactly how disappointed he was."

In other circumstances Cruz might have been able to smile at Hector's euphemism. "Passed away" seemed an odd phrase to use of somebody blown to pieces by a bomb.

"Your father wasn't straight with me. If he'd told me the truth I would never have got involved."

Hector leaned forward in his chair and his tone suddenly sharpened. "You wouldn't? Well you are involved right up to your neck and the shit you're in is going to get a whole lot deeper if you don't do exactly what you're told."

"So what is it you want me to do?"

Hector smiled. "That's better. Well, it's simple enough. You have to perform an act of penance, then we can be reconciled."

Cruz didn't feel like playing games "Just tell me straight what you want me to do!"

Like a child making a pretend gun, Hector pointed two fingers at Cruz. "I want you to kill somebody who's upset me."

Cruz's mouth felt as parched as sun-dried leather. "Who?" he managed to croak, already guessing the answer.

"Why, the bitch who gave me this of course." Hector lifted his arm stiffly and grimaced. "It's still painful but it won't bother me so much when I attend her funeral. I assume you know that Coretta and her ELR comrade are in the house next door meeting two of my military associates? I had advance warning of their little get-together which is why I was able to take over this place ready to make a move when I'm ready. Luckily for them the owners of this house are away."

Cruz gripped the arms of his chair to stop his hands from shaking. "And what if I refuse to go along with this?"

"I shoot her myself, then I shoot you. Either way Coretta dies, it's just a question of whether she has you for company."

"If you hate her so much why don't you just do the job yourself?"

"Two reasons Inspector. First I believe that you have, shall we say, a more than professional relationship with Coretta. Killing her will be your punishment for disobeying my father. Second your prints will be on the murder weapon. By an odd coincidence it's the same gun that was used to shoot Marta Albañez. Next time you're asked to do me a favour you'll carry out my wishes to the letter or that gun will find its way to *Comisario* Delgado."

Cruz's grip on the chair tightened until he felt his fingers would crack. He had an overwhelming urge to hurl himself at Hector using fists, teeth, anything to wipe the smile off the gang leader's face but a small voice in his head reminded him that outside, in the darkness, he had one Ace left to play. Right now he also needed to play for time. He hoped Hector was the kind of mobster who liked to boast about his achievements.

"Tell me" his voice still sounded odd, as if somebody else was speaking. "Who came up with the idea for this three-way deal? Was it you?"

"Let's say I had the brains to take the opportunity when it came my way."

"It was your idea then, not El Chico's?"

Hector smiled. "My father was getting a little conservative in his approach to business."

"I guess he might have been worried about how the Colombians would react."

Hector's smile vanished. "I can handle the Colombians. They're not the only ones who can run an integrated operation. We also have the skills to grow and process the stuff, not just market it."

The gangster was beginning to sound like the general in charge of the Junta's Department of Industrial Production. Cruz kept that thought to himself.

"So how did you get in touch with Diaz and the ELR?"

"A little while back, when we heard that the Black Helmets were under pressure from the *Yanquis* to start interfering in our business, my father asked me to try and make contact with one or two key officers. I found out that Colonel Diaz has a liking for very young girls. I was able to supply him with some choice cuts."

"And how did the drugs operation come into it?"

"A happy accident you might say. The Colonel found that one of his ELR prisoners, Roberto Salas, was a chemistry graduate who'd already been producing snow on a small scale. That gave Diaz the idea of making himself enough money to retire and live like a playboy. Maybe buy himself a harem of twelve year old virgins. Salas didn't need much persuading but they still needed a large-scale distributor."

"So Diaz went to see your father who told him he wasn't interested?"

"And that's when he turned to me. My father was a great man but like I said he had got a little set in his views. Sometimes it takes fresh eyes to see the big picture."

"And nerve to make a big decision like going up against the Colombians."

"As they say Inspector, a shark has to move forward or it dies: remember that. Now it's time for you to make your decision, except that you really don't have a choice. Either way Coretta is killed, it's just a question of who's holding the gun. If it's me then you end up dead as well."

Hector revealed his teeth in a smile that reminded Cruz of the dead Caiman. The gorilla standing behind him tapped his shoulder. As if in a dream, Cruz got to his feet and followed Hector out of the room into the garden then back through the gap in the hedge. As they moved through the darkness, Cruz was conscious of more men on their heels. Another of Hector's gang was waiting for them at the far side of the hedge in Gonzalez's garden. "They're still talking boss" he whispered. "Five of them sitting round the table on the patio."

"Good" said Hector. "Let's go and join the party." He pulled out a gun then turned to the *gorilla* who was standing at Cruz's elbow. "Enrico, take two guys and go round the far side of the house. Make sure nobody leaves that way."

Enrico nodded and disappeared into the darkness. Cruz glanced around, three or four more of Hector's men had stayed with them, too many even to think about trying to grab the gang leader's gun. For a few moments nobody moved while they waited for the others to get into position. Cicadas chirruped from the surrounding bushes and there was a faint sound of dance music coming from an upstairs window of the house. A tango that Cruz vaguely recognised. Who had he been dancing with when he heard it last? Felicia? Adriana?

Hector put a hand on Cruz's shoulder. "Move!" he said then led the way through the garden onto a gravelled path that followed the side of the house towards the patio. When he reached the corner of the building, Hector stepped aside. As he did so, one of the men behind Cruz shoved the detective in the back so that he stumbled forward onto the patio.

Hector had made no attempt to muffle the noise of his footsteps on the gravel so the five people Cruz saw in front of him had heard them coming. The two Black Helmets, Diaz and Araya, both in uniform, were seated at the circular wooden table that occupied the centre of the patio area. On the table was a briefcase that looked like the one Coretta had been carrying when she left *Costa Azul*. Sitting next to the two Black Helmets was a silver-haired figure in civilian dress who Cruz guessed must be the lawyer Gonzalez, the owner of the house. Coretta and Roberto Salas were standing at the far end of the patio as if ready to make a run for it. Coretta held a gun but Salas was empty-handed. Behind them Cruz could make out the dark shapes of the *gorilla* Enrico and his men.

"Tell her we're police, tell her to drop her gun" Hector hissed from behind him.

Cruz did as he was told. If Coretta was fooled into thinking this was a police ambush she was less likely to attempt a suicidal shoot-out.

Coretta stood staring at Cruz, gun pointing at him but wavering in her hand.

"Coretta, put that down, you're surrounded."

Coretta's eyes shifted to Salas who was standing beside her. He raised his hands in "Do as they say." His voice shook with tension. "We haven't a chance."

Coretta's glance flicked back to Cruz, who walked slowly towards her and held out his hand. With a shrug she gave him the gun.

"Perhaps I should have let Roberto finish you off on the *carreterra*."

"Cruz!" Enrico called out from behind Coretta. "You won't be needing that gun. Just put it on the ground and step away from it." Cruz bent down to drop the gun and as he straightened up saw Coretta's look of surprise change to anger, then fear.

"*Hola* Coretta." Hector had appeared from behind the corner of the house. "How could you think of arranging a party and not invite me?" Without waiting for an answer he signalled to Enrico who emerged from the darkness and bound Salas's hands behind him before doing the same to Coretta.

Coretta made no attempt to struggle as the gangster tied the cord round her wrists and tightened it. When he stepped back she turned to look at Cruz. "Were you working for him all along or did he buy you at the last minute? You know what kind of scum he is. You're dirtier than him, *mierda!*"

"So unpleasant when a lady uses that kind of language." Hector nodded to Enrico who pulled a scarf from his pocket and gagged Coretta before placing his massive hands on her shoulders to force her down onto her knees.

Hector leaned down and smiled at the helpless girl. "I have a little business to discuss with my associates here. While we do that you can think about what's going to happen to you once we're finished."

Hector strolled across to the table from where the two Black Helmets and Gonzalez had been watching the scene play out in front of them.

"Gentlemen, my apologies for keeping you waiting." He sat down then signalled for Cruz and Salas to be brought forward. Cruz saw that the ELR man was trembling as if he had a fever. Hector glanced at him then turned to Colonel Diaz. "Comrade Salas looks to me like a man who has had enough of the revolutionary struggle. What do you think Colonel?"

Diaz carefully placed the cigar he'd been smoking onto the ash tray in front of him, exhaled a cloud of smoke and nodded. "I think he realises it's time to make the most of his talents." His voice had the guttural, gritty quality of a *campesino* who'd worked his way up from the bottom. A rise that Cruz guessed must have taken both ability and ruthlessness.

Salas's eyes flicked from Diaz to Hector then back again. "But we brought you the money. We had a deal, a three-way deal." He had lost the tough guy tone Cruz had overheard the night before in the University library. Now he sounded less like a revolutionary than a whining teenager.

Diaz stood up and walked around the table to confront Salas and slapped him hard across the face. "Did you think I would really be part of an operation to help finance a bunch of red terrorists? If you did you're living in a dream world you stupid little fuck!"

Gonzalez, who so far hadn't said a word, leaned forward and spoke to Salas in the smooth, measured tones of a lawyer advising a client.

"Señor Salas, you are extremely fortunate in possessing technical skills which mean your well-being is of value to my friends here. If it weren't for that, your chances of survival would be remote. I would strongly recommend that you fall in with their wishes."

"What he means" broke in Diaz, his voice sounding harsher than ever, "is that if you want to stay healthy you do exactly what you're told. Forget your three-way deal. You work for us. We've got your equipment safely stashed away. You put it all back together and by next week we start production."

Salas stared at Diaz as if he was hypnotised. "And if I say no, you're going to kill me?" he finally croaked.

Diaz laughed. "You won't be that lucky. We'll just work on you a little. As you know, my friend Captain Araya here is a real expert at getting people to say yes. I believe you saw a few examples of his work in *Puente Alto*. After a couple of hours you'll be begging him to shoot you."

Salas made a muffled sound and Cruz realised that he was sobbing. He looked as if he was going to collapse until Diaz stepped forward and pushed him down into an empty chair.

"I don't think your sterner measures will be necessary Colonel" Gonzalez observed." I believe Señor Salas is ready to be cooperative, isn't that right?"

Cruz waited to see if Salas would plead for Coretta, try to bargain for her life but he said nothing, just nodded his head.

Gonzalez looked around the table. "Well gentlemen, I think that takes care of that."

Hector helped himself to a glass of whisky from the bottle standing in the middle of the table, took a drink and said "Now for the next item on the agenda, my personal piece of business."

Gonzalez pushed back his chair. "I don't think I need be here for that so if you'll excuse me..."

Hector chuckled as the lawyer retreated into the house. "Señor Gonzalez seems to lack the stomach for what's coming. Pity, it should be entertaining."

Cruz's guts tightened and he risked a quick glance at his watch. As he did so the faces around him were suddenly illuminated in a golden glow. High over the tree tops, sparks from a skyrocket cascaded downwards at the same time as another burst in a spectacular shower of red and green. A third and then a fourth rocket soared into the night sky before darkness returned.

The brief display reminded Cruz of the old custom still kept up in some rural villages: firing off rockets at the end of a wake. It seemed Hector remembered it also. His teeth shone white as he grinned at Cruz. "I see someone's celebrating. A little early, but not by much."

Hector pulled an automatic out of his pocket and held it out to Cruz who stared at the weapon as if it was a venomous snake. "Take it" Hector smiled and thrust the gun into Cruz's hand. It was a .22 with a silencer fitted. The assassin's weapon that had killed Marta. "Oh and just in case you think of trying something really stupid, there's only one bullet in the magazine. That's all you'll need."

Cruz's fingers closed round the automatic, the butt felt warm, maybe because his fingers were icy cold. "Your hand is shaking Inspector, it's lucky you'll be firing point blank. Oh and one more thing, I want you to shoot her between the eyes. I'd like to see you looking at her face when you pull the trigger. Time to say your goodbyes, Inspector."

Cruz stood holding the gun. In front of him Coretta knelt, still gagged and with her hands tied behind her. "Any last word for your girlfriend?" Hector was standing next to Cruz so as to get the best view of Coretta's face. She was making no attempt to struggle, just looking up at Cruz who was thankful that the gag she wore made it impossible to read the expression on her face. Where in God's name was Daley?

"Nothing to say? I'm disappointed." Hector didn't look disappointed, he looked as if he was enjoying himself. "What a shame and you with such a reputation as a lady's man Inspector. OK, let's not waste any more time." Hector stepped forward drew his own gun and jammed the muzzle against Cruz's neck.

"I'm going to start counting and when I reach ten, either you fire or I do."

Cruz tried to think of some way out. There wasn't one. He could shoot Coretta or leave it to Hector. Either way she would die. Was there a chance he could get his one bullet into Hector? Not one in a thousand, but if he pulled the trigger on Coretta could he live with that memory?

"One...two." No more time: he made his decision. Hector's voice almost in his ear counting off the seconds. Cruz's right leg began to tremble so violently he could hardly stand up. "Four, five, six..." Then, as Cruz's finger involuntarily tightened on the trigger, he was blinded by the beam of a powerful floodlight. The blast of a loudhailer accompanied the sudden blaze of light.

"This is the police! Everybody stand still!"

Cruz felt Hector's gun jerk away and a burning pain seared the back of his neck as the gun went off, immediately followed by the staccato crack-crack-crack of an automatic. He dropped his own weapon, slumped to the ground and blacked out. When he opened his eyes he found himself lying on top of Coretta. He rolled sideways then recoiled: he was staring straight into Hector's face. One eye was open, the other was a bloody hole. Hector Torres was obviously very, very dead.

Cruz crawled back to Coretta and managed to untie the knot holding her gag in place. She groaned and started to gasp in air. He was fumbling at the rope tying her hands when he became aware of a well-known voice.

"Why is it that whenever I get a phone call in the middle of the night, you're involved Inspector? It seems you have some serious explaining to do."

Cruz looked up to see *Comisario* Delgado staring down at him. Alongside his boss stood Brad Daley, an oddly blank expression on his face. Behind them, a squad of armed police held Diaz and Araya under guard.

Cruz's neck felt as if somebody had used a blowtorch on it. "So no commendation then?" he muttered and began another attempt to loosen Coretta's bonds. He found that his brain didn't seem to be communicating too well with his fingers. He looked up at the circle of cops surrounding him. "Has nobody here got a fucking knife?" he enquired.

MONDAY AGAIN 1: *AVENIDA LIBERTAD*

Cruz took a hand from the steering wheel and gingerly touched the bandage covering the painful area on the back of his neck. The muzzle blast from Hector's gun had scorched his skin like a blow lamp, making him wince every time he needed to turn his head at a junction. Like now, Cruz realised as he approached the *14 Julio* intersection. The traffic lights weren't working and he was forced to look left and right before gunning the engine and speeding across the junction. He swore as he saw that ahead the next set of lights at *Constitucional* was also out of action. So no red or green guidance on how his day was going to turn out. Somehow, with an irate Delgado waiting for him, he hardly needed a sign from the Gods to predict his immediate future.

Cruz slowed as he came up to the junction and at the same time saw the familiar figure of Nesto propelling his trolley to the edge of the pavement. He waved frantically at Cruz who pulled into the side of the road.

"What is it Nesto? I thought you were working the hospital beat these days?"

Nesto scowled. "Some fat bastard of a security guard there saw I was doing OK and started asking for a cut. When I told him to screw himself the piece of *mierda* had me thrown off the site."

"So back to your old territory. What is it you want this time?"

Nesto leaned into the car. "A message, as usual. Different client but we both know what happened to the last one. This time it's Rocky Jara: he'd like to see you."

"Rocky! About what?"

"Who knows? But there's a big hole in the market where El Chico used to run things and the whisper is that Rocky plans to fill it."

"He does eh?" Cruz started to chuckle. When the opportunity of expanding his empire had come up, Rocky's little homily about contenting himself with running his own *barrio* had turned out to be bullshit.

Cruz's laughter stopped abruptly as pain seared the back of his neck. "Give Rocky my very best regards but tell him that after today I don't think I'll be in a position to do favours for him or anybody else. Go with God Nesto. Working for Rocky you'll be on the right track. He's hand-in-hand with the Almighty." Cruz shut the car door and put his foot down to accelerate through the crossroads. Time to face an interview with his own personal deity, *Comisario* Delgado.

MONDAY AGAIN 2: *BAR GATO NEGRO*

"It could have been worse *amigo*. They could have sent you to the jungle." Tomas took a cautious sip of his beer and grimaced. His dark brown complexion muted but didn't entirely hide the bruising on his face and one eye was still half-closed. He'd not been too keen to come to the *Gato Negro* and display his injuries but in the end had given in to Cruz's plea for a sympathetic ear.

"At least you don't freeze to death in the jungle" Cruz replied gloomily. "*Puerto Pedroso* is the coldest place this side of the South Pole. Two years chasing smugglers and dodging frostbite!"

Cruz had been prepared for a roasting from Delgado but thought he might at least get some credit for breaking up the drugs plot, solving the manuscripts case and retrieving $250,000. He ought to have known that the *Comisario's* number one priority was not clearing up crime but ensuring subordinates showed a proper respect for his authority. Cruz was in big trouble as soon as his boss found out that a humble Inspector had gone behind his back to get help from Brad Daley.

"Two years will pass my friend. And the mountain air is good for the health. You and Felicia could learn to ski!"

"Felicia is staying right where she is. She doesn't like heights and she doesn't like snow." Since Felicia had told him she wasn't coming with him to his new posting on the Andean frontier, Cruz hadn't been able to decide whether he was glad or sorry. He would miss his daughter but the thought of being cooped up with Felicia in the grim cement-block police house that provided the only accommodation for the unfortunate senior officer assigned to Puerto Pedroso had not been appealing.

"That's too bad. Still, you'll be a bachelor again, meeting lots of young *chicas* on the ski slopes."

Cruz shook his head. "There aren't any ski lifts in *Puerto Pedroso*, just snow, llamas and a bunch of frontier police too dumb to find themselves a better posting."

Tomas decided to change the subject. "Did you get any chance to talk to Coretta yet?"

"No I didn't but that's what I'm going to do now. As soon as I've read this."Cruz pointed to a large envelope sticking out of the document case he'd parked on a corner of their table. "It's the final forensic report on the Golden Gate bomb. It might help to answer a few questions that have been bugging me."

Tomas raise his eyebrows. "Didn't Delgado take you off the case?"

"Sure he did but fuck him. I've got loose ends to tie up and what more can he do to me?"

Tomas could think of several things but decided it was wiser not to share them with his friend. "You want me to come with you to see Coretta?"

"Thanks but no. One screwed-up career is enough. Another drink then you should get yourself home. I'll tell you later how it went." Cruz signalled to the waitress for two more bottles of beer. She eyed Cruz's bandage and Tomas's battered face curiously.

"In case you're wondering" Cruz told her, "We didn't do this to each other."

She smiled sweetly at him. "I never thought you did *señor*. But your wives maybe?"

MONDAY AGAIN 3: *LA CAMPAÑA* WOMENS' PRISON

Coretta was sitting with her knees drawn up, allowing Cruz just enough room to perch on the bottom end of her bunk. She was dressed in the grey shift given to women prisoners when their own clothes were taken away. Her face was pale and there were dark shadows under her eyes.

"You would have done it wouldn't you? You would have shot me if that *Yanqui* spy hadn't turned up when he did."

The flash burn Cruz had suffered when Hector's gun went off was still painful and to make matters worse, visiting the womens' prison, a gaunt four-storey concrete block surrounded by a tangle of razor wire fencing, always made him feel depressed. The gaol stood close enough to the big rail freight yard at the western end of the city for their conversation to be accompanied by the mournful clanking of wagons punctuated by the occasional high pitched blast from the horn of a shunting locomotive.

"What's the point of saying anything different. You wouldn't believe me anyway."

"That's right, I wouldn't"

"Not that I owe you anything after you and your boyfriend tried to kill me on the *carreterra*."

"I didn't try to kill you! I had no idea until you got out of the car that it was you following us. And don't call that piece of shit my boyfriend!"

"What was Salas then?" enquired Cruz, "just another comrade?"

"A comrade doesn't betray his cause."

"Or his friends" added Cruz, wondering if Coretta had caught the whiff of jealousy in his question. "At this very moment he's singing like a cage bird. He's claiming that you persuaded him to go along with Colonel Diaz and Hector."

"And what does Diaz say about that?"

"Diaz doesn't say anything. When Delgado asked for him and Araya to be brought in for questioning he was told that they were under military jurisdiction and would be court-martialled tomorrow. My guess is they'll be quietly disposed of to protect the honour of the officer corps."

"Honour!" Coretta gave a bitter laugh. "So Hector's dead and those two Black Helmet thugs soon will be. And Roberto has turned informer. Where does that leave me?"

"I don't know. You and Salas were in possession of $250,000 when you were caught. We shouldn't have much trouble proving that was the proceeds of the manuscript thefts. Still a good lawyer might be able to convince a judge that you were just an accomplice following Salas's orders."

Coretta's laugh had no trace of humour. "A good lawyer! How am I going to afford a bad one? Even if I could find an *abogado* who'd dare to defend me."

Cruz shrugged his shoulders. It was true enough. Any lawyer who stood up in court to represent an enemy of the *Junta* would do well to check the details of their life insurance first.

Cruz pulled out a pack of cigarettes, remembered Coretta didn't smoke and shoved them back into his pocket.

"On the bonus side, what Hector said to me lets you off the hook for Marta's murder."

Coretta stared at him open-mouthed. "You thought I killed my best friend?"

"No, I didn't believe you would do that and in any case the timings didn't fit. But if Delgado had been looking for another charge to pin on you it might have been convenient. After all she did apparently disappear with $250,000 of the ELR's money."

"That wasn't how it happened!"

"So how did it happen? Was she carrying the money when I put her on the train to *Costa Azul?*"

"Yes, I didn't dare take it with me in case you searched my things. She was supposed to stay on the coast until we contacted her but I guess her boyfriend Alejandro turned up at her father's house and Hector's men were waiting. They must have forced him to ring her and spin a story that made her come back to *Independencia.*"

"But she didn't bring the money with her?"

"No, either she was too scared to carry it or she planned to go straight back to *Costa Azul* after she'd seen Alejandro."

"So why didn't she tell Hector where the money was? I know she was your friend but I couldn't see her standing up to what they did to her for long."

Coretta's head dropped and she started to cry quietly.

Cruz handed her a handkerchief. "I'm sorry but I guess you know what happened."

Coretta nodded. "Poor Marta, I don't want to think about it. You see Hector didn't know anything about the manuscripts or the money. He believed the lies the *Junta* puts around about us being funded from Cuba."

"So what was he after when he interrogated Marta?"

"I guess he was trying to find out where I was hiding and Marta didn't know that." Coretta started to cry again. As Cruz fought against an impulse to put an arm round her shoulders, there was a knock on the cell door. A moment later he heard the scrape of the bolt being drawn back and the door swung open.

Cruz stared at the burly figure of Brad Daley framed in the doorway. "Hi Amalio, no surprise to find you interviewing the best-looking suspect!"

Daley had to duck his head to come through the doorway. Finding nowhere to sit, he leaned against the wall, arms folded and stared impassively at Coretta.

Cruz glanced up at the American. Even that slight movement made him grimace. "I guessed it was you Brad. Who else would knock on the door before coming into a cell?"

"I hope I know how to treat a lady."

Coretta glared at him. "Was that part of your training course at Langley spy school Mr CIA man?"

Daley raised his eyebrows at Cruz who shrugged. "I didn't tell her Brad."

"Why should anyone need to tell me?" Coretta demanded. "You *Yanqui* spies are as inconspicuous as a priest in a brothel."

"I wouldn't know *Señorita*. I haven't visited any of your whorehouses."

Cruz raised a hand to close down the argument before it became any more heated.

"Listen Coretta, I asked Señor Daley to come along here. I just want you to tell us both how you got into all this."

Coretta shook her head. "Why should I tell this *gringo* anything?" she asked Cruz.

Daley leaned forward, towering over the girl on the bed. "How about because I saved your life when Hector was ready to blow your brains out? I guess you owe me after that."

Cruz nodded, then winced again. He must try to keep his head still. "I guess he's right Coretta. If Brad hadn't showed up we would both be dead by now."

Daley had noticed Cruz's discomfort and pulled a small flask out of his pocket. He unscrewed the cap. "Here, try some of this *amigo*. Twelve-year-old Scotch. Tastes a hell of a lot better than pills."

Cruz took a cautious sip and then another, bigger one: Daley was right. The neat whisky spread a golden glow through his stomach. He handed the flask back to Daley who carefully replaced the cap and put the flask back in his pocket.

Cruz felt the pain in his neck ease although he was having a momentary difficulty focusing on Coretta's face. "That helped. Now, why don't you tell us the real story about what happened when you stabbed Hector?"

Coretta looked wary. "I've already told you about that."

"What you mean is that you've told me a pack of lies. I have a reliable witness who saw most of what happened and she can testify that you weren't spying on that meeting between Diaz and Hector, you were part of it."

Coretta looked more than ever like a sulky adolescent. "If you know so much why are you asking me?"

"Because, just for once, I'd like to hear the truth from you. All that stuff you told me about saving your boyfriend in Puente Alto was just bullshit, right?"

Coretta shook her head. "No, it wasn't all a lie. Roberto **was** held in Puente Alto. It's just that he made a deal. Diaz found out that before he was caught, Roberto was processing coca paste to raise funds for the ELR, just in a small way, selling on the campus. Somebody ratted on him and he got arrested. Diaz had the idea to set up a big operation and he promised Roberto he'd be released if he agreed to cooperate."

"And a share of the profits?"

"Yes but they needed a way of marketing the stuff on the streets. That's where Hector came in."

"And that's also where you could make the link."

"Yes I knew Hector. When we were children I used to play with his sister Carmen and he would be around sometimes. Like I told you before, their mother was my father's cousin. I kept in touch with Carmen but I hadn't seen much of Hector for years. He spent quite a bit of time abroad, Mexico, Colombia."

Cruz nodded. "We can guess why. But he remembered you when you contacted him?"

"Of course. That's when we set up the meeting. Gonzalez's house was kind of a neutral territory and Hector suggested the party would be good cover."

Cruz shook his head. "I'm still not getting all this. You're trying to tell us that Hector Torres and two renegade officers from the Black Helmets were willing to set up a drug deal that would bankroll the ELR?"

Coretta's rubbed a hand across her eyes. "That puzzled me too. When I asked him about it, Roberto told me Diaz and Araya were undercover agents working for the Cubans and giving covert support to the ELR. Now I know that was just more lies. I think maybe Roberto had already given up on the struggle. I guess he just wanted to get out of *Puente Alto* and make money for himself. He invented this story about Cuban agents so I would do what he wanted."

Cruz glanced at Daley who shrugged. "So, if Roberto was in charge why wasn't he at the meeting at Gonzalez's place?" the American asked.

"Diaz had had him moved from *Puente Alto* to the Officer's School. He didn't trust him enough to let him go until we'd agreed a deal, so I went to the meeting instead."

"And you came to a deal with Hector and the Black Helmets?"

Coretta brushed a stray lock of hair from her face. "Yes, kind of."

"What do you mean kind of?"

"I mean we had a deal provided we put up the money for the first consignment. Luckily for Roberto we had the cash we'd raised from the manuscript thefts. It was supposed to be used for running the organisation and helping the families of ELR prisoners but Roberto persuaded us that if we used it to pay our way into the drug deal we could soon be making millions."

Cruz raised his eyebrows at Daley who grinned back then turned to Coretta. "Sounds like your Roberto was well on his way to turning himself into a good little capitalist."

The girl glared at Daley then turned her head away. "It was supposed to be money for the cause, to help the ELR struggle. And I've told you before he wasn't my Roberto!"

"What about Hector?" Daley persisted. "Didn't he have to contribute as well?"

Cruz noticed that Coretta still didn't look at the American but she answered his question.

"The deal was that Hector would be responsible for distribution. He couldn't help with the finance. El Chico kept him on a tight leash. He gave him a fat wad of notes to flash around, bought him a big *Yanqui* car but never let him get his hands on any real money. That was one of the reasons Hector was keen to come in on the deal."

Daley shook his head disbelievingly. "And he was stupid enough to think El Chico wouldn't know what was going on?"

"El Chico had put him in charge of *Sector Norte*. The market there was expanding and Hector reckoned he could start slipping in a percentage of what Roberto was processing without anybody noticing. He had his own people up there to watch his back, the *gorillas* you saw at the Guzman house."

Cruz nodded. "So what went so wrong at the meeting that you ended up sticking a knife into Hector?"

Coretta's long, elegant fingers picked at the neck of her shift. "Can't you guess? When we'd finished our business Hector suggested the two of us took a stroll around the garden to talk about old times. Being abroad he hadn't seen me for four or five years, since I was a schoolgirl in fact. He'd been drinking and maybe he'd snorted a little C. I didn't want to leave the others but I felt I had to keep him sweet. Then as soon as we got into a quiet corner of the garden he started pawing me.

He wouldn't stop when I asked him to and when I pushed him off that just seemed to excite him even more. He grabbed me and tried to rip off my dress. I managed to pull myself away and I kicked him as hard as I could, then I ran. He chased me into the kitchen and there was a knife lying on the work top. When he ran at me I picked it up and stuck it into his arm. He yelled out and I dodged past him. I didn't stop running until I got to Marta's. You know the rest."

Daley pulled a pack of cigarettes from his pocket, offered one to Cruz and lit up. "What about the brick of C the military cops found in your bag?

"Hector must have put it there. It was just the kind of spur of the moment thing he would have done after he'd lost his temper. He was like that as a kid: nasty but not too bright."

Cruz blew a puff of smoke towards the ceiling. "Bit of a coincidence the party being raided that night wasn't it? Do you think Diaz and Araya were just playing you along?"

Coretta laughed. "You think they were really honest cops just pretending to be bent? No, I'll swear they were seriously interested in making money. I'm sure they knew nothing about the raid. Either it was a coincidence or the Black Helmets had a tip off. One of Hector's men maybe, or even Gonzalez."

"Gonzalez?" Daley scoffed. "I don't think so. He's been the Torres family's pet brief for years!"

Cruz wasn't so sure. "He's been El Chico's brief you mean. Could be that when he found out what was going on at his party he rang El Chico and the big boss thought a night in the cells would teach his son a lesson. Maybe he intended that to be the first step in cutting Hector down to size but then he got blown away."

"So you think Hector arranged that?" queried Daley.

Forgetting his burned neck, Cruz shook his head and had to suppress a yelp of pain. "No, I don't think the bomb was down to Hector. Even if he'd thought about something like that he was too scared of his old man. What do you think Brad?"

"I don't know, it could have been one of the other drug bosses. How about your friend Rocky Jara?"

"Rocky? He might be interested in filling the big man's shoes but this was above his league. Besides, blowing half a dozen innocent bystanders to bits doesn't seem like his style."

Daley shrugged. "A lot of people had an interest in seeing El Chico dead. It's hard to know where to start."

"Well, I'm not starting anywhere. I'm sure you'll have heard what Delgado has in mind for me."

Daley laid a sympathetic hand on Cruz's shoulder. "Yeah I heard Amalio. It's a damn shame. You didn't deserve that after the way you worked this case."

Cruz stood up and faced the big American. "Not too many people get what they deserve."

He locked eyes with Daley. "It was you Brad, you planted the bomb at the Golden Gate. You blew away El Chico and those other people who just happened to be in the way."

Cruz heard a sharp intake of breath from Coretta but he didn't take his eyes off the American's face. Daley looked puzzled. It was a good act, thought Cruz.

"Amalio, are you nuts? I guess what you've been through the last week is catching up with you. Perhaps you should go home and take a rest for a couple of days."

"No Brad, I'll have plenty of time to take a rest when I'm stuck in that frontier post on the border. Until then I've got questions I want answers to and the biggest of all is who sent that little present to El Chico? The one that nearly fried me as well."

Daley stubbed out his cigarette on the floor and folded his arms. "OK, my friend. Let's hear what makes you think I had anything to do with it. Maybe I can clear a few things up for you."

Cruz sat down on the bed again and began ticking off on his fingers. "First, motive. As we agreed, lots of people had a reason to want El Chico dead, but if we think about who had access to explosives, then things begin to narrow down."

Daley shook his head. "Plenty of people can lay their hands on the stuff. You know it's easy enough for anyone with the right know-how."

"Such as the ELR you mean."

Daley nodded. "That fits. ELR agitators have been active in the mines for years and there's plenty of guys there who know how to handle explosives. They have to be prime suspect."

"No way." Coretta broke in. "That bomb was nothing to do with us. Military targets only, that was our policy, not slaughtering civilians!"

Cruz kept his eyes fixed on Daley and ticked off another finger. "Second, information. El Chico didn't make a habit of visiting the Golden Gate on a Wednesday afternoon. He went there especially to interrogate me about Coretta. Whoever planted the bomb was able to find out about the Big Man's movements at very short notice. My betting is on a phone tap and that points to either the Black Helmets, or you Brad."

Daley kept his smile but Cruz saw his lips tighten a little.

"OK let's play along with that. Maybe you're on track with the Black Helmets. I can see Diaz and Araya had a good reason to eliminate El Chico. That would leave a clear field for Hector and the three-way deal could go ahead without having to worry about what could happen if the big boss found out. That all makes sense"

"Plausible but wrong when we consider number three" Cruz crooked a third finger. "The forensic evidence."

For the first time Daley sounded a little uneasy. "What evidence? I've just read the forensic report and I don't remember anything unusual about it."

"You don't?" Cruz was starting to feel more confident. "Brad you made two mistakes. First off, if you wanted the ELR to get the blame then you should have used dynamite, not plastic. The ELR can get hold of dynamite from the mines but they've never used plastic."

"You can't be sure about that. Maybe the Cubans have got some through to them."

"Not impossible but very unlikely. With what's going on in Nicaragua, the Cubans have other things on their minds. In any case that wouldn't account for your second mistake."

Cruz paused. Now he was starting to enjoy himself. He waited for Daley to say something but the American simply raised his eyebrows to indicate that he was ready for whatever grenade Cruz was going to lob at him.

"Your second mistake" Cruz repeated "was the type of detonator you used."

"Soviet bloc manufactured wasn't it?" queried Daley, sounding slightly puzzled. "Czech I guess, or East German?"

"That's right, East German."

"What's so odd about that?"

"Nothing if the bomb was your idea Brad, but you see a few years back the ELR exploded a bomb outside a police station in *Aguas Calientes*. They used a Soviet detonator supplied by the Cubans. It caused a big diplomatic row with Cuba and a lot of bad publicity for the ELR which got itself labelled as a puppet of Fidel's. After that they've always been very careful to use *Yanqui* or West European detonators stolen from the mine stores or bought on the black market. You thought using East German kit would point to the ELR, in fact it points in exactly the opposite direction, straight at you my friend."

Daley shrugged. "OK, maybe not the ELR then, but that still leaves Diaz and Araya in the frame."

"It might, except that the Black Helmets are responsible for dealing with terrorist offences. Before Colonel Diaz was transferred to the anti-drugs unit he worked in the counter-terrorism branch. He was chief investigating officer on the *Aguas Calientes* bomb and at least two other ELR bomb attacks after that one. He wouldn't have made your mistake because he knew the ELR had switched from using Soviet Bloc equipment.

Daley laughed but it wasn't the easy laugh that Cruz remembered from their previous conversations. "Amalio, you'll have to do better than that. What your little fantasy doesn't explain is why I should want to kill El Chico?"

"Because Brad, you were sent here to make sure the ELR stayed down and out and to fight your President Reagan's war on drugs. El Chico was a very good customer for the Colombians and anything you can do to put the squeeze on them is bound to be popular with Washington. It must have seemed a neat idea. Blow away El Chico and put the blame on the ELR. I'm even wondering whether those dead civilians were an unfortunate accident or part of the plan. A few innocent victims would certainly blacken the ELR's name more than taking out a drugs baron."

The big man kept a smile on his face. "OK my friend, so why if I did that, did I save you and the girl from Hector?"

Cruz stared Daley out. "Because that's not how you planned it. I wasn't too delighted when Delgado turned up at Gonzalez's place, I thought you'd called him but turns out it was a surprise for you as well. When Delgado hauled me in to give me the good news about *Puerto Pedroso* he told me he'd had a tip-off from no less than Señor Gonzalez himself. Trust a lawyer to know when to rat on his friends. I think the south side boys must have got to him or maybe even Rocky Jara. It must have been a nasty shock for you when Delgado muscled in on your show. You could hardly sit back and let Hector murder two people in front of the *Comisario* of Detectives, even if I'm not exactly his favourite son. If he hadn't shown up in time, I'm guessing you'd have waited to take out Hector until after Coretta and I were both dead meat."

Daley shook his head slowly but he wasn't smiling now. "There's not an ounce of proof in anything you've told me, just house of cards guesswork."

"True" Cruz admitted. "But we both know proof isn't necessary. There are still one or two journalists in this country prepared to take risks to publish a good story. Maybe if they do a little digging they'll find out more about what you've been up to. In any case once your photo is splashed across the front page you won't be much use to your bosses."

Daley shook his head. "You wouldn't dare. Delgado would crucify you."

"As we say in this country Brad, 'Beware the man with nothing to lose' Delgado's already exiled me to the shittiest police post in the country. What more can he do? Fire me? So what? I'm just about ready to walk away myself."

Cruz saw Daley's hand slip inside his jacket. The American drew out his automatic and pointed the muzzle at Cruz's stomach.

"Give me your gun" Daley demanded in a voice grown suddenly hoarse. Cruz made no move to unholster his weapon. He could make a good guess at the agent's next move. Shoot Cruz with the detective's own gun, then kill Coretta and plead self-defence. He would claim the girl had seized the policeman's weapon, shot Cruz then tried murder him as well.

Cruz tried to keep his voice steady. "It won't work, Brad. It's too risky and it's too late. I've written a letter setting out everything I've just told you and I left copies with three different people to be posted to the press if anything happens to me."

Daley kept his gun pointing at Cruz's chest. "You wouldn't happen to be bullshitting me about that would you?"

Cruz stared back at the *Yanqui* and tried to keep his voice steady as he lied for his life. "It's the truth. If you don't believe me pull the trigger and find out. But I'd much sooner we talked about a deal."

Cruz held his breath, eyes locked on Daley's trigger finger. What felt like half a lifetime passed before the *Yanqui* gave Cruz a

very small smile and lowered his gun. "A deal? What kind of a deal?
"

AFTERWARDS

Cruz showed his ID to the sub-machine gun toting guards on the door. They checked it carefully before waving him through into the secure lounge at the capital's *Aeropuerto Internacional*. He'd guessed this was where she would be. Besides catering for VIPs, the lounge was occasionally used to hold high profile criminal or political prisoners being transported by plane.

In one hand Cruz carried a suitcase, in the other a bunch of flowers he'd just bought from a street vendor's stall next to the airport taxi rank. He paused inside the lounge entrance and scanned the dozen or so people waiting for their flights: a few higher ranking military officers in uniform, the rest prosperous businessmen or senior government officials. Finally he caught sight of Coretta, sitting in the far corner flanked by a burly woman in the uniform of a prison guard. Cruz noticed that the other passengers had avoided seats close to the two women, as if they were somehow contagious. Coretta had her back to him as she stared out of the picture window at a plane taxi-ing along the runway. He walked up behind her.

"I believe yours is the flight after that one *Señorita*."

Coretta span round and stared up at him. "Amalio!"

Cruz brandished his ID in the face of the guard. "Give us a couple of minutes." He pointed to the next row of seats.

The guard glowered at him, wearing the expression that in Cruz's experience, prison staff put on at the same time as their uniform. "I'm not supposed to leave her on her own until she's on the plane" she said in a tone that matched the face.

Cruz put some steel into his voice. "She won't be alone, she'll be with a police officer. I need to talk to her, it's official so do as you're asked before I phone your superiors and tell them that you're obstructing a state security investigation."

The woman's tough expression crumpled. "I'm sorry Inspector, I was only following my..." Her voice trailed off as Cruz impatiently waved her away and sat down next to Coretta. He handed her the flowers. She sniffed them then gave him a quizzical smile.

"And how do these fit into a state security investigation?"

"Not very convincing was it?" he admitted. "But at least she's given us some space."

Cruz took a long look at Coretta. She was no longer dressed in prison garb but wore jeans, open-toed sandals and a brightly coloured top cinched at the waist by a broad patterned belt of the kind woven by *Indio* women on the *Altiplano*. Her hair hung loose on her shoulders and even under the harsh fluorescent lighting in the lounge, she needed no makeup.

"Do you like this blouse?" she asked. "They brought me just one small suitcase of clothes from my old flat. This was the only top in it apart from a couple of t-shirts."

Cruz felt unusually tongued-tied. "It looks...you look, very nice."

"Very nice!" she teased him. "You sound like a *gringo!*" Before he could say anything else Coretta turned and pointed at the *Cubana* jet parked next to the nearest terminal gate. "You arranged all this didn't you?"

Cruz nodded. "I had a hand in it."

"How did you manage that? I was expecting to get thirty years in *Puente Alto.*"

"You heard me talking to Brad Daley. We came to an arrangement. I kept quiet about what happened at the Golden Gate and he agreed to talk to a General or two."

Coretta's smile vanished. "So your deal was that I get a flight to Cuba and the *Yanqui* spy responsible for those people at the Golden Gate being blown to pieces gets away with it! How do you think that makes me feel?"

Cruz shook his head. This meeting wasn't going the way he'd played it through in advance. "Daley was going to get away with it anyway. I could have made some trouble for him, put a black mark on his record, but that was all. There was no way he would ever be arrested, let alone convicted. The Generals wouldn't risk offending the *Yanquis* like that."

Cruz saw Coretta's expression soften. She put a hand on his. "I'm sorry, I'm giving you a hard time and you've saved my life. Not many people walk out of *Puente Alto*. I just wonder why you've gone to so much trouble for me."

A wave of melancholy washed over Cruz. He summoned up a smile. "You know very well why, don't you?"

Coretta's dark eyes regarded Cruz, then she smiled. "Yes, I suppose I do. And you never even got a kiss from me Inspector. Still, I can put that right now." Her mouth tasted to Cruz of sunlight, cool water, sweet apples. He heard a disapproving grunt from the prison guard sitting behind him but he ignored it. It was a long kiss and when it was over Cruz sat back feeling as shaky as a teenager on his first date. "That was good" Coretta observed, then giggled. "I wish you could see the expression on that old bitch's face."

Before Cruz could reply, an announcement boomed over the tannoy. "*Señores y señoras,* attention please! First call for the flight to *San Cristobal.* Will passengers please come to gate number three." Automatically he looked round to check his suitcase was still where he'd left it. Coretta's eyes widened. "Are you flying today as well? I thought you'd just come to see me off."

Cruz nodded. "I'm on the *San Cristobal* plane. It's the nearest airport to my new posting. They're sending me to *Puerto Pedroso* on the frontier." He didn't add that it had taken a large box of chocolates to persuade Natalia Hernandez to alter the date on his posting letter so that it coincided with Coretta's flight. Not to mention the excuse he'd made to Felicia that it would upset him too much if she and Laura came to see him off.

"Why are they doing that to you? Is it because of me?"

Cruz shook his head. "It's because I've annoyed too many people."

"But what about your wife? Your daughter?"

"They're not coming with me. It's sensible for Felicia to stay where she is, where her friends and family are. Then we have to think about Laura's schooling."

"And you'll be stuck up there in the snow on your own."

"It's a two year posting. I'll get through it."

Coretta smiled at him and leaned forward to whisper in his ear. "I wish I was coming with you. You'll need someone to keep you warm in those long cold nights."

Cruz stood up as he heard the second call echo over the loudspeaker. "Maybe, one day." He jerked his thumb at a cluster of army uniforms on the far side of the lounge and in a voice low enough to make sure Coretta's guard couldn't hear, added "Those bastards aren't going to be in charge for ever."

"Then let's just say *hasta luego*" Coretta put a finger to her lips and touched it to his hand.

"*Hasta luego.*" Cruz repeated then picked up his case and without looking back made for the nearest door. As he walked down the long corridor leading to gate number three a vague memory kept nagging at him: some film that his mother had been fond of, an old black and white picture with Spanish subtitles she always watched when it came on TV. Was it a *Yanqui* film? Or maybe French? The last scene was at an airport, a man and a woman saying goodbye, a man who, like him, hadn't got the girl. But unlike him the man had not walked away alone, he'd had a friend to drown his sorrows with.

"Hi boss. I just came along to see you off." Jerked abruptly out of his reverie Cruz blinked, then focused on the figure in front of him. "Tomas!" Cruz managed a smile for his old partner then gave him an *abrazo*. "Good to see you." He glanced at the big clock on the wall by the gate entrance. "Pity we haven't got time for a drink."

"That's where you're wrong *compadre!*" Tomas drew a hip flask from his pocket. "Brandy, genuine cognac, or as genuine as I could get this side of the Andes. Just the thing to settle your stomach before the flight."

Cruz took the flask, had a swig and handed the flask back to Tomas who followed his example before passing it back again. Cruz took another drink: even if brandy wasn't a miracle cure for the way he was feeling, it might help a little. And now he remembered the film and how he used to show off to his mother by repeating in English that famous line of dialogue. He raised the flask in the direction of the VIP lounge. "Here's lookin' at you kid. Here's lookin' at you."

THE END

Printed in Great Britain
by Amazon